10/15

This book is a work of fiction. References to historical events and actual locations are included for the purpose of showing the story's relevance to history. Names, characters, other events and locations are used fictitiously. Any resemblance to actual persons, living or dead, places, or events is coincidental.

To Tom Dowd
With warm regards

Dead
Men's
Bones

Stephen Boehrer

A NOVEL

Stephen Boehrer

Wind-borne Publications

Also by Stephen Boehrer

Unless a Grain of Wheat: Published by
Wind-borne Publications, 1997

Cover Design by Judy Bridges

Library of Congress Control Number: 00-132996

ISBN: 0-9660607-1-7

Published by: Wind-borne Publications
P.O. Box 733
Hales Corners, WI 53130

First Printing: May 2000
Printed in U.S.A.

To
Sister Maura Clarke
Sister Ita Ford
Jean Donovan
Sister Dorothy Kazel
Sister Dianna Ortiz

and the one-third of this world's
women who have been abused,
beaten, raped or murdered.

Woe to you Scribes and Pharisees, you frauds! You are like white-washed tombs, beautiful to look at on the outside, but inside full of filth and dead men's bones.

Gospel of Matthew 23:27

)

PROLOGUE

The frail, elderly Franciscan shuddered before the Archbishop. "They were raped, Excellency. And then murdered - stabbed again, and again, and again."

Archbishop Lucas Villariego looked up at his secretary. "You say they were human rights workers? What was their organization?" He pointed at the newspaper. "This tells me nothing."

"There are no special organizations, Excellency," the Franciscan said. "They were supported by their religious congregations who work collectively for the poor."

"Did you say that Sister Weber was from Belgium?" the Archbishop asked.

"Yes, she was a Franciscan."

"And Sister Delaney?"

"An American, a Maryknoll sister."

"And Sister Chaves?"

"She was Indian, a native. Also Franciscan."

The archbishop stood and stared out the window. "These women are so stupid to go where it is not safe. They draw hate on themselves from the men." He turned to his secretary. "Can it be of God, Father Antonio, if their work brings out such hatred?"

"The people say they help the poor...."

"Don't patronize me, Father."

Their heads turned to heated Mayan voices outside the window. The archbishop took two steps across the rich carpet and glared at the workers in his flower garden, stopping the voices. "Then why did the communists kill them?"

"The people are saying the police did it, Excellency."

"The people are stupid. General Castillo would not permit such a thing. I know this. He is my cousin."

"Still...."

"What do peasants know?"

PART 1

MAGGIE

Sister Margaret McDonough lifted the empty suitcase to her bed and walked to her closet. What to pack, Maggie? she thought. She had estimated her absence would be no more than one week, and it would be warm in Central America.

She held up a navy suit and began to inspect it for stains. Darn those Italian sauces. Turning for light, her eyes caught the picture of *Sacajawea* on the wall, the white and sorrel pinto given her by her parents on her eighth birthday. She had named the horse after one of her heroes, the intrepid Shoshone woman whose wisdom and endurance had been so critical to the success of the Lewis and Clark expedition. Over the next six years *Saca* was Maggie's most trusted confidant. The pair, accompanied always by the family's huge mongrel, *Lily*, roamed the high prairies of Montana. Her parents permitted her at twelve, on her persistent claims of competence, to camp overnights alone with *Saca* and *Lily*. She thrilled to the midnight howls of prairie wolves, and never felt fear. Riding *Saca* she had competed in races with her five brothers, and had won her fair share.

Maggie was fourteen on a crisp autumn day when they raced across the prairie for the last time. The grass-concealed maw of a prairie dog hole trapped *Saca's* front right foot and sent the pair sprawling on the dry, hard ground. *Saca's* leg shattered.

A veterinarian had euthanized the mare with a hypodermic shot to the neck. Maggie's father held her gently and stroked her hair as the wet sobs of her grief stained his shoulder. It was Maggie's first experience of loss.

Tonight, though, Maggie's nostalgia went to the happy memories. She fitted the navy suit into a garment bag and pulled a lavender suit from the closet for inspection. As packing always did, this one reminded her of past journeys, and the feelings of each: the sense of adventure and insecurity when she packed to leave Montana for Padua College in Wisconsin; her curiosity when spending week-end visits at the parental homes of boy friends; her exhilaration as a young nun at being chosen to get a doctorate in history, and the first waves of awe on wandering the halls of Harvard.

The lavender suit passed inspection and joined the navy one in the garment bag.

In her bathroom Maggie selected toiletries and a few cosmetics. She glanced in the mirror and stopped to pluck a gray hair, revealed in the bright light for its contrast to the even blackness of its neighbors. Not yet, Lord, she thought. Give me a few more years before that. Is that pride? And why can't I pass a mirror without checking myself out? Is that too much pride for a nun? She checked the hue of her aqua blue eyes and the light cream color of her face. No age spots yet. She wore a sweater and jeans, and she turned before the mirror to check their fit.

As she inspected herself, the words of a letter from Father Charles Mueller began to flow through her mind.

Dear Maggie,

'Shall I compare thee to a summer's day?
Thou art more lovely and more temperate.'
No, no, scratch the temperate.

Maggie released a soft velvet laugh at the memory. He was right. Temperate I'm not.

'How do I love thee? Let me count the ways.'
I love thee secretly -- thus far.

Maggie walked into her living room and picked up Charles' picture from the fireplace mantel. She read St. Francis' words from the memorial card tucked in the corner of the frame: "Lord, make me an instrument of Thy peace; where there is hatred, let me sow love; where there is injury, pardon; where there is doubt, faith; where there is despair, hope; where there is darkness, light; and where there is sadness, joy." You were all this to me, she thought, and placed the picture back on the mantel. Mellowed remnants of grief flooded her body.

It was still early evening when she completed her packing and nestled in an overstuffed chair to read. History or a novel? History tonight. I'll save the novel for the flight. She reached for the book and was soon lost in *Bitter Fruit* by Stephen Schlesinger and Stephen Kinzer, a history of American use of force in Central America.

The next morning Maggie followed the slow-moving line of people down the airplane's aisle, lifted her hand luggage into the overhead storage compartment, and took her window seat in the plane's tourist section. She looked out the window at the hustling flight-support workers at Rome's Leonardo da Vinci airport, and watched her black suitcase ride the elevator toward the plane's cargo area.

11

A twinge of dread filled her, as it had on every flight since the time when she landed to the news that her dearest friend, Father Charles Mueller, had been murdered. What waited for her in Central America at the end of this flight?

Her thoughts were interrupted by the arrival of a stout, heavily made-up, middle-aged woman. Bangles rode each of the woman's forearms, and a bleached streak coursed the middle of her light brown hair. After struggling to place a carry-on bag under the seat in front of her, she turned to Maggie. "Hello, my name is Trisha."

"My name is Maggie. I'm pleased to meet you, Trisha."

"I just hate airplanes," Trisha dug through her purse and pulled out a small black, velvet blindfold. She pulled it over her head and adjusted it to her eyes. "I simply can't stand to watch take-offs," she muttered, then lowered her head and slumped down into the seat.

As the plane rose into the early morning sky, Maggie looked down on the land and watched its detail give way to broader images. She felt a momentary thrill. What had Lindbergh felt as he headed out over open sea in *The Spirit of St. Louis?*

The aircraft leveled off and the sound of its engines lowered to a steady hum. Trisha came alive. She pulled off the blindfold and stuffed it back into her purse. "I've been visiting my daughter," she said, as if there had been no break in the conversation. "I swear I don't understand this younger generation...marry...divorce...live together...groupie stuff...all right out in public. Not that I haven't had my own little fun over the years, but gracious, I've always kept it private. Wouldn't you think? My goodness!"

"Yes, um, sounds wise," Maggie replied, breaking into a smile.

"I saw the Pope in Rome. Not that I'm Catholic or anything like that, but there he was up in the window, just so quaint."

"Isn't he a nice man?"

"My husband, Roland, simply refused to come along. He's just so busy. He said I'd have more fun by myself." Trisha turned and winked. "He was ri-i-ght as always. Roland's a financial planner in Philadelphia, that's where we live, and he's very successful. He just won't think of my working. He's old-fashioned that way." She put a tissue to her nose and blew. "Thank God. Do you work, Maggie?"

"I'm a nun. I work in the Vatican."

"A nun?" Trisha leaned forward, wide eyes on Maggie. "Re-e-e-ly! That's just so quaint! Were you disappointed in love?"

"No," Maggie replied, smiling, "I wasn't."

Trisha thought for a moment. Then her face lit up. "You were abused as a child!"

"No, I had a very happy childhood. I was raised in Montana, in a loving family, on a wonderful ranch. I loved to ride horses. I had the fun of being outdoors. I even loved school."

"Re-e-e-ly!" Trisha lapsed into silence.

Maggie pulled a book from her briefcase.

"You do like men, don't you?" Trisha asked. "I mean, you're not, you know, I mean...."

"I'm attracted to men, if that's what you mean," Maggie said in a matter-of-fact tone.

"Then why?"

"Why what?"

"Why did you become a nun?"

"I fell in love with the Gospel."

"Re-e-e-ly! I simply must read that sometime. Roland has an old Bible...somewhere."

"Good idea." Maggie opened her book.

Trisha pulled a paperback from her purse and opened it. "I do so love to read. It's so intellectually stimulating, don't you think?"

Maggie read the title. *Passion, Dusk to Dusk.* "I'm sure

it is," she said.

Trisha's lapse into silence lasted now, except for an occasional "oooh, oooh," until she was taken up with the in-flight movie.

Maggie rechecked her flight schedule. There would be time between flights at JFK Airport for her to make calls to friends at Highmount College. She had been president of the prestigious Highmount prior to going to Rome. Then she opened her book to a marker placed midway through its pages. *El Senor Presidente*, a novel by Miguel Angel Asturias, the Guatemalan winner of a Nobel prize for literature, traces the path of a dictator, a literary replica of the tyrants that have plagued Central America's history. Maggie was quickly captivated and saddened by the story of people living in terror under capricious, brutal and totalitarian controls.

When the pilot announced the beginning of their descent into New York, Trisha again donned her blindfold and slunk deeper into her seat.

Maggie thought of the papal credentials she now carried to Central America.

When she boarded her plane for the second leg of her journey that afternoon, Maggie felt elated by the friendly voices that had greeted her phone calls to Highmount College. Each had asked, "When are you coming back to us?" She didn't have an answer.

The flight was on time as it descended in the steamy, late-afternoon heat. The predominant whiteness of the capital city below surprised Maggie. Why did I expect pastels? she wondered. She carried her hand luggage across the tarmac to the customshouse. The rose-colored fabric of her suit quickly absorbed the heat and she was grateful for the air swirls of ceiling fans inside the building. When her luggage arrived, she rolled it along in the slow-moving line of people toward the customs inspector.

Outside the customshouse Maggie squinted under the still

bright sun. As she looked around, she spotted a young woman wearing a small black veil. Their eyes met.

The young woman approached. Her gaze dropping momentarily to the medallion that hung by a silver chain from Maggie's neck. "Are you Sister Margaret?"

Maggie smiled and nodded. "Yes, I am."

"My name is Sister Carmen."

"Thank you for meeting me, Carmen. And please call me, Maggie."

"The car is this way, Maggie." The young nun reached for the larger piece of luggage. "I can see that you are very tired."

As they drove, Maggie listened to Carmen's travelogue and watched tableau after tableau of this different culture pass by. Women walked along the dirt paths of the roadside, carrying large, round baskets on their heads. "Their dresses are so full of life and energy," she commented.

"Yes, they are beautiful. Each design is unique to a particular village. In that way we natives can identify each other's home."

Maggie watched the proud, erect bearing of the women and thought of her own ancestors, the women of Ireland. They wove their village's motif into the unbleached brocade of their men's sweaters. When a fisherman's body washed onto the beach after a storm at sea, the women knew his home from the motif.

"I forgot to tell you, Maggie," Carmen said. "The archbishop's secretary called our convent this morning to say that his excellency is indisposed, a stomach flu I believe. He said that your meeting with the archbishop is delayed from tomorrow morning to the next."

Maggie smiled. "I don't think I can object, do you Carmen?"

Carmen laughed. "Since you will be free tomorrow, I will show you the city. If you would like that. We are proud of it -- except for the poverty, of course."

"I would like that very much," Maggie replied. She shed the instant annoyance she felt at the impending delay.

Carmen pointed ahead to Maggie's side of the road. "That is Santa Maria park, where the sisters' bodies were found," she said.

"Can we drive into the park?" Maggie asked.

"Yes, of course. That will be no trouble. If you are not too tired?"

"Not for that," Maggie replied.

Carmen stopped the car near a flower bed. As Maggie opened the door, she heard the squawk of pink flamingos in the shallows of a nearby pond. She stood near the flowers, made the sign of the cross and bowed her head. Her imagination recreated the deadly scene and tears coursed the edge of her nose.

"Did you know them, Carmen?" Maggie asked when she re-entered the car..

"Sister Rosalita Chavez was of my congregation. She was so kind to the poor people. Sister Joan Delaney spoke to our convent once. I did not know Sister Miriam Weber."

"Have the police identified the killers?"

"No, Maggie. And we believe they will never do so. All of us believe the police were the killers. But, of course, we are helpless to prove that."

"The police blame the insurrectionists?"

"Yes, but to the police, anyone who tries to help the poor is an insurrectionist, a Marxist, or a leftist. And these sisters all worked for the poor. Why would those who help the poor kill others who do the same work? It makes no sense." Carmen pulled into a driveway and up to a tall wooden gate that opened instantly. Before them, the box-like convent rose in two stories of unadorned white stucco. A small statue of the Madonna rested on a plain brown adobe pedestal next to the entrance.

Inside the convent, after Carmen introduced her to the other nuns, Maggie began to feel warmth and security from their company. Later though, alone in her room, she tried to read and failed. Despite their familiar coverings of holy art and a crucifix, the thick walls of the convent were unable to hold out the strangeness of the land. She felt fearful, alien and unprotected. She knelt by the bed and prayed. "Lord, I feel so insignificant in this foreign land. Protect me. Give me courage." At length she slept.

The convent stood next to the Church of St. Francis. In the morning sun, the church's facade and bell tower bloomed in pastels of gray and pink. At mass, Maggie gathered confidence from prayer. She felt her breathing deepen and even out. Walking back to her pew after communion she sensed a growing strength and knelt with shoulders back. At breakfast in the convent she listened with growing admiration to the work stories of the sisters. These are real heroes, she thought, heroes chiseled day after day by the everyday work of feeding and educating the destitute. Their closeness increased her feelings of confidence.

Carmen drove to a market to begin the day's touring. The traffic's fast pace struck Maggie as a strange counterpoint to the measured pace of the pedestrians. At the market, Carmen led Maggie through a maze of stalls and open spaces where women, hunched down on their knees, waited behind baskets of their wares: oranges, bananas, beans, corn, glazed pottery, and more. Brightly colored clothes, hammocks and fabrics hung from wooden rods in the stalls. Maggie shopped the fabrics and selected a shawl. She stooped to the seller, a woman who sat weaving at a back-strap loom. The woman deftly moved the shuttle of yarn through the warp strings.

"How much?" Maggie asked, holding out the shawl. The woman answered in a Mayan language. They bartered then, with fingers and head shakes. Maggie, to Carmen's disappointment, made only a feeble attempt at lowering the price.

1 7

Men peddled bundles of wood as the xylophonic sounds of a Marimba band resonated with the bartering voices.

At midday they entered the Cathedral plaza. Primary colors decorated the umbrellas that rose above the strolling pedestrians. The huge bells in the twin towers of the great church began to peal their invitation to the *angelus* prayer. On entering the church, they were met by the pungent smell of incense. Inside, they walked the perimeter and studied the stained-glass windows and murals. Soon, however, Maggie's attention was pulled to the people. In a small side chapel, a man, his clothes showing his poverty, inserted a coin slowly into the slot below a tier of candles, lit a taper from a glowing candle, applied it to the wick of another, and then knelt on the stone floor in prayer. Maggie prayed that his prayer be answered. The odor of melting wax and smoke in the little chapel gradually overpowered the smell of incense. Watching the man, she sensed the mystery of the Mayans and wondered what was their blend of native and Christian beliefs.

They ended their tour with a walk through slums. Face to face with the poverty of these lovely people Maggie felt diminished by her relative affluence. Row upon row of low, crude shacks clung one to another for support. They looked to be constructed of everything dull and colorless, pasted together, absent of all symmetry. Women carried water jugs on their heads, and babies in slings on their backs. The smell of untreated sewage clung heavily to the air. Thin men, a dull sadness etched in their eyes and faces, sought any kind of shade in the afternoon sun. The men looked out at the exuberant play of laughing children who seemed unaware of poverty's claim on them.

At day's end, Maggie was exhausted. She realized it was not from the day's meager physical exercise, but from the visions of want and need whose weight she was unable to lift from her imagination.

The next morning, as Carmen drove her through the city

to her meeting with Archbishop Lucas Villariego, Maggie's sense of being alien returned. When they arrived at the episcopal palace, she stood for a moment at the car and looked at the impressive building, surprised that the sense of security it brought her was greater than her feelings toward its opulence. She was admitted to the palace by the archbishop's secretary, Father Antonio. Carmen walked to the nearby cathedral to wait and pray.

Archbishop Villariego brought his substantial bulk upright as Maggie was ushered into his office. "Welcome to our beautiful country, Sister Margaret," he said as Maggie was ushered into his office. "Beware or it will charm you into staying forever."

"Thank you, Archbishop. It is my first visit to your charming country," Maggie replied. She shook his extended hand.

Villariego beamed and gestured toward a thin, pallid cleric who rose from the obscurity of a large wing chair of soft leather. "Perhaps, Sister Margaret, you already know our papal nuncio, Monsignor Guerrolino?"

Maggie turned and extended her hand. "No, I do not believe we have met, Monsignor. I have been at the Vatican such a short time."

The nuncio mumbled his pleasure.

Villariego indicated a chair to Maggie and waited for her to be seated. "The Secretary of State informed us of your visit, Sister Margaret. He said that you come at the specific direction of the Holy Father and asked that we give you our full support. A needless request," he added. "We would, of course, do so without the asking. How may we be of help?"

Maggie leaned forward. "The Holy Father is greatly concerned, Archbishop, because the killing of nuns and priests is happening once again in your country. He had hoped this tragic scandal was history. He has directed the Congregation for Justice, for which he has given me the responsibility, to consult on these events and report directly back to him. I have decided to come personally."

"It gives me comfort that you do not delegate this responsibility, Sister. I will have the more confidence that truth will return to the Holy Father," Villariego replied. "What consultations do you plan?"

"I am pleased that I can begin with you, Archbishop and with Monsignor Guerrolino. I am hoping you can give me entry to those in power. Then I will consult with representatives of my fellow sisters, and with priests. After these consultations I would come back and share my findings with you. I am not given to secrecy."

Villariego's relief was apparent.

"It is indeed tragic, Sister Margaret, but once again the killings are the work of leftists," the nuncio interjected. His eyes, set close together on his thin face, opened wide as he looked at Maggie.

The archbishop sniffed. "As I say, Sister Margaret, it is good that you come. When you return to Rome you will be able to assure the Holy Father that we are dealing here with an exaggeration of the liberal press. It is not a problem for Central America only."

Maggie looked from man to man. "I realize, gentlemen, that crime is not limited to this country. But, surely, the rape and murder of three nuns, and the murder of a bishop, was not a fiction of the liberal press."

Villariego tilted his head back and looked down a bulbous nose at Maggie. "Hardly, Sister. But you must understand that our poor country is alive with insurrectionists. Investigations by our National Police reveal these crimes were committed by leftist insurrectionists who will stop at nothing to embarrass the legitimate government."

Maggie regarded the archbishop thoughtfully. "You seem so certain, Archbishop. Yet, many priests and nuns here seem to have a different opinion. They report that the present government will oppose any effort to help the poor, the Indians.

There is widespread belief among them that the National Police are themselves the killers."

"Then they are wrong," Villariego replied. "The police have no reason to do such things." He tugged at a heavy jowl.

"Is it possible that the police are supporting a government policy designed to bind the poor to their poverty? A policy that insures a virtual slave workforce for the wealthy landowners, perhaps?"

The nuncio turned his bland face to Maggie, eyes again wide. "But, Sister, surely you agree that the contest between labor and management is an ancient one, and again, not restricted to Central America. It is not the church's battle."

Maggie leaned forward, shoulders straight, and spoke softly. "But we're talking rape, Monsignor. We're talking slaughter, not labor negotiations."

Archbishop Villariego broke in soothingly. "Friends should not get into endless debate. Sister Margaret, General Castillo, the commanding officer of the National Police is my cousin. We are close. He is a good man, a good Catholic, a family man, a weekly communicant even. I am confident he would meet with you at my request. He can explain to you the work of the National Police better than Monsignor or myself."

Maggie was quiet for a time. Carmen had pointed out the Headquarters of the National Police on their city tour. The picture of the forbidding fortress returned. Will I be safe, she thought. Then she said it. "If we met in the National Police Headquarters, would I be safe?"

"Absolutely safe, absolutely," Villariego replied. "You will be under my protection. In fact, I will accompany you, if that will ease your worry."

"Thank you, Archbishop. A meeting with General Castillo would be a good place to start," Maggie responded, smiling her appreciation.

"It is my pleasure. I will call you when it is arranged."

The men stood. Villariego rang for his secretary, who saw Maggie to the palace entrance.

On the drive back to the convent Maggie told Carmen of her coming appointment.

Carmen echoed Maggie's earlier concern. "It is the lion's den, Maggie. Will you be safe?"

Villariego had reneged on being her companion. He was "indisposed." However, he assured Maggie that all had been prepared for her meeting with the general, and that he, the archbishop, had personally seen to her absolute safety. Carmen had volunteered to go with her, a proposal Maggie had refused. Carmen could offer no protection, and might put herself in jeopardy should Villariego be wrong in his assessment. She weighed the situation and decided to go ahead with the meeting on the strength of Villariego's assurances.

She shuddered at the sight of the cold, stone building as she emerged from the Archbishop's limousine in the heat of the early afternoon sun. A uniformed officer escorted her into the building and through long, stark corridors. Their steps echoed from the gray cement walls. A faint acrid odor stung Maggie's nostrils, but she could not identify it. She was admitted to a spacious, windowless office, bright with light, elegantly carpeted and filled with art. The apprehension that gripped her when the gate into the fortress had slammed shut faded now in the room's warmth.

General Roberto Castillo y Gomez, tall, thin and darkly handsome, rose from behind his desk and greeted her. His manner was distant and aloof, his posture stiff, his tone courteous. "The archbishop informs me of your curiosity, Sister Margaret. Do you think we are barbarians?"

"Thank you for seeing me, General Castillo. No, I do not think you are barbarians. I am here at the direction of the Holy Father. We are trying to understand why nuns and priests are being murdered."

"I too, would like to know the answer," the general said. "What I do know is that our country is infested with insurgents intent on the destruction of the legitimate government. It is my job to see that they do not succeed."

"But, those murdered nuns were not insurgents, General," Maggie responded quietly. "They wanted only to educate the poor."

"Perhaps that is so, Sister. But, I do not think it is so simple a matter. To my mind, many of the priests and nuns support these rebels by their education. As you say, they want to educate the poor, but it is this education that leads to insurrection. So, if priests or nuns would ever be shown to be insurgents, their religious garb will not protect them."

"General, what is it these insurgents want? Is it something more than jobs, something more than the ability to care for their families?"

"I think first they want chaos, Sister. They want to destroy the present order so that they can pillage the wealth of those who have worked for it. At the same time, they want to steal the land from its legitimate owners."

"Are they that ambitious? Could it not be they want only a share? Yesterday, I walked through one of the city slums. Is there no hope for those who live there?"

"That will take time. They must be patient."

"Would you be patient in their place, General?"

Castillo leaned back in his chair. "Perhaps not. But I am also impatient. I am impatient to insure safety for my wife and daughter, to insure that what has been accumulated for their well-being is not taken from them. I am impatient that my father, a strong force in the building of this country, is not deprived of what he has gained. I am impatient for the safety of my brother and his family, for the good citizens of this country. I fight for what belongs to me and to them. We cannot cure every weakness of society in a single day."

"Is this your daughter, General?" Maggie reached for a

framed portrait that sat obliquely on Castillo's desk.

"She is my life," Castillo responded softly.

"She is very beautiful," Maggie said, studying the figure. "How old is she?"

"She is just fifteen. I am very proud of her." The general's face relaxed slightly.

Maggie replaced the picture, sat back in her chair and studied the general's face. "Were those nuns killed by your police, General?"

Maggie's directness drew a long stare from Castillo. "No, Sister," he replied coldly. "The police do not murder."

"Who would want to kill them? Why were they killed, then?"

All softness was gone from Castillo's face. His dark eyes were coloring deeper. "It appears, Sister, that the insurrection is running out of steam. It needs martyrs, and so the insurrectionists provide their own."

Maggie looked at Castillo's face and squinted in thought.

"I apologize, but you must excuse me now, Sister," Castillo said abruptly. "I have an unanticipated meeting with the president. My deputy, Colonel Jorge Molina, will continue to assist you. If you will follow me, please."

Castillo led her down the hall to a door marked *Deputy for Operations.* He opened the door. The man at the desk stood and walked to meet them. He had a stocky build and a military-style crew cut.

Castillo made curt introductions. "This is Sister Margaret. She comes to us from the Vatican, Jorge." To Maggie, "This is Colonel Molina."

Molina did not respond to Maggie's extended hand.

She felt a chill from the Colonel's opaque eyes.

"Lock her up, Jorge," the General said. "Give her our most comfortable cell. But, do not kill her, yet." He turned cold, brittle eyes to Maggie. "So you see, we do not answer to the Vatican. You can go to hell."

Maggie watched the door close, then turned in shock to the colonel. His fist smashed into the center of her face and propelled her against the door. She fell, unconscious, to the floor.

****

The telephone nagged his ears, a distant irritation for Archbishop Lucas Villariego, who was focused on his entree. A servant had just placed a platter of quail before him and hints of their succulence rose in small wafts of steam. The butler answered the phone and Villariego tuned out the audible murmurs. He sniffed. Juices flowed in his mouth as he reached a fork to spear a bird and lift it to his plate. He carved one side of the tiny breast from its bone with practiced grace and brought a portion to his mouth. He closed his eyes as his tongue worked the shreds of meat for their last milligram of taste. A swooshed sip of wine cleansed his palate for the next mouthful.

"Excuse me, Excellency." The butler appeared at the door and waited to be recognized.

"Go away. I'm eating."

"I am sorry, Excellency, but the Mother Superior of St. Rita's Convent is on the phone. She sounds very worried. It is an emergency, she says."

"Tell her I'm eating." Lucas forked in another slice of quail.

"I told her that, Excellency."

"Tell her to call back." Bits of quail meat spewed.

"I asked her to do that too, Excellency. She says it is too important. She prefers to wait on the phone for you."

"Fine, let her wait."

"Yes, Excellency." The butler disappeared.

Villariego finished the first quail but the thought of the nun hanging on his phone proved to be excess salt, smothering the quail's flavor. God, these women are irritating, he thought, first that gringo from Rome, now this one. He pushed his bulk upward and walked to his office, wiping quail drippings from his mouth and fingers. "Yes, Sister, what is it that can't wait?" he asked, irritation honing edges on the words.

"Sister Margaret has not returned to the convent, Archbishop. She said she would return by five. It is now seven. I hoped that she might be with you, but your man says no. We sisters are worried for her."

Chills fastened on Villariego. "I have not seen her today," he answered. "She was to see General Castillo today, was she not?"

"Yes, Archbishop."

"Have you called his office?"

"Yes, Archbishop. I was not permitted to speak with the general. A Colonel Molina said he knew nothing of Sister Margaret. He was very abrupt."

"I'm sure there is nothing to worry about, Sister. I will make inquiries and get back to you. If she arrives there, you will let me know."

"Thank you, Archbishop."

Villariego returned to his table, sat, and looked at the food. Heat continued to rise from the quail. He raised his fork, then put it down. His appetite had flown, carried on gusts of images that blew through his mind. He ordered the food carried away. Then he returned to his office and called for his chauffeur.

"Yes Excellency, you called?" The uniformed chauffeur bowed as he entered the office and kept a slight bend to his head.

"Who do you think called for you?" Villariego asked. "Did you pick up that nun at the Police Headquarters as I instructed you?"

"I go there as you tell me, Excellency, but the soldiers tell me that the Sister had already departed. So I come immediately back here should you have need of me. Is it a problem, Excellency?"

"Bah, Idiot, get out of here," the exasperated Archbishop ordered. He watched the bent figure retreat through the door, then dialed the nuncio. "Is the nun with you?" he asked when Guerrolino answered.

"Nun? What nun?"

"That nun! The curia nun!"

"No. I have not seen her. Why"

"She is missing."

"Perhaps you should have accompanied her."

"And ruin my day?" Villariego groused.

"You were sure she would be safe."

"Castillo's word is his bond. I'd stake my life on it."

"You would like an appointment to the curia, and the red hat of a cardinal, Lucas? At the very least you may have staked those on Castillo's word."

"What do you suggest I do now?"

"You had better call Castillo."

Villariego dialed the general's personal number at police headquarters. Castillo answered.

"Ah, Cousin General, I'm so glad you are still at your office. I have been besieged by worried nuns."

"Now what?" Castillo was curt.

"The nun from Rome. Is she still with you?"

"No, she left hours ago." Castillo's voice softened a bit. "We had a very good meeting, by the way. She now understands our country very well, I assure you."

"She has not returned to her convent, General."

Castillo was silent for a time before he replied. "I can only tell you this, cousin Archbishop. When our meeting was over I asked my deputy, Colonel Molina, to drive her to the convent rather than have her wait for your limousine. I'm sure he had someone call your office to have you informed. If not, I apologize and will see that whoever is at fault is disciplined. Colonel Molina told me on his return that the nun asked him to drive her to the park. She wanted to pray, she said, at the place where the murdered nuns were found. He dropped her off at the very spot. Colonel Molina said he watched her kneel on the grass by the flowers. He is a sentimental man. He was very touched."

"Where could she be?" Villariego recognized the dead end and struggled to find a new path.

"Perhaps she is yet praying in the park, or walking there."

"She said she would return by five. She would be punctual," the archbishop argued weakly.

"It is possible," Castillo replied, "that the insurrectionists have her. They are everywhere. Perhaps..."

"Rome will be furious if she is harmed. I will be blamed." Villariego said peevishly.

"Do not worry yet, Archbishop. I will have my men begin a search for her at once. We may be lucky."

Villariego's stare was vacant, the phone still to his ear. His imagination raised specters of Vatican displeasure, obstacles to his ambition. Had he heard a derisive snort from Castillo before the phone clicked dead?

IL CERO

Maggie's flight to Central America followed, by a little over two years, an invitation from Cardinal Alberto Della Tevere. Would she come to Rome and discuss with him the role of women in the Church? Maggie had dismissed the thought that the invitation might carry any substance. Why me? she wondered. But she had long wanted to see Rome, so she went. She first met the cardinal in his office. He was taller than she expected, and gracious, and talkative. She was struck by the warmth of the brown eyes behind the perfectly round metal rim glasses.

Della Tevere had spoken of women who had graced the history of the church, but acknowledged that little recognition had been given them, except at times, post mortem. Would she, Sister Margaret, like to help change that? He must have read her physical reaction. "You are skeptical, Sister Margaret, yes?"

She leaned forward. "We've heard it so many times, Your Eminence. Women are to be honored, women are to be equal. It always ends with a bit of honor, but no equality. It just doesn't wash anymore."

"Wash?" he asked.

She was ready, had spent the previous days rehearsing and promising herself that she would not be submissive. She would instead search out the honest verbs. "The hierarchy has little credibility when it comes to women."

Della Tevere was attentive. "Tell me why you say this."

"In a word, exclusion. Down through history church leaders have excluded us from all decision-making in the Church. By doing so these men have effectively robbed us of our equality. What will happen when the day arrives that all women realize what churchmen have done to them?"

"Perhaps we can prevent that from happening."

"I doubt it, Your Eminence, at least if history is any indicator. When churchmen can no longer ignore or subjugate us, you study us. And we are tired of committees and commissions that go on interminably *studying* us. Nothing ever comes of it."

"Isn't holiness the real equalizer?" the cardinal asked.

"No!" she shot back. "That's the smoke the hierarchy blows in women's eyes to obfuscate the issue."

A sparkle ignited in Della Tevere's eyes. "Explain, please?"

"We're not talking holiness. We're talking power. We're talking participation when decisions on dogma and moral issues are made. We're talking participation in the decisions on laws that affect women, on who can be priests, on who are elected bishops and popes. We're talking honesty when the hierarchy employs the words *Sensus Fidelium*. There is no *sense of the faithful* when women's perspectives are either absent, or presumed present when filtered through male psyches." Maggie stopped and waited, expecting the typical lecture from on high. To her surprise, Della Tevere told her about a group called *Il Cero*.

"Il Cero means the candle," he said. "We are a group who seek to make the institution of the church, and its structures, a true servant of the love Christ wants us to have for each other. We study these structures, the organizational make-up, the departments of the curia, the way in which authority is wielded, the laws and rules, all to see if they truly are servants. We determine what needs to be changed. We change what we can. For now, it is little. But we wait for the day when our influence, our power as you say, is strong enough to complete our work." The cardinal then invited Maggie to meet Il Cero's members.

The meeting took place in the cardinal's spacious but austere apartment. Maggie delighted in the wit and intelligence of the group, and quickly felt comfortable among them.

A huge black mustache bounced soundlessly above the lips of Archbishop Claude Dupuis, deputy for general affairs, the number two man in the Secretariat of State. Under an insubordinate mass of black hair his face had a permanent doleful set, but his eyes gleamed with mirth. "You are this accomplished professor of European history, Sister Margaret. And yet, you have never visited Provence, the cradle of all civilization. How can this be?" he teased.

"Would you listen to that rubbish, now?" Archbishop Timothy Burns broke in. "Claude, this lady is obviously intelligent. She knows that French civilization never broke through the Neanderthal barrier. She also knows where the real cradle lies. Scotland! Of course!" Burns, a short, terrier-faced man, looked up at Maggie. "Instruct this poor Frenchman, will you, Sister?"

A tall, smooth-skinned Nigerian, Archbishop Francis Ibowale, joined the fray. "Have you two gentlemen ever heard of Africa? Any intelligent student of human evolution knows the cradle was there. Is that not so, Sister Margaret?"

Maggie looked at the men with fake seriousness. "I don't really know where the cradle was, gentlemen, but I do know this. Wherever it was, it was rocked by a woman."

Della Tevere, a listener until now, said simply, "Touçhe' Sister Margaret. Did I not tell you gentlemen that this lady will challenge us all?"

At that moment, Archbishop Frederick Patrick Sweeney entered the apartment. Maggie stared at him, then at Della Tevere. "Is he...?

Della Tevere answered, "Yes, Fred is a member of Il Cero."

For Maggie, all the memories came back in a flood, and all the feelings tied to those memories: the humiliation she felt when Sweeney engineered her dismissal as president of Padua College; her grief at the loss of her beloved Charles, his death an accidental consequence of Sweeney's inaction. The anger that continued to burn at Sweeney's name welled up in her. Face to face again, she was unable to contain her distaste for him. His presence was sufficient to discredit the entire group. She wanted to flee, and did.

The next morning in Della Tevere's office, the cardinal sounded like a replay of Maggie's speech pattern. "We're talking forgiveness here, Sister Margaret. We're talking what Jesus was all about. I know all about your difficulties with Archbishop Sweeney. And he knows now that his actions were not defensible. I know about the death of your friend, Father Charles Mueller. And Archbishop Sweeney knows that if he had acted sooner to help that priest-abused boy who shot Father Mueller, he might have prevented that killing. Do you have any idea how heavily that burden weighs upon him even today? If he could rewrite history, believe me, he would. And it is Archbishop Sweeney who recommended you to be a member of Il Cero. It was his assessment of your competence that brought you here. The important thing is that he has changed. Can you change, Sister Margaret?"

Did she have a choice? His words went directly to her hurt. "Forgiveness in the head is easy," she replied. "How do you get it into the heart?"

"If you are open to it, forgiveness will happen," the cardinal replied gently. "It is not something to force."

And it had happened. She came to know a different Fred Sweeney. With the knowledge, came forgiveness -- and respect. And from that moment, Cardinal Alberto Della Tevere had become Alberto, and she to him, Maggie. She had joined Il Cero, but not because of either Alberto or Fred. Charles was there in the decision, filling her memory with words from his letters:

Dear Maggie:

*I carry your questions home and ruminate
on them, like an old bull chewing his cud. It's one*

way I can carry you with me, inside, and hold you
there. You asked what I think is wrong with the
Church? Not much really. The problems lie at the
center, where power replaces authority at times and
monarchical nostalgia gets in the way of being
servants....

Three months after her meetings with Alberto, Maggie was back in Rome to stay. And now, nearly two years later, the Il Cero members were going to Fiesole, the village on the hills above Florence, for their annual retreat.

The Il Cero group had barely arrived in Fiesole when Alberto was called back to Rome to deal with the inquisitorial prying of Cardinal Johann Rolf. Rolf, Prefect of the Congregation for the Doctrine of the Faith, the erstwhile Holy Inquisition, a.k.a. the Holy Office. Somehow, Rolf had come upon a trace scent of Il Cero. Word had come to Alberto that Rolf was now baying to the scent and had loosed his entire pack of dissent-sniffing hounds on the trail. They had tied the mysterious Il Cero to Alberto, a scrap perhaps from Alberto's wastebasket. Alberto had left immediately.

As Maggie wandered the stalls of the outdoor Mercato Nuovo, the Straw Market in Florence, she thought that Alberto might even now be face to face with Rolf, disengaging the inquisitor's interest from Il Cero. Her mind wove tapestry upon tapestry of that confrontation as she picked and sorted her way through the leather and lace wares of the market.

From infrequent visits she had come to love Florence. And the straw market captured much of the Florentine spirit she so admired. She did not feel her usual distaste for shopping as she settled on a pair of leather gloves rather than lace table-setting mats for her friend, Kate, back in the States. She chose a black leather purse for herself. Enough.

Restless, she left the market and walked in the direction of the cathedral. What to do until Alberto returned from

Rome? Inside the cathedral she studied the Pieta by Michelangelo, so different, with the towering figure of Nicodemus supporting the Lord's body, yet diffused with the same pathos that dominates the Pieta in St. Peter's Basilica.

Next, she went to the Uffizi Gallery. Fred Sweeney had told her how frequently rooms X and XI of the gallery had called him back over the years. She was soon absorbed in Botticelli's *Allegory of Spring,* savoring the mood and feel of the Renaissance. After a time she moved to the *Birth of Venus.* Out of the corner of her eye she caught sight of a head with the same color hair as that of Venus, sandy red. It belonged to Fred Sweeney. She walked over.

"Hello, Maggie," he said on seeing her.

"Hi, Fred. You're back again?"

"I love this painting," he replied. "The young woman, blown to shore on the half shell of a giant scallop, evokes a personal meaning. I know what it is to be born again as an adult, to emerge from one's own calcareous husk a different person."

Maggie thought of the price he'd paid for that rebirth.

Fred looked at his watch. "It's about time I get back to Fiesole," he said.

"Can I catch a ride?" Maggie asked. "I took the bus down the hill."

"Sure," Fred answered. As he turned toward the door his right foot seemed to catch something that made him stumble. He caught himself and scanned the floor looking for what had tripped him. He found nothing.

Back in Fiesole, Fred locked the car and stood, looking out at the cypress-dotted hills.

"I think I'll take a walk in the gardens," Maggie said. "Care to join me?"

The convent of Santa Maria Dolorosa sprawled along the edge of a hill. The convent gardens overlooked the city of Florence. They walked into the main entrance of the convent, through the foyer and out again through a back exit into the gardens. Bubbling fountains and ancient busts of Roman unknowns, probably appropriated centuries earlier from the ancient theatre near the church, lined the travertine paths. Both Maggie and Fred were quiet as they walked toward the garden's edge.

"Beautiful day, you two, is it not?" The thin figure of Claude Dupuis emerged from its blend with the trunk and foliage of a cypress tree.

Maggie was momentarily startled. "Sorry, Claude, I didn't see you there." She looked at the doleful set of Claude's face and saw the absence of mirth in his eyes. "You're thinking of Alberto, like Fred and I are?"

Claude nodded. "What to expect? I do not know. My body, it runs hot and cold. One moment I am fearful, and I feel the chill of the mistral that blows down the Rhone valley of my home. The next moment I am confident, and I feel the heat of a Provence summer afternoon. You see, Maggie and Fred, it is my problem. I discover at age sixty-five that I do not yet possess the virtue of perspective. If we could only get our bodies tuned to the perspective of our faith, there would be no anxiety, is it not so?"

They stood there, by a low wall at the garden's edge, and looked down, taking in the panoramic sweep of Florence on the plain eight hundred feet below. Maggie scanned the landmarks that rose above the city's red-tiled roofs: the cathedral's round red cupola; Giotto's white, green and rose marbled campanile; and the crenelated ramparts and tower of the *Palazzo Vecchio.* So beautiful, she thought, so free in its appearance from the blood and sweat, disease and death that were part of its making. She turned to Claude. "I've finished the report you wanted," she said.

"Bon. We are ready, I believe," Claude said. "When Alberto returns, we will have the quick review, and then..." he stopped in thought.

Maggie and Fred let the silence stand for a time. Claude was Il Cero's number two, the organizer. He had taken the conclusions of the group and fashioned an organizational structure that could execute those conclusions.

At length, Fred asked, "How long do you think we have?

"The Holy Father is ill beyond recovery, this much we know," Claude responded. "But no one knows how long it will be. If his body keeps pace with his will, it may be...." Claude lifted his forearms.

Who would inherit the power? They had talked of it so often. Alberto might be elected, but only if the front runners, Cardinal Johann Rolf, number one at The Holy Office, and Cardinal Marco Gattone, *Camerlengo* of the Holy Roman Church, held each other to a draw. Then, Alberto was the logical one to rise through the pack as a compromise candidate. They had done their own count, and Alberto's election seemed to be a solid bet. Or were they only naive and blindly hopeful? All their work had been predicated on getting the power to implement.

That night Maggie couldn't sleep. Restless, she turned on the light and read from a biography of St. Francis. That's it, she thought suddenly. Assisi! The idea flooded in and flushed out her restlessness. I'm going to Assisi. It will be at least three days before Alberto returns.

In the morning she was packed and headed for her car. She met Fred in the parking lot. "I forgot to give my report to Claude last night," she said. "Would you give it to him if I get it? I'm off to Assisi. And I don't want the report lying about."

"Sure," Fred replied. "What's with Assisi?"

"Back to my roots. I need to fill my tank with the spirit of Clare and Francis. It'll be a retreat."

Maggie ran back to her room for the report, returned and handed the manila folder to Fred.

Fred reached for the folder, but it slipped from his fingers. "Butterfingers!" he said aloud as he knelt to retrieve it and push back the papers that had protruded. "I'll see that Claude gets it first thing," he said. "And while you're filling your tank, don't forget to put some good Tuscan Chianti in it. It'll fuel your walks on Mount Subasio."

"Take care, Fred. I'll be back on Friday." She put her hand on his arm. "You look as if you didn't sleep. Get some rest."

Fred stood and watched Maggie drive off, his fingers on the spot she had touched.

Maggie drove down the winding road to Florence and entered the busy traffic of the city. Three quarters of the way through the city she stopped for a red traffic light in a residential section. As she started to pull away when the light turned, the passenger door opened suddenly and a man jumped into the front seat.

"Go, Lady, go," he commanded. "We are in danger."

Maggie reacted automatically and pressed the car's accelerator. "Who are you?" she demanded. "Why are you in my car?" She looked over at the gasping man whose face was turned to the rear window.

"My name is Giulio," he said, catching his breath, his eyes fastened to the road behind them.

Fright took hold of Maggie. She pulled to the side. "You just get out of this car, right now!" she ordered.

"Please, Lady, it is not safe. I am sorry that I have placed you in danger, but the danger is from other men. Do not be afraid. With me you are safe. I am a very moral man. But, please to drive on. We are not safe yet. I will explain."

Maggie hesitated, but then pulled back into traffic. "What are you running from? What is the danger?"

"I run from bad men, Lady, from men who have just now shot my good friend and would have shot me."

Maggie absorbed that information in silence and gave attention to the narrow streets and the traffic. She looked over at Giiulio, who had submerged into silence beneath intense dark eyes. She sensed his controlled feelings of outrage. Unsure of what to say, "I'm sorry about your friend," she said.

"Thank you, Lady," Giulio responded, surfacing.

"How did it happen?" Maggie asked. "Or can't you tell me?"

"I can tell you, Lady. Today is the wedding day of my friend, Salvatore. It is a magnificent celebration. Salvatore is very wealthy. But, like me he grew up poor in Naples. Today he marries into very old patrician family of Florence. They go so far back as the Medicis. After the wedding, I am standing with Salvatore in the study of his palazzo. We are both feeling so good. Below us in the courtyard there are many, many people, all smiling, all drinking the champagne. Salvatore's bride is below us also, beautiful in white gown and pearls. She sees us and flashes her black eyes at Salvatore. I say to Salvatore. You should join your bride. She gets so much attention she may forget who you are. Salvatore runs his finger along the zipper of his pants. 'She will not forget, I promise you that, Giulio,' he says. 'I have made the lasting impression.'"

Maggie felt a blush warm her cheeks.

Giulio continued, "Salvatore turns to me and says, 'But you are right, Giulio, I must return. You are coming?' "No," I say, "I am enjoying this wonderful scene--and my espresso. I will come soon." I watch for Salvatore to emerge below me. And then I see what I will never forget. I see faces of men I know to be enemies. I see their guns. I see the smoke and hear the bark, bark of the guns. I see Salvatore's face pain, and then Salvatore falls, so slowly it seems. I see a smile on the face of the bride's father. And then I run. Me. Fifty years old. I feel like I am running like a cat. I run through the front door, and lucky, I run into a man with a gun, knocking him to the ground. Perhaps he waits for me. I continue to run. There are many people on the street so he cannot shoot at me. I run to the intersection and jump in your car. I do not know what else to do. I can run no farther. I am not so young anymore."

"I'm sorry for your friend," Maggie said.

"Thank you again, Lady," Giulio said. "I will grieve him very much, but no more for now, not until justice has been done to his killers."

"Are you a policeman?

"No, Lady, I am too honest for that."

Maggie's eyebrows raised involuntarily. She took another look at Giulio. "Government?"

"No, Lady."

"Mafia?" Now, why did I ask that, she thought.

Giulio sat forward, his head tilted and turned to Maggie, giving the impression that he was looking up at her. "No, Lady. They are in Sicily. I am from Naples."

Maggie took the time to look at him carefully. The genuine distress in his swarthy face disarmed the last vestige of her fear. "Where do you want me to take you?" she asked.

"Where are you going, Lady?" he countered softly.

"To Assisi."

"Bene, I will go with you to Perugia. It is on your way. I will pay you well, Lady."

"There is no need to pay, Giulio."

"I like the way you say, 'Giulio,' Lady. But I do not know your name."

"Maggie. It's short for Margaret."

"Maggie, Maggie," Giulio repeated slowly. "Guh, Guh. It sounds too harsh for such a pretty lady. Margaret is softer. It fits better."

Maggie laughed. "You don't know me, Giulio. The hard G's fit, believe me."

"Do you live in Florence or Assisi, Maggie?"

"Neither. I live now in Rome."

"Ah, Rome, bella. I am often in Rome." He looked at the

ring on Maggie's hand. "I see you are married. Do you have children, Maggie?"

"No, I'm not married, Giulio. I'm a nun."

His native superstitions took hold of Giulio and he pulled in a sharp breath. He moved the fingers of his right hand to touch his belt buckle, a move to protect his virility, or whatever it was, he couldn't remember exactly, that needed protection. "A nun? You are a Sister?" he asked, his eyes wide. "Yes."

Giulio leaned forward again and turned to Maggie, his eyes moving up and down to examine her. "But, you are so pretty. And you have wonderful legs."

Maggie's skirt had hiked up several inches. She pulled it taut to her knees as her face reddened slightly. "Isn't it all right for nuns to be pretty?" she asked, turning onto a ramp of the Autostrada del Sole. With a deft sureness she pulled out onto the autostrada and increased the speed of the car.

Giulio shook his head. "I have not ever talked to a Sister, except when I was a little boy." He pulled the sun visor down and fixed its mirror so that he could view the road behind. "Do you believe in fate, Sister Maggie?"

"I believe in Divine Providence, if that's what you mean," Maggie responded. "Why?"

"Because I have this feeling inside. It is a feeling that fate, or your divine providence, has brought us together for a reason."

They stopped briefly at a service center for Giulio to make a telephone call. As they drove on, Giulio's curiosity led to a series of questions that kept Maggie busy responding. By the time they reached Perugia an hour later, Giulio possessed a mental dossier on Maggie. She realized later that she knew no more of him.

Giulio again leaned forward and turned his face to Maggie. "You have done me a favor, Sister Maggie, that I cannot fully repay. You do not know how big is this favor. But I know.

And I tell you this, Sister Maggie. I am your friend whether you are my friend or not. But I would like you to be my friend." It was a question.

"I would like that, Giulio," Maggie responded openly, looking into Giulio's face.

"Bene," Giulio said quietly. "Today I have lost a friend who was like a brother to me. But I have gained a sister--a sister who is a Sister. I must tell you, I am not yet believing this. I will come to see you in Rome, Sister Maggie. Now, if you will please to take the next exit, I will direct you. It is not far."

"There, that is the road," Giulio said shortly after they left the autostrada. "My friends will meet me down that road. You can hear their helicopter now."

As they drove slowly down the road, a helicopter descended cautiously to a field at the edge of the road, a short way in front of them. Giulio was quickly airborne.

In Assisi, Maggie walked down a small flight of stairs to the crypt of the Basilica of St. Clare. There, she looked at the shriveled body of Clare in its gold and glass casket. Unaccustomed to visual displays of corpses, she shuddered and felt an immediate revulsion. She prayed silently, asking for Clare's support, and then let her imagination bring Clare alive. She pictured Clare walking the slopes of the Assisi hills with St. Francis and wondered about the love between them. Had it been like her love for Charles Mueller, and his for her? Had it been as affirming and strengthening as Charles' love for her?

Only after his death had she admitted to herself that she loved Charles. Had he known? Had he been equally affirmed by her love? She had learned, also after his death, of his love for her. It sailed the pages of his letters. Charles had never mailed the letters. They had been delivered to her, unopened, by Fred Sweeney at her office in Highmount College.

She summoned the memory of Charles's image, the shock

of auburn hair, the smiling hazel-green eyes, the strong line of his jaw. She watched him take a lemon drop from the bowl on her office table, his eyes dancing with laughter.

She had never speculated on where their love might have led them. They were both committed to their religious vocations. But she felt his love for her as the crown of her achievements, a gift that let her look at herself in a new, more confident way. It brought more confidence than her rise to the presidency of Padua College in her mid-thirties, more even than the success she had in raising the college to a recognized first rank. It gave her a greater sense of strength than her survival when she was dumped from that presidency through the connivance of Bishop Sweeney and his cronies on the Board of Trustees. I hope Francis's love did as much for you, Clare, she thought.

Two days later, Maggie joined Fred and Claude in the convent's guest dining room at Fiesole. The simple rectangular room had plain white-painted walls and a red tile floor. Small red squares garnished the white oilcloth coverings on the two tables that allowed space for sixteen. The windows looked out on the garden. Claude had celebrated an early mass for the three and they waited for breakfast. The smell of bacon drifted into the room.

Maggie sipped hot chocolate slowly. She looked up from her newspaper and held up her cup. "The two of you must make me a promise," she said. "When I'm dying and can no longer eat, you will instruct the hospital staff to feed chocolate to me intravenously. Promise?"

"Bon," Claude replied, his eyes merry in the melancholy frame of his face. "Let us make the pact, the three of us. When I am at that point in my life, you will see that they fill my veins with the red wines of Provence, say vintage Chateauneuf-du-Pape, or Cotes-du-Rhone. What will it be for you, Fred?"

"Coffee," Fred replied, "thick black coffee. I want to be

wide awake for my going forth."

"You're good sports," Maggie said, laughing. "We have a deal."

The three returned to their newspapers. Maggie read *Corriere della Sera.* The paper had become the main source of her Italian proficiency. Claude buried himself in *Le Figaro,* Fred in *The International Herald Tribune.*

Maggie's eyes caught the small headline. "Florentine Notable Found Dead." It was a family tragedy. The wealthy and titled man was found floating, face down, in the Arno. Preliminary medical examination had found no sign of violence. The death followed by only several days the shooting of the man's son-in-law on his wedding day. The bereaved wife and daughter were in seclusion. It was speculated that the man had taken his own life in a moment of despondency. Maggie raised her head over the newspaper. "I didn't tell you of my meeting with a man who called himself Giulio. It was most unusual. I was driving through Florence on my way to Assisi...."

Dead Men's Bones

ALBERTO DELLA TEVERE
-- CARDINAL

Cardinal Alberto Della Tevere relaxed his tall slender body into a comfortable window seat on the *Eurostar Italia*, and his long, slim fingers massaged a late afternoon stubble. His face, thin and ascetic, and accented by round, metal-rim glasses, was at contrast with the vitality of his frame. He was barely seated when a gentle jolt signaled the train's start on its swift run to Rome.

When the train was clear of Florence Alberto was soon caught up in memories evoked by the rolling countryside, its fields and vineyards. Born into a patrician Milanese family, the second of four sons, he was nonetheless connected to the countryside and its soil. His father, titled, had been both a banker and a landowner. The family estates dotted the Po Valley. And they owned extensive vineyards in Tuscany and Veneto, and land in Sicily. Alberto recalled the hard labor in Verona vineyards required of him and his brothers during their vacations from school. Wealth did not excuse them. Count Della Tevere understood work as connected to the soul's growth. When his sons were old enough, they could choose their own work, but while under his roof they would do the work he chose for them. The Contessa chose the work for their two daughters.

Alberto thought of that labor, and of the calluses he had earned, and acknowledged his father's wisdom. He had learned respect for all honest work, and for the workers. Still, he had been happy to escape into the work of academia, and the labor of the mind. As a child he received private schooling from carefully selected tutors. Then he had gone to Oxford, his choice, for university. There, by the simple chance of watching a debate, he became acquainted with the writings of Cardinal Newman. As his interest in Newman grew, so did his Catholic faith. He returned from England intent on entering the seminary. The count, cool but accepting, had cautioned him. "It is perhaps easier to save your soul as a lay person, Alberto." The Contessa was thrilled. "He will be pope someday," she predicted.

Alberto's attention was snapped back to the present as a tall, dark-haired young woman entered the eight passenger compartment. She stood at the doorway and inspected the compartment walls until her eyes came to rest on a small plaque. Its message: "*Vietato Fumare*" and the design of a lit cigarette crisscrossed by an X. She took a seat, opposite Alberto, but several seats from the window. Alberto fought the urge to stare. The woman was a near replica of his sister, Gina, of thirty years before.

The image of Gina, who was next to Alberto in descending sibling order, filled his imagination as he turned back to the window. He saw the two of them, inseparable as children, playing "Mass." He saw the nine year old Gina announce at dinner to the entire family that she would be a priest when she "grew up." He heard again the ridicule aimed at Gina by another brother. He heard again the patient explanation from his mother that only men can be priests. He saw again the stunned look on Gina's face, and heard the simple logic of her reaction. "It's not fair." That scene was always the first to come to mind whenever Alberto thought of Gina. She never mentioned it, but Alberto knew that from that moment she was suspect of the church.

Gina's rebellion at being sent to a convent school, her behavior there so outrageous, had been traumatic both for the school and for her parents. In the end, Gina attended a non-sectarian school in Switzerland, and then studied at the highly-rated law school of the University of Michigan. She now practiced corporate law at a prestigious law firm in New York City.

4 6

They were still close, Gina and Alberto. But her disappointment with the church showed at times. At his episcopal ordination celebration she had stood next to him before a wall of mirrors. He wore his episcopal cassock, complete with red piping. With one arm held high she turned before the mirror in a slow elegant circle. "Caro Alberto, if the church wants someone to wear dresses, don't you agree that women wear them better?"

Alberto knew how many layers of cultural assumptions he had shed before he saw what Gina had seen at age nine....

"Would you care for some?"

Alberto turned to see the young woman holding out a paper plate toward him. His eyes lit at the assortment of cheeses and crackers. "Ah, how kind of you. I must tell you that I love cheese, every kind of cheese." He reached for a slice of cheese and a cracker. "My name is Alberto Della Tevere."

"Mine is Lisa Martini." She stood and moved to the seat directly opposite Alberto. "You are a priest?"

At his core, Alberto had a thirst for simplicity. He was a questioner, always searching for the simple heart of complex problems and of people. He was simple also in his life style. He loved people most, and would listen with full attention to anyone's story. "Yes, I am a priest. Are you a university student, Lisa?" By the time they reached Rome, Alberto had listened to a new story, and Lisa knew that besides cheeses, Alberto loved wit and all kinds of music, especially jazz, and that he played the piano.

In his office on the *Piazza Pio XII* Alberto held a narrow, three-ring binder and slowly revolved it in his hands. So small, he thought, so very small after so many years of work. He opened the binder and began to file through the pages. As each conclusion registered, the image of its originator came to mind: Claude Dupuis, Fred Sweeney, Maggie. Maggie's image lingered. It has been so difficult for her, he thought, so much more difficult than for the men.

He recalled that first meeting with Maggie in his office, how history had filled the room, an overflow from her vast memory. He had always felt a hazy debt to history for its lessons, but never had its importance been displayed with such vivid examples.

When, finally, she consented to join Il Cero and come to Rome he felt compelled to warn her. "It is clear from history is it not, Maggie, that a simple declaration, even an infallible one, won't create equality for women in the church? We already have such declarations. They are, as you say, already on the books. But they accomplish nothing. So, it is equally clear that the equality we seek will require a political solution, a change in institutional structures. And that means we must have the power to change those structures. Is that not another lesson of history?"

"Yes, of course."

"Along the way to this power, you will be personally tested. Can you see that as well?"

"I have been tested before," she replied.

Alberto had seen the question rise in her eyes.

"How will I be tested?" she asked.

"In a number of ways. First of all, you will be bored. In this Vatican culture you will be excluded from activities done with bare adequacy by men, activities that you could perform with greater efficiency. At best, you will be allowed to watch. Can you bear that?"

"I've been bored before. I'll find a way around it. How else will I be tested?"

"Here in the Vatican you will be ignored, invisible to all but Il Cero members, invisible like a kitchen drudge to the lord and lady of the manor. This is a culture of men who give honor only to Mary, and sometimes to their mothers."

"Invisible is not all bad," Maggie replied. "I can handle that. Any other tests?"

"Yes. You will be insulted by clerics who will truly believe they are complimenting you."

Alberto smiled at the recollection of one such event. It occurred in his own apartment where he was entertaining a group of clerics. Maggie was there. Johann Rolf, Cardinal Prefect of The Holy Office approached Maggie. "Would you agree, Sister, that women find their nobility as wife and mother?"

"Yes, of course, Cardinal Rolf. Just as men find their nobility as husband and father. But I wonder where that leaves you and me. I am neither wife nor mother. You are neither husband nor father. Is there no nobility for us?"

"I am a cardinal," Rolf sputtered.

Maggie smiled sweetly. "Well, then, I guess I get the short straw." She left the holy inquisitor staring quizzically after her.

Maggie had herself laughingly reported other such incidents to Il Cero members. "You are reported to be an excellent grammarian, Sister Margaret. Would you be interested in managing our word processing pool?" "The food at our college suffers terribly, Sister Margaret. Would you consider taking over our kitchen?" "Would you believe, Sister Margaret, we get requests from women asking to be dispensed from their womanhood so they can be priests?"

It had taken Della Tevere's personal intervention to insure that Maggie had free and complete access to the Vatican archives. She had buried herself there, emerging periodically to furnish Il Cero with her historical insights.

Alberto picked up his phone and dialed Cardinal Rolf at The Holy Office. Rolf was out, but his deputy, Angus Dilford, took the call. No, there would be no problem, Angus had declared after examining Rolf's calender, for Della Tevere to meet with Rolf at 10:00 the next morning.

The colorless Palace of The Holy Office sits to the left and front of St. Peter's Basilica and lies hidden behind Bernini's expansive colonnade. Alberto's long legs carried him down its halls in graceful strides. His energies surged in moments of challenge. Today was no different. He was escorted into an office where Cardinal Johann Rolf rose to greet him.

"Johann, it is so good of you to see me." Alberto made himself the petitioner, Rolf his benefactor.

Rolf was gracious. His tanned, handsome face broke into a bland smile.

"It has come to my attention, Johann, that you are making inquiries concerning a mysterious Il Cero. It is true, is it not?"

Rolf said it was incidental, of no consequence, but yes, he had inquired.

"Ah, good if it is incidental only, because, of course, it is. I will explain it. There is no mystery. Il Cero is but a group of retreatants. I, myself, am a member of this group. We call ourselves Il Cero with the naivete of children, hoping to be a light to others. We have been making retreats, studying and meditating together for years. You, yourself, might be interested to join us. I invite you. We are about to make such a retreat at a convent in Fiesole. The good archbishop, Claude Dupuis, whom you know, is our retreat master." Alberto saw the hint of disappointment in Rolf's eyes.

Rolf declined the invitation, but Alberto persisted. "Johann, we are soon to lose our Holy Father. We both know this. Everyone says that you will succeed him. As your friend, let me tell you this. The only concern I have ever heard about you is a slight doubt about your spirituality."

Rolf's eyes widened.

"Please do not be disturbed by this. I am sure it is not so. But not everyone knows you as I do. It is only a perception by how many, I do not know. But, trust me, a retreat now, at this time, would erase any doubt. Where was he when the Holy Father died? they will ask. You will have been called back to Rome from your retreat. Everyone will know this. Come, join us."

Alberto's smile was welcoming, but Rolf again declined. That evening, Alberto responded to the doorbell of his apartment. He opened the door to the grinning, pocked face of an old friend, Cardinal Marco Gattone, *Camerlengo* of the Holy Roman Church.

"Alberto, it is always good to see you," Gattone said as he removed a cape and threw it over a chair. "But, as we are always truthful to each other, I confess it was Benito's cooking that lured me here tonight."

"Welcome, you old cat. Benito runs my life. Watch out or he will be running yours."

"If I could steal him from you, I would."

"Now you scare me, Marco. That is too much honesty. Did you know that Benito has named a dish after you. He calls it *Melanzana Gattone di Trastevere.*"

"I know this. It is what brings me here this evening. That and the martini you are about to get for me."

They took chairs, like old friends, without formality. Benito's short, thin figure appeared with cocktails already prepared.

"How did you know what Benito is serving tonight?" Alberto asked

"When I received your invitation, I called Benito immediately. Thank you, Benito," he said, reaching for his martini. "You make the best martini."

"*Prego, Eminenza.*" Benito bowed. Punctilious and proudly so, he was a servant to his core.

Gattone continued. "Do you imagine for a minute, Alberto, I would have you determine my supper? What would I eat, then, Benito, bread and soup?"

"Benito," Alberto said, "this crotchety old cat says he wants to employ you. Beware, he smiles but he is a tyrant."

Benito nodded, chuckled and left for the kitchen. He had heard it all before.

At dinner, the two men grew serious.

"How long, Marco?" Alberto asked.

Gattone held up his arms. "A day, maybe ten. Certainly not more. He is desperately ill."

"Is he in pain?"

"No, the doctors control that."

"Is he alert?"

"Oh yes, he is still in charge."

"How is his mood?"

"Ugly. He does not yet believe that, like for the rest of us, death is his portion."

"And then?"

"Then we elect a successor."

"We had better eat this soup before it cools. Have you now convinced Benito to name it *Minestrone alla Gattone.* Save room for your melanzana." Alberto dipped his spoon and tasted. "Ah, it is very good, the beans and vegetables."

When Benito had collected the soup dishes, Alberto turned to Marco. "They say that it will be a close race between you and Johann Rolf, Marco. Do you see it that way?"

"That is what I hear, my friend. But I also hear that should Rolf and Gattone deadlock, Alberto Della Tevere may well rise to take the prize. Do you agree?"

"Yes, I think that is possible. I wanted to tell you, Marco, that I would be immensely pleased to kneel for your apostolic blessing."

"Thank you, Alberto."

"But," Alberto continued, "I will also accept the office should it be offered me. I need to be open with you on that as well."

Gattone reached a hand to Alberto's arm. "We understand each other well, my friend. Whatever happens, we shall be friends."

****

Back in Fiesole, the checkered oilcloths were removed from the dining tables, and Alberto presided from the head of one of the aged plank tables. "My friends, we no longer have the worry of Johann Rolf making capital of Il Cero. Before I left Rome this morning I talked with him one last time. He has declined my invitation to join with us in our retreat, but was leaving Rome for a retreat at the monastery of Monte Cassino."

Alberto looked around the table at the six others. Together with Maggie, Claude and Fred were Archbishops Timothy Burns, Francis Ibowale and Antonio Sanchez. Burns, a short, fiery Scotsman; Ibowale, a tall, thin, majestic Nigerian; Sanchez, a short, pudgy Brazilian. All except Maggie held second-tier jobs in the Curia. All smiled a knowing response to Alberto's success at disarming Rolf.

Alberto never gave the impression of hurry. His warm brown eyes met the eyes of his companions one by one. His long slim fingers tapped gently on the planking. "My friends, we are soon to see if God will bless our labors." He consulted the thin three-ring binder and held it up. "It seems so little, does it not? After all our labors? Our shovels have been busy. We have discarded so much more than we saved. But this little that remains shall be like the mustard seed. We shall together watch it grow. Still, as small as this is, I have a summary for you. Fred found it for us." He held up a scroll and his long thin fingers slowly pulled it open. "This poster was used several decades ago, in 1970 to be exact, as a symbol of Earth Day in the United States. Earth Day was a day set aside to promote protection of the environment. The creatures you see are the creations of one Walt Kelly. They live in a swamp called Okefenokee. This one on the poster is called Pogo. Alberto lifted a second cartoon from the table, "and this one is his friend, Albert. Do you think he looks like me? I think his nose is longer than mine." Alberto turned his head aside to pose.

"I see the slightest resemblence," Claude responded, to the group's delight.

Alberto waited for the polite laughter to subside. "What is important is Pogo's words. *'We have met the enemy and he is us.'* It is beautiful, don't you think? It captures so much of our work."

"Now," Alberto continued, "I must remind all of you that it is forbidden to campaign for the papacy. One does not publish his intentions in this regard, nor does one publish a platform on which he intends to make his run. However, as we know, there are ways to make oneself known to the cardinal electors so that one's visibility is enhanced. We have already done that in many ways. I only wish the candidate could be one of you and not me."

There were murmurs of dissent from the six. Claude spoke. "Only you have a chance. Only you are a cardinal. And we know the next pope will be chosen from the cardinals. Also, from among us, you are our choice."

"Thank you," Alberto replied, regret audible in his voice. "And I will try. If we are to succeed there is much work to do. We have done all we can for now. The rules are very strict. And I want you all to be aware of them. You must all read the Apostolic Constitution, *Universi Dominici Gregis* of Pope John Paul II. I will later give you copies. For now I will summarize for you two pertinent sections, 79 and 81. Those sections forbid anyone, including even the cardinal electors, to plan for a papal successor, or to promise their votes, or to make any kind of decision in advance of and in regard to a papal election. The penalty of excommunication is imposed for violations of this directive. The document does not, however, forbid an exchange of views concerning the election during the period when the Holy See is vacant."

Alberto put the constitution on the table with slow deliberation, then looked up. "Cardinal Gattone informed me last night that it is a matter of days, perhaps only hours, for the present Holy Father. We can do nothing now but we should be ready for the nine days of mourning, the *novemdiales,* and for the other days before the opening of the conclave. After the Holy Father's death we will have a minimum of fifteen days, a maximum of twenty before the conclave begins. Each of you, Maggie excepted, will have many contacts to make with the cardinals of your respective areas of influence. Fred: the North American contingent; Timothy: the Commonwealth; Francis: Africa and Asia; Antonio: Central and South America: Claude: Europe, except for Italy. I will deal with the Italian cardinals. The purpose of our meetings will be the 'exchange of views.' We will gather again in Rome before the conclave. Maggie will continue her research and support us as we have need. Someday, God willing, we will return the favor. Are there any questions? If not, we will go to the chapel now for the conclusion of our retreat."

The convent chapel's simple Gothic interior was lined on its outside wall with stained glass windows. In the afternoon sun their Giotto-like figures ripened into bright colors as Claude Dupuis rose to close the retreat. He stood at the center aisle's front, his audience of six clustered in the rough pews to one side. "Our retreat, it comes to the close," he said. "If I may leave you with one thought, it is this. It is the virtue of freedom, the freedom of love, that we must cultivate in ourselves and inspire in others. The virtue of freedom is the power, the ability to be for our fellow humans for their own sake. It is freedom from the self. It is the freedom of love. Only the person who is able to love is truly free. It is in the exercise of this freedom, by loving others, that we are most fully spiritual and most fully human. We are not called to be puppy dogs who lick their master's hands and wag their tails *because* they are fed and cared for. And, if we are to lead, we must not treat out fellow humans as puppy dogs. We must impose no other tether, and request no other bond than a love that springs from freedom. May God bless our journey."

JOHANN ROLF -- CARDINAL

Cardinal Johann Rolf raised his eyes to the tall, gangly figure in his doorway. "Come in, Angus," he said.

Archbishop Angus Dilford's long legs carried him awkwardly but quickly to a seat in front of Rolf's desk. As he opened a notebook on his lap, he peeked up at the Rubenesque nude on the wall behind Rolf.

Rolf, catching the movement of Dilford's eyes, winked a mischievous eye. "Did she wiggle her tush at you, Angus?" he asked.

Dilford's face reddened slightly as his hand moved to cover a muted cackle.

"What's on the menu for today?" Rolf asked, pleased with himself at snaring his subordinate's voyeuristic act. Since he did not generally invite visitors to his office, he had placed the painting on the wall some months before for this amusement.

Dilford, looking up from his notebook, replied, "Barcos!"

Rolf leaned back in his chair. "Ah, yes. Tomas Barcos, our heretical Brazilian. What has he done now?"

"He declines, 'respectfully' of course, to provide the explanations we have required of him. He will, he says, provide them when he is not so busy."

"Which is when?"

"Barcos is always busy." Dilford used an index finger to push thick spectacles back up onto the bridge of his nose. "I believe that Barcos will always be too busy."

"Refresh me on Barcos. I can't track all these cuckoos."

"Exaggerated focus on the importance of a non-corrupt clergy. Preaches against the 'minor extortions,' his words, stipend for this, stipend for that, the fat priests. Wants to cleanse the clergy of their worldliness. A throwback to the Albigenses, Waldenses, and Hussites. He has personally embraced a real poverty, and so have the clergy who follow him."

"How will we get him for that?"

"He advises people to go to priests who are worthy. We read that as an attack on the validity of the sacraments when performed by the, ah, unworthy."

"I haven't seen his writings yet," Rolf said, a touch of irritation in his voice. "Weren't you going to bring them to me?"

"That's the catch. He hasn't written anything. He only preaches. We have tapes now, and they've been transcribed. Do you want to see the transcriptions?"

"No writing? What influence can he have? If we went after every pipsqueak local preacher who talks crazy because he doesn't know any better, we'd need an army. Why do we even bother with this cuckoo?"

"He's not all that small. Right now he's limited to the city, but he and his clique are pulling in people in large numbers -- some in churches, but mostly away, in the open. He may be isolated now, but this could easily spread. It has a contagiousness about it."

"Do we have anything else on him?"

"Barcos has a woman and lives with her."

"Cardinal Jimenez should crack down on him."

"He'd like to. But his eminence, whose limitations you know, feels trapped." Dilford again pushed up his glasses and directed magnified eyes at Rolf. "If he hammers the guy on the basis of discipline, he's afraid of the popular response. And he can't hit him on the woman thing either. In South America, as many people as not respect priests who shed their celibacy. And the people do respect and respond to the poverty thing. It makes Barcos one of them. So, in short, his eminence wants us to do his dirty work on a fact-finding of heresy. Then he feels he can safely follow up."

****

A continent away, in Brazil, Tomas Barcos, his slight frame dressed in worn jeans and a T shirt, walked slowly along a litter-strewn alley. He stuffed his hands into the pockets of his jeans and placed his feet carefully to avoid cuts from the jagged glass and metal that had accumulated over years, debris that was rejected again and again by the gleaning hands of even the city's most destitute. Movement in a small cleared space next to the wall caught his eyes. He moved toward it, only to stop as a rat popped its head above the surrounding rubble. He continued along the alley, his heavyset companion, Francisco, silently dogging his footsteps. Suddenly the fetid odor of decaying animal matter filled his nostrils. He stopped again, his eyes straining in the poor light. Near the alley wall he could make out the outline of a small foot, emerging from the edge of a covering layer of filthy cardboard. He worked his way through the debris to the spot and reached down. "Francisco!" He motioned his companion to the other end of the cardboard.

Francisco reached for the cardboard. Together they lifted it aside and faced the terror-stricken face of a young woman, a girl really, who clutched a tiny baby to her breast.

"You are safe," Barcos said to her immediately. "I am Padre Barcos. And this is Brother Francisco." He pointed to his companion.

For a moment hope glimmered in the girl's eyes, followed quickly by a mix of skepticism and fear.

Barcos knew her fear was rooted in abuse. It was always so. "You are safe now," he repeated, kindly. "We are here to help you." He smiled. "And we are not from the government."

She tried to raise a smile on her smudged and dirty face, and failed.

"Come now," Barcos coaxed. "We will take you to a place

where you and your baby will be safe, and where there is food for you." He reached out a hand. "What is your name?"

"Rosa," the girl replied hesitating, and then reached out her hand. On her feet, unsteady, she held on to Barcos' hand. "Don't hurt my baby," she pleaded, and held the child tightly in her other arm.

Francisco reached out for the baby. "Let me help you," he said.

"I will carry him," Rosa replied, unyielding of the baby.

"Your baby is safe, and so are you," Barcos soothed. "We will let Francisco carry the baby. I will tell you this about Francisco. He has ten younger brothers and sisters, so do not fear. Francisco knows how to take care of babies. Now, you lean on me."

Slowly, they worked their way carefully through the mounds of trash.

****

Johann Rolf sat in his office chair, his eyes looking out over the head of Dilford. His mind calculated the value of a favor to Jimenez and the number of votes in his corner at the soon to happen conclave where the next pope would be chosen. "Do it," he snapped. "Excommunicate Barcos! Anathematize him! Chop the beak off that cuckoo!" As Dilford left to execute this directive, Rolf picked up his phone and directed an assistant to put through a call to his eminence, Cardinal Jimenez in Sao Paulo.

The next morning Rolf's limousine purred a slow pace up the hairpin turns of Monte Cassino's steep slope. The driver's eyes focused on the road. From the back seat, Rolf scanned the countryside. On the downslope side of the road, cement and steel pillboxes from World War II held empty surveillance over the valleys. Here German soldiers had held up the advance of the Allies on their way north from Sicily.

Rolf's own father had commanded German forces somewhere in these mountains. The Allies, unable to forge their way beyond this place, had at last bombed the monastery into rubble in a final, and successful, attempt to dislodge the German troops.

Near the top of the mountain, Rolf ordered the driver to stop on the traffic-free road. His eyes were directed out toward the mountains, but he was looking now through the eyes of a fifteen-year-old boy at the stiff back of his uniformed father. He heard again the denigration. How could any son of Colonel Jacob Rolf enter the spineless world of the clergy? Rolf had experienced his entry into the seminary as his first act of spine, a raised fist to an unfeeling, unforgiving parent.

He ordered the driver to proceed, and shortly the car pulled to a stop at the entrance of the monastery of Monte Cassino. Rebuilt with American money after the war, this perfect replica of the bombed-out monastery once again graced the summit of the mountain.

"Welcome, Cardinal Rolf! Father Bernardo is expecting you. Please have a seat. I will call him at once." The aged porter shuffled back into his stone office.

A few minutes later, his nostrils filled with the smell of damp stonework, an already bored Johann Rolf heard the echo of his retreat master's approaching steps.

****

Bianca Pavona had cleaned Rolf's rented Villa near Caserta and had prepared the evening meal which was ready for the oven. She tested the hot water of a bath with her wrist, then spilled bath salts into the flow. She pinned up the flowing strands of her hair, removed her robe and lowered herself into the water. There she luxuriated in the water's warmth and scent.

How long had it been? Four years now since he had discovered her in the back streets of Naples. Her protector had demanded an enormous sum for her freedom, but he had paid it without hesitation. Half of that sum awaited her should she choose to leave him. He had taken her to Rome and responded to her compulsive need for direction. He had convinced her of her special vocation, a privileged way to work out her salvation. He was so intelligent, and handsome, and rich. And he was always kind to her. She had never imagined living in such splendor. This was so much better than the dirty men of the dirty streets of Naples. She did not dream of leaving.

When the water began to cool, Bianca reached for a towel and stood in the tub. She toweled her face and neck, and then caught her image in the full length mirror. He had told her how beautiful she was, how exquisite her legs, how firm her thighs, how perfect her breasts. She believed him, of course, but also the mirror.

In the bedroom, she pulled on a silk robe emblazoned with frolicking kittens. Then she went barefoot down the stairs to the kitchen. She heard the car in the drive, the curt dismissal of the driver, the house door open, and the signal sound of the latch. She ran from the kitchen to embrace him. "Was it a hard day? she asked.

"No."

"Was it a good day?"

"No."

"Come, let me help you out of these clothes. Here is your robe. Sit here now. Here is wine." She ran her fingers through his hair and kissed his cheek. "You must relax now. I will help," Bianca soothed. She slipped out of her robe and knelt in front of him. Parting his robe she leaned forward and, having gently coaxed him to firmness, bobbed once again at the work of her salvation.

Johann Rolf leaned back. His fingers roved through Bianca's silky hair.

Later that evening Rolf called the monastery to inform

them he would be indisposed the next day and that they should inform Father Bernardo. Next he called the limousine service to tell them the limo would not be required tomorrow. "We are going sailing, Bianca," he said. "I have had the *Bella Bianca* sailed from Porto San Stefano. It will be waiting for us in the morning at Pozzuoli. We will take your auto."

As they drove into the ancient city of Pozzuoli, Rolf recalled that, as Puteoli, this city had been the harbor city of Rome long before the time of Christ. The *Acts of the Apostles* reports that after his shipwreck off Malta, St. Paul had arrived at this port on his way to Rome for trial. Now the relic of an ancient amphitheater was left as a reminder of those times. And only two kilometers further west was Baia, the sin city of Roman Emperors.

Their sleek yawl, its port side gleaming white in the morning sun, slipped past the breakwater into the gulf of Pozzuoli and past the promontory that hid the city of Naples from sight. The jib sail's shape bleached white into the blue sky as it pushed the forty-four-foot luxury craft into the open waters of the bay of Naples. Rolf engaged the winch to raise first the mainsail, and then the mizzensail, and felt the boat lean to starboard as it gathered speed. They skirted Ischia on their starboard side and sailed southwest toward Capri. Bianca went below and emerged a short time later in a two piece aqua-green swimsuit. She joined Rolf at the wheel.

Off Capri, Rolf gave wide birth to the dozens of motorboats and other craft there to disgorge hundreds of tourists to swarm like ants to the famous *piazzetta* and there sit at tables to drink their espressos and liqueurs and gaze starstruck at each other.

Bianca used binoculars to study the grottos and cliffs, and the towering pillars called 'the Faraglioni rocks.'

Rolf looked at Bianca with appreciation. "Get your sun now," he said, and turned his attention to the sails.

Bianca went forward, untied her bra, and stretched out on

63

a cushion to the sun side of the jib.

A pod of dolphins joined the boat and played, darting forward, retreating aft, swimming back and forth under the craft, and breaking water in arched leaps. Rolf gave himself to the spell of the breeze, the dappled shine of the waves and to the silence. This is my back door, he thought, my escape hatch. Should Rome ever disappoint me, I can disappear.

He led his mind over the details of this alternate life. The family wealth, now his, was concealed in Switzerland. There were industries under corporate titles that had increased in value to a point where he need never again query costs. There were alternate passports, now also for Bianca. And though he never uttered the word love, his attachment to her had strengthened over time to an enduring stability. Losing her is unthinkable, he thought.

After a time he was unable to keep his thoughts focused on either Bianca or the sea. The thoughts of the coming conclave intruded. This institution has endured through time, he mused, because of strong men. History shows that only strong men, the nobility, are capable of holding imperial authority. Call it self-serving if they want, but only men like me are strong enough to thwart the frequent thrusts toward fickle change. If there is a God, He will forgive my other peccadillos if I remain stalwart in this. And He is about to give me this papal throne. I know it! Already my lieutenants are busy: Pustkowski from Krakow, Sullivan out of New York, Dougherty in Armagh, Jimenez now for South America. Rolf traced the list to its end.

Ordinarily Johann Rolf was not given to day dreaming. But for a moment, words attributed to Pope Leo X became real to him in the spell of sea and waves. "The papacy is ours. Let us enjoy it."

A PAPAL FUNERAL

Cool breezes are usual in the Alban Hills in summer. On this day, however, no breeze stirred the yellow, red and blue pleats of their uniforms as the two Swiss Guards stood watch at the palace entrance. Unusual also were the full-dress uniforms of the guards. The summer heat embedded itself in their shiny metal helmets and breastplates and emerged in the perspiration on their faces. A lone fly seemed to delight in buzzing their impassive faces, flying from one to the other, and back. Car wheels thrummed a cobblestone staccato as they passed through the piazza, but raised no dust from the well swept stones.

As it did in the twelfth century when the Gondolfi family built their palace here, the hill town of Castelgandolfo stands on its volcanic rim and looks down over four hundred feet into the volcano's voiceless throat, the dark waters of Lake Albano. The Via Laghi around the lake's six-mile circumference leads to other hill towns, but it was here in Castelgandolfo, in the seventeenth century, that Pope Urban VIII built his papal summer palace. Larger by a quarter than Vatican City itself, the estate contains both a farm and a park.

The two guards abruptly raised their arms in salute. An ambulance moved quickly through the gate and into the courtyard. Two black limousines rode its wake. Their passengers emerged and bustled with purpose. Soon a body-laden stretcher was muscled gently but efficiently into the palace.

He had come home, to this favorite of his homes, to die. Neither doctors nor the sanitary technologies of the hospital could hold him any longer. His staff had set up a hospital bed in the throne room where he had held so many private and semi-private audiences. The hall allowed ample room for doctors, other medical professionals and members of his court family. Head and shoulders raised by the bed's mechanism, he wondered at the brazen insolence of his affliction. He suffered the doctors now. For too long he had diagnosed his own illnesses, contrary to their diagnoses. For too long he had dictated his own treatment, contrary to their prescriptions. And now, here at last, he knew he had been wrong. It was his first and only experience of a limit to his infallibility. He dozed, in and out of sleep, guarded closely by the attentive eyes of his most trusted aide, Cardinal Marco Gattone. Gattone was *Camerlengo,* the papal chamberlain.

Gattone's eyes held on the papal face and his ears tuned to the labored breathing. What a man you are! he thought. A wolf pack leader, disabled for two years now, but stubborn, unable to relinquish power and lick the muzzle of a successor. You were an outsider, but you became a media-smart, globe-trotting populist, a consummate politician. You ignored completely the evidence that this world is not all Catholic. Every human is your child, your son or daughter, ignorant all, and in need of you, all poor in some way, and in need of you. Never free men and women, never brothers and sisters, equal, they are complete only when tethered to you, the tether a necessary part of their being. Those untethered, unwilling to grant you absolute authority or unable to accept the limits you imposed, you ignored or excluded. They ceased to exist. It is this tether that is worrisome. Gattone reached for a tissue and sponged a spot of drool from the papal mouth.

At 3:00 a.m., Gattone woke himself with his own snort and took a moment to orient himself. He looked at the face of the pope, peaceful, silent. The silence spoke the news. He leaned forward and felt the still warm forehead, tracing on it the sign of the cross. Taking a tissue he wiped spittle from the dead pontiff's chin. He called the doctors and watched as they confirmed the death. Then, removing a small silver hammer from the drawer of the bedside table he gently tapped the body's forehead, the ancient ritual confirmation of death. Next, Gattone walked to the dead pope's office and retrieved the fisherman's ring from the papal desk, the pope's fingers having been too swollen to wear it. He stared silently at the ring's signet, an engraving of St. Peter fishing from a boat. Since the twelfth century fisherman rings have been used by popes as their seal. This ring will seal no more, he thought, and placed the ring in his pocket. Later, the ring's signet would be publicly shattered. A new ring would greet the next pope. Gattone moved to a chair. Tears in his eyes, he began to pray.

The word quickly escaped the palace and soon all of Italy and the world knew. *Il Papa e morto. Viva Il Papa.*

On the following day, about mid-morning, seminarians from the English and North American Colleges were relieved of their watch around the pope's bier. A short time later, as Swiss Guards knelt on one knee, their halberds to the fore, the bier was carried to the courtyard. Red suited porters gently pushed their burden into the hearse. There, like a relic in crystal, the pope's body was visible through windows that surrounded the compartment. The shiny black hearse, crowned on top with a large golden tiara and four golden angels, left the courtyard quickly with a two car escort. Traveling down the hill it turned onto the *Via Appia Nuova* and moved at moderate speed the scant fifteen miles to the ancient walls of Rome.

A somber and silent crowd of thousands greeted the hearse as it moved through the ancient gate into the square of St. John Lateran, the pope's cathedral. While the body was carried into the church for a brief ritual blessing, the thousands of clergy, priests, bishops and cardinals, companies of the Italian army, Swiss and Noble Guards of the Vatican, Papal Gendarmes, and dignitaries were formed *modo Italiano* into a procession.

Past the tear-stained and the curious, staring faces of thousands, the procession began its two-hour march to St. Peter's Basilica. Down the *Via Merulana* and the *Via Labicana* it rounded the Colosseum and into the *Via dei Fori Imperiali.* The silent procession, traveling roads mounded on their sides by crowds of thousands, carried the sovereign's body past the ruined glories of his models, the ancient Roman emperors.

Shouts of "Papa! Papa! Un miracolo, Papa, per favore!" were aimed at the prostrate figure of the pope. No miracles were apparent. Flower petals strewn by hundreds on the path of the procession were gradually ground to bits by the thousands of marchers. Some of the bystanders ran to touch the hearse and sign themselves with the cross.

They entered the *Piazza Venezia* where the showman, Mussolini, so often shouted an illusion of glory to his countrymen. Then into the *Corso Vittorio Emanuelle II* and on toward the Tiber.

****

Maggie returned to Rome from Fiesole as the pope's body was receiving its blessing in the cathedral of St. John Lateran. She was puffing when she reached the fourth-floor landing of her apartment building. She set her briefcase and suitcase on the floor and retrieved her apartment keys from her purse. Opening the door she turned back, picked up her luggage and backed into the apartment. The fragrance filled her nostrils before she kicked the door shut. She turned and stared in wonder at the exuberance of colors that confronted her. The floral arrangement seemed to fill her living room. Surely a mistake. Lucia, the building manager, who alone had a key, should have known. Maggie wrestled her suitcase to her bedroom and returned to inspect the flowers. A small envelope was partially hidden in the blooms.

"*Benvenuto a Roma,* Maggie! I will call you. Giulio."

The phone rang. She picked it up, her senses still drinking flowers.

"Ciao, Maggie. It is I, Giulio."

Maggie checked her watch. She had to run if she was to catch the procession. At Giulio's request, she arranged to meet him for lunch several days later. She left her luggage unpacked and quickly left her apartment. She walked into the *Piazza Campo dei Fiori* thinking of her flowers. In the mornings this piazza held a sea of umbrellas spread over vendors, their flowers, and their produce. She shopped here daily for the freshness. Now, in the early afternoon, the market was closed. Giordano Bruno's statue, on its tall pedestal, overlooked the square near where she entered. She admired Bruno, burned at the stake here in this papal execution square, for daring to confirm that Copernicus' heliocentric theory was correct and that the Bible has nothing to say about astronomical reality. As she smiled up at the statue she thought of making him her patron saint. We are both so impolitic, she thought.

She hurried on, not wanting to miss the procession. She crossed the square and walked the short length of the *Via Baullarai* to the *Corso Vittorio Emanuele.* Crowds had already assembled, alerted by the tolling of bells from every direction. She stood on the curb and waited.

A tightly drawn phalanx of gendarmes headed the procession. They were abreast of Maggie before she could see the army units and then the long line of clergy. Fred, Claude, Tim, Francis and Antonio walked some distance in front of the hearse in a large group of bishops and archbishops. As they passed, Maggie caught Francis' eye. The tall Nigerian gave a wink and a nod but kept his somber face and cadence. Alberto walked directly in front of the hearse with a small group of cardinals. She saw Rolf, and Gattone, all grimly silent. She wondered at their thoughts. So many cardinals were too feeble for this walk. Were these here to show their fitness?

The next morning, Maggie joined the snaking line in the piazza of St. Peter's Basilica. It took an hour before she was inside the church. As the coiled line of mourners moved slowly forward, she began to catch glimpses of the dead pope on his raised bier. The bier had been placed just in front of Bernini's intricate *baldacchino,* the bronze canopy that covers the main altar and the stairs that lead down to the crypt. The tomb of the apostle, Peter, is believed to lie beneath the crypt. And the tombs of many popes are housed in the crypt.

The body of the pope seemed to grow larger as she approached. At the bier she stared at the body, clothed in purple, pontifical vestments, at the stern face beneath the white miter, and at the thin, tightly pursed lips. He had never seemed to listen.

That evening Maggie received a call from Larry Mulligan, a fourth-year seminarian from the North American College, the living quarters for priesthood candidates from the United States. They had met months before in a coffee shop near the Trevi fountain. Larry had introduced himself. He was, he said, skipping a boring class at the nearby Gregorian University. "There's this guy talking Latin in a heavy French accent," he explained, "and he's teaching Hebrew. Can you believe what that's like?" She had liked him instantly and he had done volunteer work for her at the office.

"Would you like to join me for the pope's burial tomorrow in the Basilica," he asked. "I've got great tickets."

At 1:00 a.m. the next day, Maggie and Larry entered the church. The interior of St. Peter's Basilica had been partitioned with four-foot high barricades into holding sections. The color of the ticket determined the section to which mourners were allowed to advance, if they were lucky enough to have a ticket. On a first-come basis, several hundred people had already been admitted to the vestibule and the very rear of the church's nave. Forward of that, a gendarme stood at the entry to each holding section, and examined tickets closely at times, but mostly by color. Maggie had a ticket that allowed her presence, but no view. Larry said they could do better. Noting ticket colors as they advanced deeper into the

Basilica, Larry reached into his cassock before each gendarme and casually waved tickets of the right color for a section further on. Maggie soon realized that Larry had as many tickets as there were sections, that they were tickets from past papal events, a part of Larry's collection, and not for this event. They advanced section by section up the nave to the swirling columns of Bernini's *baldacchino*. The mass of burial was to be conducted in the apse, behind the main altar and at the Altar of the Chair. Larry headed for the bleachers that lined the apse. The gendarme at the entry motioned for the tickets. He stared at the forgeries with widening eyes, then at the pair. Oh Lord, Maggie thought, we're caught. What happens now? Her face reddened in embarrassment. Larry calmly met the guard's stern gaze. Dignitaries crowded up behind them. Suddenly the guard smiled, shook his head, and waved the two into the seats.

"They like Americans, and they admire chutzpah," Larry whispered to Maggie as he led her higher into the bleacher. They took space on an unmarked bench.

Maggie lost herself in the ensuing spectacle. The bier, still bearing the pope's body, had been moved during the night into the apse and placed in front of the Altar of the Chair. A cortege of cardinals processed up the center aisle of the Basilica and took seats in the apse, directly across from Maggie. Maggie caught Alberto's eye, and returned his surprised smile.

The afternoon sun shot yellow-golden rays onto the bier through the Holy Spirit window, the famed golden window with its white dove. Cardinal Gattone celebrated the Mass, after which he and the other ministers gathered near the body of the dead Pontiff and prayed the ritual prayers of burial. Maggie watched intently as the pope's body was placed into a casket, actually into three caskets, one inside the other, one each of cypress, lead and oak. She gave herself to the sound of Gattone's Latin prayers, to the choir's assurance of death's defeat and to the scent of incense that filled the apse as the casket lids were set in place and sealed one by one. The closing completed, the ministers rolled the casket to the stairwell at the main altar that led down into the crypt. There, with the aid of a crude, noisy windlass they lowered it into the crypt.

"Goodbye," she whispered.

Several days later, halfway through the traditional nine days of mourning, Maggie and Fred Sweeney drove to an eating place in the center of Rome. Popes create the mood and feel of the Vatican, whether that mood be joyous or morose, light or heavy. "It's like a city of the dead," Maggie commented, "I'm glad to get out of there for awhile."

They were seated when Giulio entered the Trattoria. Maggie caught his split-second display of disappointment when he saw she was not alone.

Giulio approached the table and bowed slightly to Maggie. "Ciao, Sister Maggie. It is good to see you."

Maggie held out her hand. "It's good to see you again, also, Giulio. This is Fred Sweeney."

"I'm pleased to meet you, Fred," Giulio said as he shook Fred's hand.

"Fred is an archbishop in the Vatican," Maggie added as Giulio took a seat.

Giulio's fingers moved slowly to his belt buckle under the table. "Fred? In Italian that is Federico, is it not?" he asked.

"That's correct, Giulio. In English the full name is Frederick," Fred responded.

Giulio's eyes showed his appreciation as they scanned the pert waitress who appeared to take their orders. "Not so pretty as Sister Maggie, yes, Fred?" he asked when the waitress departed. "But, okay, yes?"

Fred's face reddened, but he laughed, nodding his agreement.

"So you are an archbishop, Fred. You must be very rich,"

Giulio said, holding up his right hand and rubbing his thumb over the other fingers.

Fred laughed. "No, not rich, Giulio. Why do you think I'm rich?"

"It is the way things are with bishops. It is our history," Giulio responded.

"Are you a Catholic, Giulio?" Fred asked.

"As they say, *sono Cattolico, ma non sono fanatico.* You have heard this saying? It is said much here in Italy. My mother told me I was baptized in church of San Gennaro in Napoli. You know this San Gennaro? He is one whose dried blood turns to liquid twice each year. Or most every year. I go to see this once. When it does not happen we are in trouble from Mount Vesuvius. So, you see I am Cattolico. But most of my life I live it, how you say, without the formalities. I have read the gospel, and I like this Jesus. And if I marry someday, I will marry in church. And when I die, they will bury me in church. I think that will be enough for me of the rich priests."

"It sounds like you don't think much of priests and bishops," Fred said.

"Is better to say, I don't think about them much at all. Sister Maggie is first nun I talk to since I am a little boy. You are first bishop I ever talk to. I talk to a priest when I was in school. He was a good man, good to the poor people. He had a woman. I liked him."

A wine steward appeared. "May I choose wine for us?" Giulio asked. "I promise, is very good. I, myself, am exporter."

"You are in the export business, Giulio?" Maggie asked after Giulio placed the order.

"Yes, Sister Maggie, I...."

"Call me Maggie, please, Giulio."

"Yes, Maggie, I am exporter with some friends. We export wine, and olives, and olive oil, and sometimes other things. I am also in construction business, and some other businesses. I like to be busy."

"You must be very rich yourself, Giulio," Fred said, "a man who commands helicopters...."

"I am not so rich like the clergy, Fred, but I do okay." Giulio laughed his enjoyment of the exchange. "What do you do, Fred?"

"Sister Maggie and I are studying ways to make the church...." Fred paused. "Perhaps a good way to say it is, we are trying to find a way to make this Jesus whom you like more visible in the church leadership and organization."

"Ah, you try to change things. I think I like you better already, Fred. Do you think you can succeed in this?"

Before Fred could answer, the wine steward appeared with the wine. Giulio waved away the offer to taste it and motioned the steward to fill all the glasses. He lifted his glass first to Maggie and then to Fred. *"Salute,"* he said.

They responded, "Cheers."

Maggie looked at Giulio. "Giulio," she asked, "how would you change the church?"

"I never think of this before," Giulio replied. "Let me think a moment."

The waitress arrived with their food. The three began to eat and the conversation lagged.

After a time, Giulio dabbed his lips with his napkin, looked upward and announced thoughtfully, "I would take away the *palazzos* from the bishops. I would take away the titles, the *eccellenza* and the *eminenza.* I would have the bishops live as the poor live. You cannot love people from so high up. You must live where you can give the *abbraccio.* And when you are down in the dirt and there you make the rules, they will be rules that help people." Giulio stopped, his eyes unseeing. "I think that would be enough for me to see Jesus in the church."

Maggie and Fred looked at each other, then at Giulio.

Giulio continued. "But I also think it will be the very cold day in hell before we see such a thing."

"The church has changed before, Giulio," Maggie said.

Giulio twisted linguine around his fork. "Maggie, I know you are historian and doctor. I am not university person but I read, I see, in my own life I experience." He set the full fork on his plate and looked from Maggie to Fred. "For hundreds and hundreds of years, pope was monarch, king of papal states. Bishops were rich aristocrats, like dukes and princes. Clergy were, how you say, like lords. The poor, they were poor. Then, only hundred years ago or so, people take papal states away from pope. So is pope poor? No. He makes new kingdom for himself. The church is now kingdom. Pope then say he is infallible. Everybody must obey *him* to get to heaven. He makes rules to control people. Bishops continue to be aristocrats. Let me give here the example. In south of Italy, in Sicily too, after the war, do bishops join the poor? No. They join with rich landowners. I know this. Is in history books. They pretend it would be *comunismo* to help poor. What they really say is, it is not our job to help poor. The clergy abandon the people. So people abandon them. People do not abandon Jesus. Perhaps they know Jesus better from being poor."

Giulio gulped a mouthful of linguine and washed it down with Valpolicella. "You think you and Fred and your friends can do what loss of papal states could not do -- take aristocrat from bishop? I do not think so. The bishops are very clever. The people do not believe them so much anymore."

∗∗∗∗

Later that same afternoon, Fred Sweeney's steps echoed down the corridor of the Vatican Palace to the entrance of the secretary of state's offices. Inside, he went directly to Claude's office where Claude looked up from a pile of correspondence, his desk as disorderly as the unruly mass of black hair on his head.

"His name is Giulio Giuliano, Claude, the man Maggie told us about in Fiesole. He's taken quite a shine to Maggie, says she saved his life in Florence. He says he's in the export and construction businesses. Maggie would club me with a crucifix if she knew I was checking this guy out. Can't help it, I guess."

"Where does Giulio Giuliano live?" Claude asked quietly, his black mustache bobbing with the words.

"Naples, he says."

"I can check to see if he stands out from the crowd there. If he does, I can check on which side of Mother Justice he walks. That's your point?"

"Yes." Fred said. "Just between us?"

Claude nodded. "I, too, had the protector role stamped on my gray cells. My mother! She was *formidable* in her expectations of the courtesies."

Twenty-four hours later, Fred and Claude again faced each other across Claude's desk. "This is what I have, Fred," Claude said, handing Fred a sheet of paper.

The report was brief: "There is no record with the Naples Police or with Interpol that Giulio Giuliano has membership in any known underworld organization. He is well known in Naples, wealthy by standards of property and lifestyle. He has many friends in the upper ranks of government, in the business community and among the police. He has been observed dining with members of the Camorra, the Naples version of the mafia, but has never been personally connected to any crime. He has never been married, at least of record. He is reputed to be a ladies' man, but there has never been a complaint of anomalous behavior."

"Thanks, Claude," Fred said as he returned the report. "We can tear that up. Maggie can handle him, I'm sure."

"How does Maggie seem to you?" Claude asked. "I mean,

how is she handling her lack of involvement?"

"She is bored," Fred replied. "I wish we could use her wit on some of these cardinals."

****

Maggie was bored. She had spent the past few days helping at a shelter for homeless women. Her desk was clear. She knew the Il Cero office would be empty for the *interregnum.* The rest of the gang all had other offices and would be too busy to even stop by. She squelched resentment at her lack of a role to play and escaped to the Vatican Museum. Inside she passed by the Picture Gallery and the Sculpture Galleries and went deep into the museum. At the stairs leading to the Sistine Chapel a gendarme blocked her entry.

"It is closed," he said, pointing at a sign.

"But I only want to see what it looks like for the conclave," Maggie replied. "Is it ready?"

"Yes, it is ready, but it is closed."

She remembered the advice of Larry Mulligan. "Just wait them out," he said. "Keep talking. They'll cave in, take my word for it."

"I'm sure you won't do security checks until just before the conclave," she said to the guard. "You could stand at the door while I take a peek," she added, and then waited.

The guard averted his gaze.

"Now, what bad things could I do in there?" she asked and continued to stand in front of the guard. "I work for Cardinal Della Tevere."

Shrugging his shoulders, the guard grinned and gave in. "Follow me," he said. He walked her up the stairs, opened the door to the chapel and beckoned a guard from the interior. "Let her in for ten minutes," he said.

It had always been the majesty of Michelangelo's ceiling

that drew her attention. This time it was the canopied rows of chairs and cloth-covered tables that lined the sides of the chapel. Two guards in full uniform stood one at each side of a canopied altar. The altar stood at the chapel end where Michelangelo's gigantic fresco of the Last Judgment covered the wall. Except for the guards she was alone, feeling the solemnity and the personal importance of the impending election. "Dear God, let it be..." she prayed. Then the quiet of the chapel struck her. How unlike the rest of Italy, even the churches, she thought. The memory of Charles invaded her mind, the words of a letter:

Dear Maggie,

It is so quiet here in the countryside. The quiet seems to stretch time. Even as I go about my work there is more time for reflection.

Reflection is both good and difficult for me. You are a constant intruder. Your image, the memory of your voice and your laughter, invade my thoughts. I am forced at times to lose myself in activity in order to break free from the hold you gain.

Back in her apartment that evening the phone's ring broke the hold of a novel she was reading. Fred asked if she would help arrange an evening dinner for the American prelates. She was grateful for the chance to do something. It took her twenty minutes.

The phone rang again. It was Larry Mulligan. He was persuasive in his invitation to crash the final funeral mass of the *Novemdiales.* "Lots of bigwigs there," he said. "U.S. secretary of state, the French president, royalty, you name it.

I've got the tickets ready to go."

Maggie declined. "Thanks, Larry, I'll pass on this one. I've seen enough of the morbid side. Get busy on those tickets for the coronation. Who are you betting on?"

"I think Gattone will come out on top," Larry answered. "He's a good guy, moderate. Doesn't make waves. Who's your candidate?"

"I'm hoping for Della Tevere. What's your word on that?"

"Good man, too, from what I hear. But I don't see where the votes will come from. Then, what do I know? Take care, Sister, and don't worry about the coronation. We'll be right up front."

What will I do if Alberto doesn't win? she wondered, and then felt surprise that the question had never surfaced before with the same stark reality.

The next afternoon she walked to St. Peter's. Inside, she turned to the right to see the *Pieta*. The sight of Michelangelo's beautiful Madonna, holding her dead son on her lap, always brought a sense of awe. What suffering this woman endured! Is there meaning there? she wondered. Is there power in suffering?

THE ELECTION

Cardinal Marco Gattone felt his seventy years. From a table at the head of the room the stout, genial prelate looked out at the assembled cardinals. They were gathered in the large Consistorial Hall in the Vatican Palace. As *Camerlengo* he had not lost his job at the pope's death as had all but two others of the Roman cardinals. As dean of the College of Cardinals, elected by his peers, the rules decreed that he preside over the general congregations, the daily meetings of cardinals as they governed the church during the *interregnum.* Though tired he met the various requests of his peers for information with unfailing grace. He had read them the oath of secrecy and, one by one, they had taken it. Now he listened to a lengthy and boring report on the Vatican's financial health prepared by a subordinate. He already knew the details. It was now his bailiwick.

You are an alley cat, Gattone, he thought. You've come a long way from that poor hovel in *Trastevere.* You've survived in these deadly marble alleys, had more lives than you deserve. Now they say you are *papabile.* It is this that keeps you sleepless. Do you want another life? One thing is certain. They will not say that I used this chair to promote myself. *Che sera, sera.*

While it dabbled in petty administrative matters, the general congregation had no authority to make significant change. Gattone knew that their real agenda was several days away, when the entire membership would finally arrive in Rome. Today there are ninety-three. In a few days all one hundred twenty cardinals will be here to elect the next pope. Then they will speak, circumspectly to be sure, but each to his vision for the coming pontificate, defining the next pope not by name, but by agenda.

A few days later, early in the second week of the

interregnum, the cardinals were again congregated in the Consistorial Hall and set the conclave for seven days hence, fifteen days after the pope's death. There were 127 of them, 120 eligible electors and 7 cardinals over the age of eighty, the age that disqualified them from the conclave, but not from the general congregations. Marco Gattone looked out at them from his table. We are courtiers, all of us, he thought. We have learned our craft playing to a single monarch. Now, without him, we are cautious, less artful in playing to each other. We sit, not in cadres according to our loyalties, but interspersed so as to give the illusion of neutrality.

The cardinal from Krakow began the fundamental agenda. "We live in desperate, evil times," he said from the lectern. "Our dear, sainted, departed Holy Father was a bulwark against the evils of our times. A champion of orthodoxy, he faced every enemy, ready to cut them down with the sword of righteousness. He was fearless. Can we find one so fearless among our number?"

Managua's cardinal, eighty-four years old and visibly unsteady on his feet, was strident, his face grim, his thin lips barely opening. "The enemies of truth are not dead. Modernism greets us with new and dangerous faces. The church is beset with rampant relativism. Communism, yes, my brothers, what we had hoped dead, communism lurks yet today behind new facades of concern for the poor. Materialism, that curse of modern times, is everywhere. We are the fortress church, strong, guileless. We must remain strong. We must strengthen our ramparts. We will protect the precious gems of truth in our treasury from the thieving fingers of these 'isms.' We must continue to be uncompromising."

These were voices for Rolf. They continued. Manila's cardinal walked to the podium and adjusted the microphone downward. "We recall the many deceptive voices of theologians lately trapped and silenced by the careful scrutiny of the Holy Office. We recall the fearless intransigence of this

Holy See on the matter of sexual mores, and on other examples of the moral decay of our times. We must hold firm."

Armagh's cardinal spoke quietly, a pious bend to his head, but steel in his eyes. "What has happened to obedience? Why are we losing that quiet, holy docility of our people? Are we not now paying the price for the liberal spirit of the last council?"

Gattone's eyes moved from man to man around the hall. Are you looking into a mirror, Marco? he asked himself. How stoically we conceal ambition. We feel the tension but mask it. We convey the impression it is the Holy Spirit Who will guide us to His personal selection. If it were so, our history makes Him valet to bribers, bullies, libertines, even murderers.

Brasilia's cardinal, bald and rotund, moved to counter the present thrust, to stop a ground swell that built only to Rolf. "Our late Holy Father was indeed fearless," he said, calm and smiling. "And a fearless man should succeed him. But is it fearless to isolate ourselves from the world, or the people of this world, friend or enemy? How can we say we love the sinner if we refuse to talk to him, or listen to him? Never again must we erect the barricades."

The cardinal from Bologna, gesturing with long slim fingers, supported the new thrust. "Are we to hide within walls because 'isms' are at the gate? Does truth become inarticulate before error? Do we fear dialogue with anyone? Might there not exist paths to new understandings?"

The diminutive cardinal of Jakarta questioned. "Can we ever allow abstract formulations to take precedence over concrete justice? Surely not, if the law above all laws is love of neighbor. Truth must serve love or it is vacuous."

The voices of conciliation came last. Barcelona's cardinal rose, tall and imperial. "My brothers. It has been said of my Spain: 'the multitudes have deserted the church, but not before the church deserted them.' We must learn from this.

We must be brothers to each other, or we shall surely fail the brotherhood of mankind."

The cardinal of Shanghai, peering at notes through round glasses, switched from agenda to character. "The universal church desires a pontiff who has attained a universal perspective, who peers at humanity from above the powerful inner voice of his own culture, his own nationality, his own race."

Gattone smiled inwardly. If nothing else, this conclave will be entertaining..

The week passed quickly. Standing in the *portiere* office doorway off the hotel foyer, Gattone watched and listened as his fellow cardinals entered. The Hotel Saint Martha, in the Vatican's *Piazza Santa Marta,* would be their living quarters for the duration of the conclave.

"I am sorry, Eminenza, but it is forbidden," a gendarme said, and reached for the small radio under the Bangkok cardinal's arm.

"But, it is only for the music," the cardinal sputtered.

"I am sorry, Eminenza. We have strict orders."

The gendarme placed the radio on a small table next to the conveyor where another officer screened luggage through X-ray equipment. Bangkok walked through an adjoining screening device.

Gattone had himself given the instructions to the gendarme's superior officer. "You must examine each cardinal with care. No radios, no television, no newspapers, no magazines, nothing that gives contact with the outside." At his instructions, technicians had been busy removing all telephones from the rooms.

After each cardinal was screened for electronic contraband he was asked to draw an envelope from a small box. The envelope contained a key and the number of his room.

"What do you mean, I am to have a single room? I demand a suite!" the New York cardinal sputtered. "Do you take me for some missionary bishop?"

Gattone heard the cardinal's attack and saw the gendarme's consternation. He moved to assist. "Is there a problem, *Eminenza?*" he asked.

"This hotel was built with American money," the New Yorker replied, punctuating his words. "There should be some consideration!"

Gattone thought for a moment to exchange the suite he had drawn for the American's single, then decided against it in the face of the American's arrogance. "There are only one hundred eight suites, *Eminenza,* and we are one hundred twenty electors," Gattone replied calmly. "Twelve of us must occupy single rooms. What could be more fair than to draw the lots for our rooms? It is the American way, is it not?" He moved away from the distressed prelate.

The cardinals had begun their entry into the Vatican under the Arch of the Bells at 8:00 in the morning. Gattone had them settled in comfort, not luxury, by 10:00 a.m. Assistants carried their luggage and then departed. Men accustomed to the aloneness of standing above, now found themselves in an unaccustomed aloneness, the absence of staff, the absence of all communication, in rooms where even the windows had been clouded to prevent visual communication with the outside.

By chance, Marco Gattone and Alberto Della Tevere drew adjoining suites.

At eleven o'clock Gattone had the cardinals gathered in the apse of St. Peter's for the prescribed mass for electing a pope. As the prelates listened to the first meditation on the solemn duty before them, Gattone knew that technicians were sweeping both their living quarters and the Sistine Chapel for listening devices. At lunch they would mix haphazardly at tables, coming and going as they chose. After lunch, many would nap, preparing themselves for the possibility of a long imprisonment.

The captains were busy however, those electors enlarged

enough in their own egos or the respect of enough others to fancy themselves king makers. Krakow for Rolf, Bologna for Alberto and Barcelona for Gattone himself. These men would send out probes and suggest the superiority of their candidate to whoever was available. They would rarely depart these encounters with certitude. It was too early in the game, and the usual response would be, "Be assured, he will receive my most prayerful consideration."

Some of the cardinals remained aloof, alone in their rooms, dreaming against reality. Genoa's cardinal, Giuseppe Colombo, remained closeted in his suite, on his knees. He had this feeling. Was it of God? Was it an inspired vision? He foresaw an oracular event. The cardinals would be gathered in the Sistine Chapel for the election. Suddenly, a clap of thunder would compel their attention to Michelangelo's great fresco of the Last Judgment on the altar wall. There they would see bolts of lightning shoot from the cloud on which stands the judging Jesus. "My brothers," Jesus will say, "As I chose Peter to be your first leader, so now, in these dire times, I choose my servant, His Lofty Eminence, Cardinal Giuseppe Colombo, to be your next leader." How could they refuse? It will be unanimous. Colombo imagined the disappointed faces of Rolf and Gattone, and strove mightily to not take excessive enjoyment from the picture.

At three o'clock that same day, the cardinals gathered again, this time in the Pauline Chapel of the Apostolic Palace under the piercing eyes of Michelangelo's *St. Peter Being Crucified*. They lined up in order of seniority and proceeded to the nearby Sistine Chapel singing the *Veni Creator Spiritus* as they went. Inside the Sistine Chapel they kept silence and occupied their chairs under red canopies along the walls. Here there would be no discussion, argument, or politics.

Marco Gattone moved to the altar, turned to his peers and read an oath in which they pledged to observe all prescriptions for the election, to maintain complete secrecy concerning the proceedings, to resist any outside attempts to influence the election, and to serve faithfully if elected.

Gattone was the first to place his hand on the gospels and pledge:

"And I, Marco Cardinal Gattone, do
so promise, pledge and swear, so help me
God and these Holy Gospels which I touch
with my hand."

The only staff members permitted in the chapel at this time were papal masters of ceremonies and a cleric designated to give the second meditation on the grave duty facing the cardinals.

Gattone groaned inwardly at the predictable meditation. "...solemn duty....eyes of the world upon you....the well being of Holy Mother Church hanging in the balance...."

Finally, the names of nine cardinals were drawn by lot, three to serve as *scrutineers* (men who would count the votes), three to retrieve the votes of ailing electors if any became ill, and three to serve as *revisers* (men who would double check the vote count). The papal masters of ceremonies distributed the ballots, small rectangles two inches high with the words *I Elect as Supreme Pontiff* printed on the top half, the bottom inch, blank. That task completed, the remaining staff left. The door was shut *con clave,* with a key. The *conclave* had begun.

Each cardinal bent over his ballot and wrote his selection on the bottom half of the ballot and folded it. One by one, they then carried their ballot to the altar.

At the altar they took their second oath. Gattone was again the first:

"I call as my witness Christ the Lord who will be my judge, that my vote is given to the one who before God I think should be elected."

A golden plate and a large golden cup had been placed on the altar. In turn each cardinal placed his ballot first onto the gold plate, and then taking the plate, dropped the ballot into the cup, all the while observed by the scrutineers.

Outside, the piazza was jammed with people, colonnade to colonnade, from the steps of St. Peters to the white strip of travertine that marks the Vatican's border. The Il Cero members stood near the strip on the piazza's left side. They had a clear view of the small pipe chimney protruding from the roof of the Sistine Chapel. They waited, their eyes unconsciously coming back to focus on the chimney every few seconds.

How many times had they reviewed the meaning of the smoke, if it is white, then....if it is black, then.... Maggie, more occupied with tasks at hand, had given it little thought. Now she asked Claude, "What do we want to see?"

"We want to see black smoke, Maggie. If it is white that means election on the first ballot. It means Rolf or it means Gattone. Time is everything for us."

Inside the chapel, they counted the votes. First the scrutineers counted to see that the ballots matched the number of electors. Then, at a table in front of the altar, the first scrutineer opened a ballot, wrote the name down, passed the ballot to the second scrutineer, who also wrote the name down and passed the ballot to the third scrutineer. This man read the name out loud and also wrote it down. Each elector kept his own tally as the process was continued. As he read each ballot, the last scrutineer ran a needle through the word "elect", collecting the ballots on a single thread.

Marco Gattone listened stoically as the third scrutineer read "Johann Cardinal Rolf" repeatedly. Rolf received nearly half of the required two-thirds votes before half of the ballots had been counted. But then it was Gattone's turn in the counting of the second half. At the end the two were almost even. The count stood at:

Rolf	(Curia):	38
Gattone	(Curia):	36
Daladier	(Dakar):	28
Bachman	(Utrecht):	9
Della Tevere	(Curia):	7
Cipriani	(Retired):	1
Zimny	(Retired):	1

The three cardinal revisers double checked the ballot count and found it accurate. They placed the ballots in a small pot-bellied stove. A master of ceremonies collected all of the notes and tallies taken by the cardinals during the balloting and placed them in the stove with the ballots. He then added a mixture of chemicals and set them afire. Black smoke billowed from the tiny chimney.

That evening Alberto Della Tevere answered a knock on his door. "Come in, Marco. What did you think of the vote?"

Gattone settled his bulk into one of the two chairs, rubbed his eyes, and looked at Alberto. "We both think the same, Alberto. Nine Europeans parked their vote on Utrecht until they see how the wind blows. Most third world electors parked on Dakar. Two gave honorary votes to their mentors. The rest, I think are stable for Johann, myself and you. Is it not so?"

Alberto smiled his respect at the broad, slightly pocked face of an old friend. "Perhaps, Marco. Perhaps the votes given me are also in the parking lot, as you say. If so, there are enough votes in the parking lot to give either you or Johann a sufficiency. Perhaps tomorrow will tell."

"I fear we are in for a long stay, Alberto. Thirty-three more voting sessions and the rules will allow for a simple majority to elect the next pontiff. Were it not for that rule we would already be looking for a compromise candidate. That would be you. The rule may cost you the election. My guess is the fourteenth day." He reached into a valise and withdrew two snifters and a bottle. "It has been a tiring day. Will you join me in a cognac?"

Alberto nodded an assent.

Gattone poured them each a portion. "I feel my years, Alberto. Have you heard the recent slander?"

"Yes," Alberto replied quietly.

Gattone continued, not hearing. "They have spread a report that I am careless with rules, inept with finances and lacking in faith. They cite events, the half truths that, manipulated, become lies."

"Marco, few will give any hearing. I think it will work against whoever spread them, if it becomes known."

"It was Krakow."

"Then, Rolf will pay the price. I'm surprised they didn't attack me," Alberto said.

"No need to take the risk, Alberto. If they knock me out they have the papacy, or so they think." Gattone raised his glass. The smile on his broad mouth showed gold fillings at the edges. "I think it would not be so bad to kneel for your pontifical blessing, Alberto."

The four ballots taken on the second day showed little movement. One complimentary vote from the first session went to Alberto, one to Gattone. The rest held firm. I was correct in my assessment, Marco thought. The rule to reduce the two-thirds requirement to a simple majority after 12 more days will lead the electors to hold firm for now.

Black smoke billowed on the third and fourth days, after which Marco Gattone, as prescribed, called for a day devoted to prayer, discussion and a spiritual exhortation.

Dakar, hoping to reap benefits for his third world colleagues, freed his supporters without qualification. After the fourth and last ballot of the sixth day the count stood at:

Rolf: 52
Gattone: 44
Della Tevere: 15
Bachman: 9

That evening Rolf's captain, Pustkowski from Krakow, and other Rolf supporters roamed through the halls of the hotel and spread the scent of victory. They came to Alberto and to Bachman. "Now is the time," they said. "You can be the ones to give victory to Johann Rolf. You can be the one to reap the rewards for doing that. If you fail to do so now, it may be too late for you."

On the seventh day, Bachman released his supporters. But all nine votes went to Alberto. "We do not need another autocrat," Bachman said to Alberto that evening. He meant Rolf. And now, the burden fell to Alberto and Gattone.

The eighth day was another day of prayer, discussion and spiritual exhortation.

There was no movement on the ninth and tenth days and tempers began to fray. Rolf personally put a halt to threats being made in the name of his candidacy . He came to Alberto's suite on the eleventh day, another day set aside for prayer and discussion. "It appears, my friend, Alberto," he said, a silky confidence in his voice, "that the voters are at a standstill. Perhaps you and I together can solve this impasse."

"What do you recommend, Johann?" Alberto responded amiably.

"If you recall, Alberto, you yourself told me of your expectation that I would be the one elected. Is it not so?"

Alberto held up his hands, palms upward. "That is indeed true. I did say that to you. And the voting seems to agree with me. You are far in front."

"But not far enough ahead to win, Alberto."

"Allegiances will quickly break down, don't you think?"

Rolf sighed, wearily leaned back in his chair, and closed his eyes. "Yes, they will break down, Alberto. But they will break down more quickly if you lead the way."

"What would you have me do, Johann?"

Eyes open now, Rolf leaned forward. "Announce publicly that you are withdrawing as a candidate. Release those bound to you and endorse me."

Alberto studied Rolf's face silently.

"I will make you secretary of state," Rolf added.

Alberto smiled. His placid eyes looked into those of Rolf. "Johann, you are aware, I am sure, from your lieutenants that I have chosen not to endorse anyone, neither you nor Marco. Marco, too, is my friend. As for releasing those bound to me, no one is bound to me. I am not campaigning for the papacy. You have not seen me soliciting votes."

"Others do it for you."

"That may be so, but that is at their own initiative. What's more, I do not know for sure even who they are who vote for me. So, I assure you, if you can identify them, their votes are yours if you so persuade them."

Rolf stood, and his suave demeanor turned dark. "If you refuse to support me now, you may not have another chance, Alberto," he muttered, his voice low. "You cannot stop me. No one can stop me. Think about what is in your own interest. And remember that I will remember!"

"I wish you no ill fortune, Johann," Alberto said, and rose to escort Rolf to the door. As he began to close the door on the fuming Rolf, he said quietly, "*Buona fortuna*, Johann."

****

At the Il Cero office there was no sign on the door to

divulge the kind of business transacted there. Giulio opened the door and walked in.

Maggie looked up from her book. Her desk was clear. "Come, Sister Maggie," Giulio insisted. "You are bored. All you do is wait for smoke. Let us go see the fountains. I will get you to the Vatican for the next smoke."

"Giulio, I'll come if you promise to stop sending flowers. You are scandalizing my pious landlady. She thinks I am a fallen nun."

"Tell her they are from your brother."

"You're not my brother, Giulio."

"Ah, but I made you my sister. I treat you like sister. So I am, yes, a brother. It is not a lie."

"No more flowers!" Maggie insisted.

"Ah, Maggie, you drive a hard bargain."

"*Piazza Mattei,*" Giulio directed the taxi driver, and cautioned him to drive slowly. "We want time to see. It is one of my favorite things, fountains," he said, turning to Maggie. "Some day you must come to Naples for a holiday. I will take you to Caserta. The Bourbons built their own Versailles there. And in the castle park there is the *Fountain of Venus and Adonis*. It is something."

An intertwining grace of dolphin, human and turtle shapes captured their attention as they walked the circumference of the *Fountain of the Turtles*. "Taddeo Landini make this around 1581," Giulio instructed. "Magnifico. Come, there are many more." He opened the taxi door.

They meandered from Bernini fountain to Bernini fountain. The *Fountain of the Rivers* in the *Piazza Navona*, the boat-shaped *La Barcaccia Fountain* at the foot of the Spanish Stairs, the famous *Fountain of the Triton* in the *Piazza Barberini*. They escaped the taxi and lunched along the *Via Veneto*. They played a game of identifying movie celebrities, which Giulio easily won. Later they tossed Giulio's coins into the *Trevi Fountain.*

At St. Peter's, Maggie thanked Giulio for the delightful diversion.

"I have no influence there," Giulio said, pointing at the Apostolic Palace. "But out there," he swept his arm to Rome, "I do. It is yours if you need. You will remember this? Also, if you need anything, I am your brother. Money, anything."

****

Black smoke from the four ballots on the twelfth day.

Over a cognac that night, Alberto Della Tevere talked to Marco Gattone. "Tomorrow is the last day of voting before the requirement drops to a simple majority. When that time comes, I do not think Johann can be denied. I can see that stress is reaching some of our supporters. I suspect that they, too, have been threatened. And the temptations to ambition are many. I propose to get word to those who have been my supporters and suggest they give their votes to you tomorrow. That will give you the momentum and the simple majority. If there are only a few defections the election will be yours the next day."

"That is very kind, Alberto," Marco replied, his face showing no elation. "But, I have this sense that you had a certain agenda if you would win. Can you share it?"

They talked late into the night. Gattone departed with the words, "The race has been entertaining. But, I am old. This time you must let me make the decision."

Black smoke again on the thirteenth day.

The Il Cero members stood together in the piazza and waited for the first smoke signal of the fourteenth day. They knew the importance of this day and the sense of dread they felt almost overpowered the hope they each harbored. If Alberto was to rise to the top as a compromise candidate it should have happened earlier. They were nervous. Rolf or Gattone? Gattone might work with them. Rolf, never. "*E bianca*, the smoke is white," was murmured through the crowded square. A pope had been elected.

An hour after the white smoke had billowed and disappeared, the great doors on the central loggia of St. Peter's Basilica were opened. The cardinal deacon, Bologna, appeared and declared.

> "*Annuntio vobis gaudium magnum...* I give you joyful news... *habemus papam...* we have a pope. *Eminentissimum ac Reverendissimum Dominum Albertum Sanctae Ecclesiae Cardinalem Della Tevere...* the most eminent and reverend cardinal of Holy Church, Alberto Della Tevere... *qui sibi nomen imposuit Francesci Primi...* who has taken the name, Francis the First."

ADJUSTING SAILS

Maggie's rich laughter filled the papal library. "You won," she exclaimed. "Yippee!" She raised a glass of water to Francis the First.

All seven were together again for the first time since the election. It had been nearly a month but their elation had not subsided.

The new pope, standing as equal in the group's circle, bowed slightly at Maggie's gesture. "The Lord has blessed us," he said. "Each day we must thank Him." Then, turning to the tall Nigerian, "Francis, I hope you don't mind that I took your name."

Ibowale replied first with his high pitched giggle. "Your Holiness, I think...."

"You must call me Francis, Francis. All of you, when we are together, please call me Francis."

"Am I intruding?" The wide, slightly pocked face of Marco Gattone wearing a broad, warm smile, appeared in the doorway.

"Come in, Marco," the pope said. "I have waited until you are here to tell these friends about you."

Gattone joined them as the group opened its circle to admit him.

The pope's attendant, Benito, was there almost immediately, and handed a martini to Gattone.

Francis the First continued. "I have invited Cardinal Gattone to join us. You should all know this. Marco knows all about Il Cero. He knew before the election. He knew because I told him. And I tell you this now in confidence." He paused a moment. "At the conclave, as the voting procedure came close to the fifty percent sufficiency, matters became bleak. Our information, Marco's and mine, indicated that Johann Rolf would win quickly when that time arrived. I owe my election to Marco. At the end, he alone was the engineer. And he did this knowing the full Il Cero agenda." Again, a pause. "In every detail."

Everyone clapped politely.

Maggie impulsively crossed the circle to Marco and hugged him.

Marco pointed his finger at her nose. "I know about you, too," he said, smiling.

At dinner, Pope Francis apologized "that it has been these many weeks before I could gather you in. It has been a busy time, as Marco and Claude can attest. Now, however, we have matters to share. First of all, there are appointments. Claude, will you name them, please."

Claude's unruly hair dropped in his face as he reached down to the side of his chair and pulled a manila folder from a briefcase. His black mustache bounced as he opened the folder and said, "His Holi..., ah, Francis has made the following appointments for members of this group. Letters of appointment will be delivered tomorrow. Also tomorrow, the list will be delivered to *L'Osservatore Romano* for official publication."

"We do not expect serious opposition at this time, " Pope Francis interjected.

Claude continued. "Marco retains the position of *Camerlengo*, but also will hold a newly created position, that of *Deputy* to the Roman Pontiff. It will be the number two position. Marco will insure each of us access to Francis."

"Tim," Claude looked at the fiery Scot, "you will head up the Congregation for Bishops, responsible for the selection of bishops worldwide, replacing Francis in that position. Antonio, you will be second to Tim."

"You two will have the hot seats as our plans are disclosed and implemented," the Pope commented.

Claude continued his list. "Francis Ibowale, you will head the Congregation for the Evangelization of Peoples, responsible for spreading the gospel to the third world. I will be appointed Secretary of State, responsible for governmental relations. Fred, you will take my present position as Deputy for General Affairs in the Secretariat. We will work closely with Tim and Antonio when the time arrives."

The pope broke in. "Let me continue, please, Claude. As you all know, several cardinals have resigned their curial posts, some because of age. Others have asked for other specific assignments. For the most part, though, the appointments for people outside this group will remain much as they have been. You can read them all in *L'Osservatore Romano.*" He turned to Maggie. "Maggie, you will not be surprised at the next position. As we planned, I am creating another congregation in the curia. It will be called the Congregation for Justice. We have all become painfully aware that this institution has no appeal procedure for complaints against members of the episcopacy. Currently, anyone with a complaint of injustice against his or her bishop has recourse only to that very bishop. My first Apostolic Constitution, *Justitia Pro Omnibus Beata,* (Blessed Justice For Everyone) which establishes this congregation will be published tomorrow by the Secretariat of State."

Francis paused and looked at Maggie. "It may surprise you, however, Maggie, that I am appointing you as the first president of this new congregation. I trust that you will accept?"

Maggie's face showed her surprise. "I'm honored, Francis, by your trust. But, I'm not a lawyer," she said.

"That is true," Francis answered. "But, it is not a concern. You have a wonderfully keen sense of justice, and you are a proven leader. That is what is important. As for lawyers, you will have a staff of them to assist you with the technical matters. What is more important yet, you know the course we are attempting to set for this huge bark of Peter. And justice must be visible before love can be visible."

He turned to the others. "We all know that the appointment of one woman, Maggie, to the Curia will not solve the problem of equality for women in the church. And we are determined to make that happen. At best, the appointment is a signal raised to the top of this bark's mast for all to see. This signal will surprise many, it will annoy others, and will leave a question in all. What does it mean? they will wonder. Another way to say it, it is but a single candle held to the wind, by itself insufficient to make women's participation equal, and able to be quickly snuffed out by another pontiff."

He turned back to Maggie. "You did not say, Maggie. Will you accept the position?"

"Yes, thank you," Maggie responded in a low voice.

Francis again addressed the group, looking around the table. "Maggie has herself counseled us to take slow, deliberate steps in this matter. We are to seek a method that will not place a shoal or reef in the water on which our bark might flounder. I have faith, and so does Maggie, that we will find the best way to make women's equality systemic in the church. It will be a way to make women's equality so engrained in the church that it will be a light that cannot be snuffed out, and yet a way that keeps deep water under our hull. In the meantime, we will all observe how this one candle holds its flame in the wind. Does anyone have doubts?"

Fred, a hint of humor in his voice, said, "I can already picture the dismay of the first bishop who stands before Maggie in court and learns for the first time that power is not infallibility. I hope I'll be a bystander. The last time she taught that lesson, I was the pupil." He held his glass up to Maggie.

"I have one more bit of information for you," the pope said. "I am calling for a consistory of cardinals to be held next month. There, we will move the tiller of this bark another inch toward its new course. Keep that meeting in your prayers, please. When that is over, I shall begin my travels, the travels Il Cero planned."

****

On the opening day of the consistory, Marco Gattone watched as the *Sala del Concistoro* in the papal palace filled with the low buzz of male voices. Cardinals, robed in their red-piping-trimmed cassocks, walked about greeting one another and then took their places at narrow tables. At the front of the hall a throne, a table and a podium faced them. They rose at the soft tone of a bell as Swiss guards entered, followed by Pope Francis the First. Claude Dupuis and Fred Sweeney walked with the Pope, one on each side. The assembly of cardinals broke into polite applause as Francis walked to the podium, electing to speak from there rather than from the throne. Marco, Claude and Fred sat at the table.

The applause increased with his greeting. "My brothers, *buon giorno*." He waited for the applause to quiet and motioned the cardinals to sit. "Yes, you are my brothers, indeed. With you at my side we will strengthen our beloved church. I know you to be herculean in your faith and devotion. My heart tells me, and I know this to be true, if suffering could be transferred from the sick and the poor to others willing to bear it, you would be the first to volunteer. It is this certitude that gives me confidence."

Again, applause answered the pope's words.

Marco Gattone showed a placid face to the assembly. Not too thick, Francis, he thought. Some of these guys will want to piss on your grave when you are done with them today.

"Allegations are being made, my brothers," Francis continued, "about the leadership this church has provided over the centuries. These allegations, true or false, attach themselves to, and befoul our credibility. We must nurture our credibility, is it not so? Let us look at these allegations."

The scrape of chair legs could be heard as cardinals edged

101

forward in their seats.

Gattone spied Johann Rolf, who sat with his arms folded, a derisive look on his face. I'd wager that Johann's stomach is in difficulty, he thought.

"My brothers," Francis continued. "It is alleged that we have led the church in the past from premises of our western European culture, overshadowing the universality of the Gospel. God does not emigrate from any particular country."

The cardinals were attentive, silent.

"It is alleged that we leaders have led the people deeper into a religion of externals for fear that leading them to the core of love might despoil us of our own self-interests. It is alleged that we leaders have been the primary stumbling block to Christian unity, not from a concern for truth, but because unity might compromise our prerogatives."

The audience stirred.

Gattone observed the audience closely, seeing which faces revealed growing hostility.

"It is alleged that we bishops have excluded women from positions of power, and from power itself, out of our own fear of losing power. It is further alleged that we leaders share a predilection for exclusion over inclusion. We attack rather than embrace."

Gattone saw Johann Rolf's face redden. A vein protruded on Rolf's forehead and he gripped his chair so tightly his fingers whitened.

Pustkowski of Krakow blurted out, "No, no, no."

Francis ignored the outburst and continued calmly. "It is alleged that we view the world only through a celibate eye which inhibits our ability to understand non-celibate perspectives. It is alleged...."

****

A short distance from the consistory, further upstream and

across the Tiber river, Maggie and Giulio sat on a bench by a small lake in the gardens of the Villa Borghese.

"What is this thing, consistory, Maggie?" Giulio asked.

Maggie handed a sandwich to Giulio. "It's a meeting of the pope with the cardinals."

"Why are you not there? You are big person in curia now, bigger than some of these cardinals, I think."

"But I am not a cardinal."

"You should be cardinal!" Giulio produced a bottle of red wine and glasses from the picnic basket.

"It's not my thing, Giulio."

Giulio cocked his head. "How you mean this?"

Maggie finished the first bite of her sandwich. "The institution has been modeled after a royal court. Cardinals are princes in that court. It was not always so, and I don't think that model fits the Christian idea of leaders as servants. So, no *princess* for me, thank you. Oh, look at the swans."

Giulio ignored the swans. "What is the pope telling the cardinals today? Or is it secret?"

"No, no secret. All of the documents will be public as of today. First, he is telling them much the same as you yourself once suggested. They are to join the ranks of the poor with the hope it will bring them credibility."

"I know this poverty. The monks do this, too. The way it works is this. The monastery is very rich, but, since no single monk owns it, they say they are poor, poor, poor. Always they say, give us money. But, they live better than I, and I am rich. It is a joke to the people."

"Not this time, Giulio. When Pope Francis says poor, he means poor. But, he doesn't mean destitute. He means that from now on they will not have unlimited and unaudited access to money. He means dependence on the laity who contribute the money. Ultimately, it means that bishops will have to live on a budget they must present to, and have approved by, a board constituted by members of the laity. The pope's

Apostolic Constitution spells it out."

"All cardinals? All bishops?" Giulio asked.

"Yes, all of them."

Giulio chomped on his sandwich and took a swig of wine. "I do not think this being poor and dependent will make them very happy," he said, thoughtfully.

****

Francis the First stood calmly at the podium and continued. "It is alleged, my brothers, that we leaders are mongers of fear, that we prefer the safety that control by fear gives us over the insecurity of no control, the insecurity of rendering only an invitation."

Gattone saw the contortions on the face of Dougherty of Armagh. Could the man be suffering a stroke? He wondered.

"And so, my brothers, if we are to address the problems of the church it is essential that we first address the problems of our own credibility. How can we preach Jesus if our motives are in question? That is why we will take our example from the poor. Perhaps then we might regain what we have squandered, our credibility. By relinquishing control we will say to the people that we have no other interest but their interest."

Gattone listened to a lengthy silence fill the room.

Francis paused. "In my heart I know that you will join me enthusiastically as we imitate Francis of Assisi who embraced Lady Poverty. At this time," he continued, "our Apostolic Constitution, *Pauper Misericors,* (The Compassionate Poor) will be distributed to you. It tells in detail how we shall join the poor. When it is in your hand, I shall speak with you further."

The applause was restrained as Francis walked to the table, sat and took a drink of water. "How do you think it goes?" he asked Marco quietly.

"You have most of them with you," Marco replied. "But it is painful, what you ask of them."

Back at the podium, Francis continued his explanation of the new rules. When he finished he moved to the doorway so that he could greet the cardinals individually as they departed.

Pustkowski's attempt at a weak smile emerged as a snarl. "You are still a king, but we are no longer princes, is that it?" he muttered.

"I will not be a king, Chester," Francis replied. "I will be a servant. Won't you join me?"

Many of the cardinals appeared stunned, but weakly expressed their willingness to accept the new conditions, acknowledging a need.

Johann Rolf acidly questioned, "Who dares make those allegations?"

Francis smiled at Rolf. "Among others, Johann, I do."

****

"What will happen, Maggie, if all the bishops rebel against this budgeting control?" Giulio leaned his swarthy face into the sunlight.

Maggie finished packing used napkins into the picnic basket and reached for her glass of wine. "We are confident they won't rebel, Giulio. They have been so trained, so stamped with loyalty to the pope. At least, most of them. Also, we believe that most bishops will see in this a lessening of the power of the curia, and a heightening of their own, although a different kind of power. Finally, we believe that the people will shame recalcitrant bishops into compliance. The people, except for some of the very wealthy whose consciences seem more comfortable when bishops share their status, are tired of seeing bishops with unlimited access to money and living lavish life-styles."

"I think I will enjoy watching all of this," Giulio said,

leaning back and closing his eyes to the bright sun. "I never think about church much before. I am surprised I think about it so much now. It is your doing. But, tell me about the women now. I do not yet see how the women come out so good in this."

"Giulio, you like to eat. Do you also cook?"

"God forbid, Maggie. People would die if I try to cook."

"Do you know what marinade is, Giulio?"

"Yes, I know this marinade. One puts it on tough meat to permit the teeth to enter."

Maggie laughed. "I'll accept that. Well, most women are cooks. They understand marinades. This brand of poverty is the marinade that Pope Francis is pouring on the minds and hearts of the bishops. He is hopeful that as poverty softens their fibers, bishops will come to a changed view of how religion blends with life. He hopes, we hope, that it will give them an understanding of what exclusion and oppression have done to the poor, to minorities, and to women. Our church institution is far from blameless...."

"Is that enough to make them change?"

"Hopefully. It is a start. We will see...."

OPPOSITION

The coronation of Pope Francis was over. Johann Rolf sat in his apartment and hurled the snifter. Its glass lay in shards around its overturned target, a white marble nymph-based lamp.

"That was the last glass, Caro mio," Bianca said. She leaned over from behind his chair and caressed his forehead. "Be tranquil now. It is over." She had watched for more than a week as a black mood held him, his eyes dark and brooding. He had not been to his office since the election.

Rolf broke his bleak silence, his voice soft. "That bastard! That lowborn mongrel cat, Gattone!" His voice rose. "That fat, gutter-kissing ass! He did it to me, Bianca. Without his treachery the election was mine. I know it! I know it!" He pounded his fist against the chair arm, his brown eyes burning bright with anger. "He will pay. They both will pay, he and that puke, Della Tevere."

"Caro, Caro, be tranquil," Bianca persisted.

"Francis! Francis? Can you imagine taking the name of that insipid moron from Assisi, Bianca? 'My name is Francis,' he said."

"Come, Johann. It is beautiful out. Perhaps a sail?"

"My name is Fra-a-a-ancis," Rolf simpered." "It fits, Bianca. It fits that puke. Can you believe they chose that pot of pablum over me?"

"Johann, Caro mio."

"One thing is for sure, Bianca, that vanilla pope won't have the guts to interfere with the curia. He will pontificate. He will utter pious piffle to the crowds. He will piddle around aimlessly." Rolf punctuated the alliterative consonants. "But, we will still be in control."

"Johann," Bianca pleaded.

"The coronation made me nauseous. It is too much to

bear, this burden of putting on a placid face in public." Rolf was silent for a moment. Then, "You are right, Bianca. Pack up. We will go sailing. The sea breezes will dispel this smell of vomit."

The next morning, its hull and sails glistening in the morning sun, the *Bella Bianca* cleared the harbor of Porto San Stefano.

Rolf turned the boat northward and began to relax, releasing gradually the anger but not the memory, the dark mood but not its portent.

Several days later, the yawl crept into Monaco's harbor under engine power. Rolf deftly brought the yacht to its reserved dockage and Bianca skillfully secured the lines. He cut the engine. Its sound died to the mewing of crying gulls. The sun was directly overhead. They went below.

That evening he wore a striped business suit, she a revealing cocktail dress, as they left the taxi in the *Place du Casino* and walked up the stairs to the casino of Monte Carlo.

The doorman bowed slightly and opened the casino door. "Ah, Frau Boehm, Herr Boehm, how nice to see you back again."

Only minor adjustments had changed him from Rolf to Boehm. A small amount of oil gave a different order to his hair. His contact lenses turned his eyes from brown to blue. And, of course, the clothes. He had never been challenged for a likeness to the famed *eminence grise* in Rome.

Inside, Johann went directly to the cashier.

"I hope you are lucky tonight, Herr Boehm," said the uniformed cashier. Not bothering to check the line of credit, he handed over the requested stack of chips. "We have more if you need them, Herr Boehm."

Johann walked to a roulette table where Bianca had already taken a seat. He handed her several of the chips. "Good luck, Bianca," he said indulgently. "If you need more I will be in the baccarat room." He walked away as Bianca, cashing one of the chips for forty of lesser value, leaned forward over the table to lay chips haphazardly onto the numbers.

Seated at the baccarat table, Johann felt a rising anticipation as the banker shuffled the decks of cards and placed them in the shoe. Life is a gamble, his argument ran. To gamble, to live on as many edges as I can find, to always keep my balance, is to win at life. If there is a God, He, too, is a gambler. He would understand my mistress, and my mischief.

From time to time Bianca's frivolous play depleted his supply of chips. Even so, two hours later Rolf quit the table, his stack of chips tripled.

****

Rolf was back in Rome when the curial appointments were announced in *L'Osservatore Romano.* In his office, he fielded questions and concerns from his allies.

Cardinal Chester Pustkowski of Krakow was the first on the phone. "Johann, I have almost choked to death on a piece of toast when I heard the news. What is going on in Rome, Johann? A woman? A woman in the curia? At that rank? I thought that issue was dead. Perhaps we need an infallible statement from the Holy Office that a woman's place is in the home. And what is all this fuss about justice? The people get justice from us, their bishops. There is no need for a new congregation. And certainly there is no need for a woman to lead it. I tell you, Johann, we may have elected a madman. In just a few weeks he has already put the church on a dangerous course. Where will it end?"

Cardinal Dougherty of Armagh called. "Why does this pope try to fix what is already fixed? Complaints from women about their position in the church have been minimal. And when they rise we simply wait them out. The complaints go away. Why raise the issue? Why bring this plague down on us? Does he think he's Moses?"

Cardinal Rivera from Santiago: "I have received the notice that he has called for a consistory. Why so? He has not named any new cardinals. He has appointed new men to the curia. Why does he not make them cardinals? Will he try to make that woman a cardinal? Does anyone know what this man is planning?"

****

After the consistory, Rolf responded immediately to the new poverty. His apartment occupied a top-floor corner of a building owned by the Zurich-based Boehm Industries. The building was a bountiful square, a five-story structure that, like so many Roman buildings, hid its interior elegance behind uninspired exterior facings. The apartment was served by a private elevator.

Rolf inspected the two small barren rooms and the tiny bathroom, a sardonic smile on his face. Carpenters had sliced the space for these two rooms from his former apartment. They had been formed from a spare bedroom which had never been used. The far greater space of the original apartment was left intact. These two rooms were just as he ordered. Next, he would have Bianca find second-hand, damaged furniture: a bed and small bedside table for the bedroom, a lamp, a simple bookcase, and two thread-worn chairs for the sitting room. In appearance I will out-poverty the Cure' of Ars, he thought. I must remember to tell Bianca to get a crucifix for each room, ugly ones. He mentally scripted his note to the *Camerlengo,* Gattone, on his lodgings. "And the rent is even donated," he would conclude. Thank the gods I'll never live here. I will put on that face, but I will not submit. He winced at the ugly brownish-yellow walls.

A private hallway, concealed by a locked door marked "employees only," ran from the side of the newly formed apartment to the rear exit of the building. There, another private elevator served the apartment that occupied the remainder of the floor, now enlarged by the remaining space of Rolf's former apartment. Rolf inserted his key into the lock and entered the apartment. They would share, as they had before, snug as rabbits in this private warren. He found Bianca curled up on a sofa, surrounded by catalogs and celebrity magazines.

She looked up as he entered. "Caro mio, just look at this beautiful dress." She held up a photo catalog.

Rolf walked behind the sofa and looked, caressing her neck. "Get it if you like," he said. He had long ago stopped asking, "Where will you wear it?" She would wear it here, for him. He went to their bedroom and picked up the suitcase she had packed for him.

Bianca followed. "I will miss you, Johann," she said, lifting her face for a kiss. "When will I see you again?"

"Tomorrow night, if all goes well," he replied.

The flight to Krakow was uneventful except for the movement of Rolf's designing mind. His anticipation rose, much like his feelings at baccarat, as the LOT Polish Airlines jet followed the downslope of the Carpathian foothills into the Krakow airport. The feelings intensified as he cleared customs and was led by a uniformed chauffeur to a waiting car. It is the same, he thought, only magnified. The stakes are so much larger. The driver spoke only Polish and they drove in silence.

The episcopal palace stood imposingly above him as he entered. The chauffeur carried his luggage to his room while a butler led him to the library. Waiting there were Chester Pustkowski, the resident cardinal, and Cardinal Michael Dougherty of Armagh. They rose to greet him.

A fire held down the chill but the thin Dougherty pulled a cloak tighter around his shoulders. "This Francis is crazier than a Sassenach lover," he exclaimed as the three sat in stiff high-backed chairs. "We've got to save Holy Mither Church."

"We are a church built on tradition," Pustkowski sput-

111

tered. "And this man has shown contempt for tradition. He is dangerous, an anarchist. Imagine, demanding that we live as peasants do. The man has no sense of class, no regard for the nobility." He paused and coughed, holding a stringy hand to his mouth. "And, a woman in the curia. Were there women apostles? Will she want to be a priest? Offer mass? How can someone without balls dare say, 'This is My Body?' We must save our traditions if we have to die for them."

Rolf seized the thread. "None of us would grieve if the man suddenly died. However, we can't depend on that. He's healthy, even if he is a wimp. We must turn this around before these unnecessary and unwelcome reforms, he calls them reforms, get out of hand. Otherwise, it may take a century to return to our traditions. Are we agreed?" He looked at the others as they responded with nods of agreement. "So, then, first we will need money, a great deal of money. And we curialists are poor as church mice, as you know. Michael," he turned to Dougherty, "your coffer has always been bulging over, so if defending pedophiles hasn't emptied it...?"

"I can help," Dougherty said, a pinch to his voice. "How much?"

"A million pounds," Rolf answered, "at a minimum."

"So much? I thought...."

"A million!" Rolf's voice was firm.

"So be it."

Rolf turned to Pustkowski. "Chester?"

"I will give an equal amount. God wills that we succeed," Pustkowski replied, signing himself with a cross.

"Good," Rolf continued. "Fran-a-a-ncis says he will begin his travels soon. God only knows what he plans to say out there. When I return to Rome I will set up a meeting for us with Francis. We will go as a delegation with others of our friends. One more time we will try to reason with the man. If we cannot dissuade him from this madness we will need that money."

THE CASTILLO FAMILY

Her toes and heels clicked a flamenco beat as Luisa Angela Alvarez de Castillo skipped and danced on the veranda of her country hacienda. Her thoughts followed the course of last night's party. Her brilliant white teeth glistened in her smile.

The archbishop, Villariego, had been at the buffet. She had flirted. "Such broad shoulders, Excellency," she said, ignoring the enormous paunch, "how did you ever escape into celibacy? Surely, there are sad women everywhere." She touched his arm and watched a spark of lust intrude eyes normally reserved for food. Then she moved on, unwilling to compete with smoked salmon.

It was her favorite sport, playing her power over men. She relished the feeling that came with the conquest of their attention. It is better than being a queen, she thought. My subjects submit freely. She had given her husband, the general, a public kiss and embrace when he was unexpectedly called back to the capital at the height of the party. But, with Roberto gone she reveled in the freedom to play her game.

Dancing with the men at the party, Luisa read the level of their lust with a practiced ease. She finally settled on Juan, a handsome young deputy, simply because he had tried to hide his interest. "How do you survive those congressional battles? I am so afraid of conflict," she complimented. "What a strong jaw line," she said, touching his cheek. She danced to fit his body. Now, her face brightened as she remembered the pout on Juan's face when she left him, burdened with urgency, just outside her bedroom door.

The clatter of hooves on the drive brought Luisa from her reverie. She watched as Ana Alicia Castillo y Alvarez, her fifteen-year-old daughter, dismounted from Nevada, her snowy white stallion. Luisa had chosen "Come Ride Nevada," as a password for Ana Alicia's protection. The times were dangerous. Kidnappings were on the increase. Guards were necessary. Ana Alicia was instructed to entrust herself only to known friends or to military who came bearing the password, a password known only to the girl, her parents and to Colonel Molina.

Luisa returned Ana Alicia's wave and, watched her daughter's blossoming body stride toward her. More beautiful than I, she thought, without jealousy. She recalled the simulated sadism that accompanied Ana Alicia's conception, and, that later occasion when the general used a real whip with real vigor. Luisa, as wealthy and connected as the general, had closed her bedroom to him forever, and now their public warmth was affected. Their sole reason to stay together was this girl, and the strength of their combined wealth. If there is any warmth left in Roberto, she thought, it is saved for this daughter. I pity the women Roberto uses.

****

In the city, General Roberto Castillo carried a box of havanas to his father and then helped himself. He flicked a silver lighter for both cigars, then looked at the lines that pulled his father's face downward in a constant frown. He is aging quickly, and weakening, the general thought, and felt a rare twinge of sadness mix with his affection for the old man.

A slightly larger version of the general, the older man stood and grabbed a cane to assist his stroke-affected leg. "Come, Roberto, we will talk outside." As they walked slowly to the door, they passed a servant who was polishing brass. Gaspar Jeronimo Castillo whacked his cane on the back of the unsuspecting man. The servant gasped and fled.

"I love this place, Roberto," Gaspar said as the pair entered the spacious gardens. "The capital is where the heartbeat lies. Here, I can track things. This is my home." The old man breathed deeply.

"Should you be walking, sir?" the son asked.

"Yes, I should walk even more than I do. The leg comes back. But, tell me, you have matters in control?"

"Yes sir," the general replied. "There are only spots of rebellion left, and we destroy them as we find them. It gets boring."

"That is as I see it. You do good work, my son. I am proud of you -- and of your brother, Luis. He sees that the National Congress responds to our interests. Now, if your brother, Fernando, only..." Gaspar swung the cane and whacked a rose from its stem.

Roberto knew his father's thoughts. The old man had intended Fernando for the church. If Fernando had listened he would be where Villariego is now. Fernando had rebelled, made an Indian girl pregnant and, to the family's complete disbelief, married the girl and fled to the United States. He was a brother now dead to his father.

Again the cane cut the air. A second rose went flying.

"Villariego preaches from our script and sings our hymn, sir."

"I know," Gaspar replied. "But it is not the same. The Castillos would control the government, the military and the church. What is ours would be safe."

"It is safe, sir. Villariego has not the nerve to defy us."

"What then of this bishop of Japala? He makes dangerous talk. Agrarian reform he calls it, just like all those reformers have called it. It is not reform, Roberto. It is theft they advocate." Gaspar's agitation increased. "In the past we have rid outselves of even presidents for their 'agrarian reform.'" He spat the words. "And the church was with us then. The Vatican joined with us and the American CIA and we threw the reformers out. Why is this bishop now singing a different hymn? It is dangerous, Roberto." Gaspar sucked in a breath.

"I will take care of it, sir. Do not concern yourself. I will talk to Villariego, and I will take care of it."

Gaspar put his hand on his son's shoulder. "You are a good son, Roberto. Remember, what you protect is yourself and what is yours!"

Later, the general watched the parade of buildings from the back seat of his chauffeur-driven limo, his mind still on his father. Gaspar has indeed built a kingdom worth protecting, he thought. It started with bananas, established with American help. Now, it is coffee plantations, beef ranches, lumber and chicle, hundreds of thousands of acres, and the family-owned bank. He recalled the raw Gaspar, the father of his young manhood, whose whip kept 'his' Indians in constant fear and control, the Gaspar who raped the Indian women openly. He closed his eyes and found the vivid memory of the first time Gaspar had placed the whip in his own hands and ordered him to thrash a young woman. He had bent into the beating hesitantly at first, but then with vigor as a new sexual excitement awakened in him. He had struck repeatedly as the girl's life dwindled away.

The driver stopped in front of the episcopal palace and opened the rear door, saluting as the general emerged. Castillo strode to the door. It opened before he rang. The servant bowed. The archbishop is this way, please, General. The nuncio, Monsignor Guerrolino, is with him."

"What have you done about this pipsqueak in Japala?" Castillo demanded as he entered Villariego's office. "News of this bishop's stupidities has even reached my father. I will not have my father upset. And I am at the end of my patience with this madman."

"Ah, General, come in." The archbishop rose from his desk chair. "Have a chair, please. Havana?" he asked.

"No, thank you." Castillo sat down and gave a curt nod to the nuncio. "Japala!" he demanded again.

Villariego sat down. "I have talked to him, personally,

General. I have tried to show him that he does a disservice to the poor Indians he hopes to help. My argument did not persuade him, I'm afraid."

Castillo bristled. "Does he understand this land reform he preaches only incites the peasants' greed? Does he realize his preaching may incite them to revolt? Does he want their blood on his hands?"

Villariego gave a helpless shrug. "I have also had the nuncio talk to him." He looked at the nuncio for help.

The nuncio remained silent.

"You are an archbishop," Castillo roared. "He is only a bishop. You do not try to persuade. You command!" Castillo's voice was hard, unrelenting.

"I cannot command him. He is not my subordinate, General," Villariego advised. "He has complete authority in his own diocese. He reports only to Rome. I have complained to Rome. The nuncio also has complained. Rome has not replied. They do not do things quickly in the Vatican, you know. We are both waiting to see what changes our new Holy Father may bring about. If we have patience, maybe..."

"So you can do nothing!"

Another helpless shrug. "I have done all I can."

****

When the general had left, Villariego breathed a long sigh. "He is difficult at times, my cousin is," he said to Guerrolino. He reached for a bowl and crunched a chocolate-covered coffee bean in his teeth. As if tasting wine before serving it, he nodded his head and passed the small crystal bowl to the papal nuncio. "From Hawaii, they're good," he said. "Now, where were we before the good general barged in? Oh yes, tell me, Mario, what do you know of our new Holy Father? A lesser light, is he not?"

Guerrolino studied the bowl of chocolates as if to distinguish which of the identical delicacies was worthy of selection. Finally, he honored one, set the bowl on a side table, and relaxed back into the chair's soft-leather comfort. "I have met him on several occasions, Lucas. He is from wealth. His family is titled. I know that much. I do not know his..." Guerrolino searched for a word, "philosophy? I am bothered that he took the name, Francis. It is a departure. Perhaps he means to signal a change. So, I would be more comfortable with his election if he had taken a stronger name, a Boniface, a Julius, a Gregory, a John Paul." Some feeling and color awoke in the nuncio's bland exterior. "Yes, I am apprehensive that Francis the First has chosen his name with an eye on Assisi. It may be that he will launch an attack on class and wealth."

"If that is the case, Mario, we have nothing to fear. It would not be the first time someone tried to change the system. They always fail. It is simple-minded, even if well intended."

"Mark my words, Lucas. Francis the First, Alberto Della Tevere, is not simple-minded."

"You know best. Now back to my interests. How do you advise me? What approach do I now use in my humble quest for the galero, my red hat?"

"You are not concerned for Bishop Reilly?"

Villariego shrugged. "My cousin gets upset easily. But inside he is a pussycat. You can trust me there. Bishop Reilly is safe."

****

Sean Reilly, Maryknoll priest from Chicago, bishop of Japala, visited the Franciscan Sisters' school east of his see city. He joked and played with the children, but his jolly exterior contrasted with a constant ache within. These poor children, he thought, with their bare feet and their minimal diets; this rotting school with its dirt floor and makeshift furnishings. It is only the nuns that make this worthy to be called a school. How do we bring some of this country's resources to these children? I have tried to embarrass the rich. They do not embarrass easily, I fear. And where is the church? Are we afraid the powerful will close down our churches if we speak for the rights of the poor? Sometimes I think we are more afraid they will close our palaces. God help us!

Tired at the end of a long day with the children, the bishop rested with his eyes closed. He sat in the front passenger seat as a catechist drove him homeward through the hills. Coming over a rise the catechist spied the military van on the side of the road ahead. With an automatic reflex he slowed the car. He did not see the concealed marksmen in the trees. Suddenly, the car windows exploded under the fire power of automatic rifles. The two occupants slumped forward. The old Plymouth, out of control, swerved into the trees.

Colonel Jorge Molina walked to the wreck and fired a final bullet into the head of the catechist and another bullet into the head of the bishop. He then led his squad back to the van.

****

General Castillo picked up his phone and listened to the caller. "Yes, I heard the news this morning, Archbishop," he said. "I have sent Colonel Molina to investigate. However, I fear we will not find the killers. They lose us in the hills."

On the other end of the phone Villariego felt a cold chill. "Who would do such a thing, General?"

"The insurrectionists, of course. I fear the good misguided bishop was stealing their message, and their thunder. They can never permit this. It is sad, yes. But, perhaps now we will have peace."

The chill stayed on Archbishop Lucas Villariego for days.

THREE NUNS

The front doors of the late-model van carried round decals of a fish symbol and the words *Our Lady of Guadalupe School.* Sister Joan Delaney drove. Two other young nuns, Miriam Weber and Rosalita Chavez occupied one of four rear seats.

"It's wonderful. Drives like a dream," Joan enthused.

"Thank God for our sister parish in the United States," Rosalita replied. "They are so generous."

Joan looked into the rear view mirror and caught the eyes of a nun in the back seat. "You drive on the way home, Rosalita. You'll love it."

"I don't know when I've felt so free," Miriam said. "Not to be stuck in the parish all the time." She drank in the countryside.

"How did we ever get along without a car?" Joan replied. "It's like getting your first watch. Once you get used to it, you can't seem to live without it."

Miriam looked at her watch. "We don't want to miss the festival parade," she said.

"We're fine. We'll be in the capital in fifteen minutes," Joan said. She slowed the van and pulled toward one side of the narrow highway to let an oncoming van pass.

"It's a police van," Rosalita commented as the military vehicle sped past them.

Joan resumed her speed. A minute later she saw a van similar to the police van approaching from the rear. Could it be the same one? she wondered. She checked her speed. It was okay. The vehicle pulled close, tailgating. "We've got the cops on our tail," she said, unconcerned.

The two nuns in back turned around to see the grinning faces of two soldiers. They waved.

The police van bumped the rear bumper of the nun's ve-

121

hicle.

"Now what are they trying to do?" Joan asked aloud.

Again the police van bumped their rear bumper, the force jostling the nuns.

"The bullies."

Suddenly the police pulled alongside. The nuns turned to see leering soldiers. One of them, a calloused cruelty in his face, made obscene gestures. The police vehicle sped forward and turned suddenly, forcing Joan to brake and pull to the side. Four soldiers were quickly at the side of their car. One opened the driver-side door and shouted the order, "Out!"

When the nuns were out and lined up on the side of the van, the sergeant demanded their papers. Joan Delaney and Miriam Weber produced theirs from purses. Sister Rosalita said, "I have no papers. I am a citizen."

The sergeant gave a cursory scan of the papers and declared, "There is a problem here. You will come with us."

"What's the problem?" Joan asked.

The sergeant ignored the question and motioned to his men.

"There's no problem," Joan insisted. "Those papers are in order."

"You will come with us," the sergeant ordered. He issued the order and his men herded the nuns toward the back of the police vehicle.

"You will hear from the archbishop on this," Joan declared.

A soldier grabbed her shoulders from behind and forced her into the van.

"You will be disciplined," she screamed at the sergeant.

The sergeant grinned and slammed the door.

The drive was short, less than fifteen minutes. The nuns sat behind the paneled walls of the van, unable to see, unable to be seen. The van pulled to the rear of the police headquarters and the nuns were hustled inside. They were taken to a rectangular room. The room was barren of any kind of furniture. Its floor and walls had been freshly painted a brilliant white and the paint's odor lingered in the room. A seatless white enamel toilet stood at one end of the room. The soldiers left. The door, solid and metallic looking, locked automatically. The nuns stared around the sterile-looking room, then at each other.

An hour later they were still alone, the smell of the paint filling their nostrils. Two hours. Three hours. They relieved themselves, two standing as modesty guards between the toilet and the door. They knocked on the door and got no response. They waited, mostly silent. Fear began to etch imaginings in their minds, and then into their eyes.

The day passed, slowly, tortuously. Night came. Suddenly the door opened and three officers entered.

Joan Delaney said, "Oh, thank goodness you've come. There's been a terrible mistake."

The men did not introduce themselves. They looked from nun to nun. "Pretty enough, eh, General?" one of them said.

Miriam Weber recognized him then. "You're General Castillo. They were your men. Please help us."

Castillo pointed at Joan Delaney. "Mine," he said. "You two take yours out. I'll stay here."

Alone with Joan, Castillo approached her, drew a switchblade from his pocket and opened it at her throat.

Joan recoiled, her eyes filled with terror. She tried to scream, but the fear choked off any sounds.

Castillo grabbed the hair on the back of her head and held her as his knife slit the front of her dress. The knife severed the fabric between her bra cups and, at the end of its downward swoop, drew a slow ooze of blood from her thigh.

****

Jorge Molina's laughter was laced with scorn. "She was

123

a cherry, Manuel! Can you believe it? I saw the blood. And when I put the knife in her, Manuel, I came -- like I never come before. Jesus Christ, Manuel, the Sierra Madre rumbled, a nine on the scale. We must arrest for us more nuns."

The unmarked van wound through the curving road of Santa Maria Park. It pulled to the curb and the colors in a bed of flowers leapt briefly alive in the headlights' sweep. The two men walked to the rear of the van and opened the double doors. They carried the bodies, one at a time, into the flowers, then got back into the van and sped off, unobserved in the curfew's solitude.

"Like lilies in a pond, eh Jorge?" Captain Manuel Hernandez slapped his knee as his laughter spirited the night. The van pulled into the lot behind the gray fortress headquarters of the National Police. "I'll order the van cleaned, and I'll report to General Castillo, Jorge. You go home and get some sleep. You must be tired after your earthquake." Manuel doubled over, laughing. "How did you ever survive, Jorge?"

****

News of the nuns' deaths reached Claude Dupuis at the Vatican Secretary of State's office two days later. Claude sat at his desk reading the report from the nuncio, Monsignor Guerrolino. "Will it never end?" he murmured aloud. "First a bishop, now three nuns." He picked up his phone, dialed and said, "Sister Margaret, please."

Maggie stood at the window of her new office. The Congregation for Justice was assigned space in a building on the Piazza Pio XII, on a floor above the Congregation for Bishops. She watched the unmistakable form, unruly hair and huge mustache, cross the piazza and met Claude at the door.

They sat in a small conversational area of her office. The small round table, adorned with a vase of flowers and a painted bowl, full of lemon drops, was a Maggie trademark. Claude sat facing her, and accepted coffee. He handed her Guerrolino's report. "Read this. Then we'll talk." He took his coffee and stood at the window, admiring its overlook of St. Peter's Piazza and Basilica.

After a few minutes Maggie set the report on the table and said quietly, "God help us."

"What do you think?" he asked.

"I think the murder of Bishop Reilly is not likely a matter of chance violence. I think the same for the rape and murder of the nuns. It is clear they were abducted, their van left on the country road. Their placement in a bed of flowers is macabre. It may suggest something of the killers' minds. A display meant to intimidate!"

"Both Guerrolino and the archbishop there, Villariego, lay the blame on insurrectionists," Claude said. "Their reasoning has for me too much of the coziness."

"What's the background of Guerrolino and Villariego?" Maggie asked.

"Villariego comes from the landed aristocracy. He is related to the wealthy Castillo family. They are *formidable* and have much to protect. Guerrolino comes from the courtly set here in Italy, pretentious, but no longer wealthy. Both men have a natural affinity for the ruling class."

"You have brought this to me for a reason, Claude. What are you suggesting?" Maggie asked.

"We need a clearer picture, do we not? State already has its man there, Guerrolino. It would be awkward to send another. Besides, it is a matter of fundamental justice, is it not? Because the victims are all religious, there is an opening for your *Justice.* I know that you are working hard on the Constitution and other matters, but I think this would give your congregation an opportunity to put your hands into real mud. Perhaps you could send someone?" Claude let the question dangle.

Maggie thought for a moment. "We're dealing with high

125

level officials there. It would be best if the person from our side had status. I hope it doesn't sound puffed up, but I think I'd better go myself, as president of this congregation." She checked her calendar. "I have one very important meeting tomorrow, but after that I can switch a few things, make the arrangements, and leave the next day. Would you inform the archbishop there, and the nuncio. My religious order has an affiliated order there. I'll stay with those sisters."

The next morning, Maggie left her staff meeting feeling a deep sense of satisfaction. She walked out of the conference room with her deputy, Bishop Peter Van Antwerpen. Peter had been her first recruit, a recently ordained auxiliary bishop from Amsterdam. He came with a worldwide reputation in canon law, and held advanced degrees in both canon and civil law. Aware of his intellectual reputation, Maggie had spent much of their initial interviews looking for the direction of his heart. He had quickly displayed a passion for justice and a keen sense of justice as an essential prerequisite to both peace and love of neighbor. She had just as quickly taken the steps necessary to bring him to Rome. Together they had recruited a staff for the new congregation.

"What do you think, Peter?" she asked when they reached her office.

"You mean the staff?"

Maggie nodded

"They're strong," the stumpy, bespectacled deputy replied. "They're bright and they're strong. They won't be intimidated easily. And they've just shown us a sample of their analytical strength."

Several months earlier, Maggie had requested suggestions from the universal church for a Church Constitution. Replies had flooded in from all over the world. National conferences of bishops had submitted drafts. Drafts came too from lay reform groups, groups like ARCC, the *Association for the Rights of Catholics in the Church,* a group from the United

States. The drafts submitted by the bishops generally contained little variation from the status quo. Catholics should trust their bishops to administer justice with a fair hand. The drafts from lay groups reflected a different perspective rooted in a different experience. Justice for individuals was too often subordinated to the "good of the institution," and sacrificed on that altar. The laity produced drafts generally included strong sections on individual rights and individual protections.

Only weeks earlier, Maggie had placed the stack of these draft constitutions on the table for analysis by her staff. This morning's meeting had been the staff's first response.

"By the time you return from Central America, we'll have a single draft ready for your review," Peter said to Maggie.

At lunch that day, Maggie and Giulio were already seated when Fred Sweeney entered the restaurant. Fred walked over, shook Giulio's hand, and sat down. The waitress came. They ordered lunch. Fred ordered a cappuccino in place of wine.

"I'm so glad you could meet us, Fred," Maggie said. "Giulio's in town for the day on business."

"You were working all night, Fred? You look tired," Giulio commented.

"Actually, last night was the first good night's sleep I've had in weeks," Fred replied. "I've been on the road."

Giulio's eyes opened wider. "On the road? What means this?" he asked. "It sounds like you sleep on highway."

Both Maggie and Fred laughed. "No," Maggie said, "it means Fred has been traveling."

"For the last six weeks," Fred said. "North America, coast to coast, north to south."

"How did it go?" Maggie asked.

"What did you do?" Giulio asked.

"It went well. I've been checking on the progress of Pope Francis's reforms, Giulio. We split the job. Tim Burns -- has Maggie introduced you to Tim?"

127

Giulio shook his head. "No."

"Tim is head of the Congregation for Bishops," Fred said. "I took North America, Tim took Europe. Francis Ebowale -- has Maggie introduced you to Francis?"

Again a negative head shake.

"Francis is Nigerian. He heads up a congregation here also. He took Africa. We asked the archbishop of Canberra to take Australia, the cardinal of Brasilia to take South America, and the cardinal of Jakarta to take Asia. We report this afternoon to Pope Francis."

"Can you spare a preview?" Maggie asked.

"It was heartening," Fred answered. "Most dioceses have already transferred financial control to councils of the laity. And most bishops are happy about it. They say they can give more time to spiritual matters."

"What about the palazzos?" Giulio asked. "Do they give these up with the smile?"

"As a matter of fact, Giulio, most do. Many bishops have been living like hermits inside those mansions. But people don't see that. They see only the mansions. Those bishops will be happy to see them turned to other uses."

"Tell us about the ones who are unhappy. What are they doing about all this?" Maggie asked.

Fred sipped his cappuccino. "The milk in this coffee will put me to sleep," he said. The waitress came by and he ordered an espresso, then turned to Maggie. "Some of the bishops are unhappy, of course. There are those living the high life as if it is theirs by divine right. They entertain lavishly. I used to be into that lifestyle myself. Remember, Maggie?"

Maggie nodded.

Fred continued. "It's too bad. They appear pathetic to the laity, but don't realize it. They stretch infallibility from a papal prerogative to themselves and to the way they get their eggs done. A few are into the lordship thing, but they're beginning to look silly."

"What can you do about those?" Giulio asked, his eyes bright with interest.

"No need to do anything, Giulio. The people are doing it. They know what Pope Francis has prescribed. And the vast majority are in agreement. They're beginning to put on the pressure. Tim was telling me last night about Cardinal Pustkowski in Krakow. The cardinal told Tim: 'I am a prince first and I am a bishop second. I am the prince archbishop of Krakow. And I intend to live as such.' But, most bishops are changing away from that attitude."

"The marinade is working," Maggie said thoughtfully, and smiled at the two men.

Giulio stood. "I must run to a meeting. Perhaps we can meet tomorrow for breakfast? I must tell you, I am very interested in what you say."

"I can't, Giulio," Maggie replied. "You and Fred get together. I'm off in the morning for Central America."

Giulio raised his thick eyebrows. "Ah, Maggie, so you also go on the road. What do you do there?"

"Bishops, priests, and nuns are being killed there, Giulio. I hope to find out why. I don't know what I'll find. Frankly, I'm a bit nervous."

"You'll be fine," Fred assured.

"Still, I think I'd rather have breakfast with the two of you," Maggie said. "But, I'll see you in about a week."

Fred and Maggie left the restaurant together. "I'll drive you to the airport tomorrow," Fred said. He stumbled at the restaurant door, but steadied himself.

"Fred, you promised that you'd see a doctor about that foot. Have you?"

"Not yet."

"Will you make an appointment?"

"Okay, sure."

"Today?" she insisted.

Fred hesitated. "Okay."

"Cross your heart and hope to be a cardinal?"
"Okay, okay. I'll do it today. So stop now."
"Maybe it's only a nerve in your foot."

****

Guerrolino handed the message to Villariego. "They're sending that woman, the one appointed to the new justice congregation."

The archbishop swiveled his chair to gain more light from the window. He read the message and handed it back. "Ah, my friend, how easy for us," he said. "A papal favorite. A woman. She will be like putty in our hands. We will have her back on the airplane in two days time. And she will carry a message that serves my cause. How fortunate we are. God is good."

PART II

IN PRISON

Maggie edged back to consciousness and to a throbbing pain in her face. She opened her eyes to the dim light of a single bulb on the ceiling above her. Where am I? she thought, fighting for clarity. She was lying on a hard surface, her fingers grasping links of a chain. She struggled to sit up only to lie back down as unrelenting pain stabbed at her face. Then she forced herself to a sitting position and sucked deep breaths to quell the pain and beginning nausea. She saw that she had been lying on a narrow board bunk, one side hinged to the wall, the other held level by heavy chains angled from the wall.

She looked around the room. It was a cell, about six by twelve feet. The cement block walls and cement floor were wet, as if someone had hosed them down. They were stained with brownish blotches. The entry door was solid metal except for a four inch square window. A four inch gap opened between the floor and the bottom of the door. A squat toilet sat at the back wall. As her eyes cleared she saw the dark crack, a jagged wound in the toilet's side. A sink clung to the wall next to the toilet. She could see no mirror.

What time is it? she asked herself. It took time for her eyes to focus on her watch. Then she saw the 6:20. Morning or evening? How long have I been unconscious? She touched her face gently and felt the dried blood. Tenderly, she traced the shape of her nose. Swollen, but not broken, I think. She stood, legs against the bunk until she was confident of her equilibrium, and then walked to the door. She tested the knob but it wouldn't turn. She walked to the sink and turned on the hot faucet. Nothing came out. She tried the cold spigot and was rewarded with a trickle. She carefully washed the blood from her face, wetting her fingers frequently. As she worked the clotted blood from her nose, she caught the water's unpleasant odor. Sulfur? Dabbing softly, she dried her face with a kerchief from her waistband.

She walked back to the bunk and sat down. The bunk was too low for easy sitting. And it was too wide for the wall to serve as a backrest. She held her arms stiff and, leaning back on them, braced herself. Why? Why would they do this? What can they hope to gain? She gave up trying to find a logic that could tie her to such treatment. Are they demented?

For the first time since childhood, she felt the interminable length of an unoccupied minute. Eons later she heard boot steps further down the hall, squeaking sounds, and a tinny clanging. The sounds were repeated and came closer. She guessed at their cause. By the time they were outside her door she was sure the squeaking came from un-oiled wheels, perhaps a cart. Only when the metal tray and cup were shoved under her door did she identify the tinny clanging. An eye appeared at the window, and then moved on.

Maggie walked to the door and stooped slowly to pick up

the tray and cup. The cup was empty. The tray held a single tortilla and a small portion of beans. She carried them to the bunk. She had little appetite but pulled the tortilla apart with her fingers and managed to eat about half. It was cold. She left the beans and bits of tortilla on the tray, took the cup to the faucet and watched it slowly fill with water. She tried a sip, but its tainted odor and taste brought back the nausea. She poured the water down the drain and pushed both tray and cup back under the door.

She sat, waiting. Again she tried to find a sane purpose to her imprisonment. Again she failed, but the failure opened a door to fear. Imaginings flooded through the opening, wild, horrifying imaginings. She prayed, hurling her fears at God, replacing the imaginings with the intensity of her prayers. Finally, weariness and fatigue won the final skirmish with fear, and she slept.

She woke to the sound of boot steps, squeaking wheel and tinny clanging. The pain in her face had subsided. She watched the tray and cup appear, and the passing eye in the window. She retrieved the dishes. Another tortilla, no beans. She had no appetite. She tried the water again and managed a few swallows.

Waiting! She felt alone and helpless. She paced the cell. The long minutes evolved into longer minutes. She prayed. Fearful imaginings returned and she fought them again with prayer. She added mind games. She realized that she even missed some of the pain in her face. It too had been a diversion. The words of a letter from her deceased friend, Father Charles Mueller, came back:

Dear Maggie,

*...Sometimes I look at the cross and realize
I've never known real suffering. I've always
had enough food...clothes...shelter. I've always*

133

had good friends...the luxury of books and study.
I have a profession where I can give myself to
life's essential meaning...or so I think now.

I've had problems, sure, small tastes of suffering.
Like in my growing attraction to you, the pain of
so many kinds of distance between us.

But, I've never known the burdens of the poor,
the totally destitute, or the burdens of those
denied basic justice, or the sting of hatred,
the list goes on.

Somehow, I believe that suffering waits down
the path for all of us. I wonder if I will
have the strength to bear it. Do you ever
wonder about that?

She knew it was evening because cold beans were once
again on the plate. She ate the tasteless tortilla and about half
the beans. That night she slept, memory and dreams turned
toward Charles.

The next morning Maggie began a vigil at the tiny window. Once, a soldier walked by, but the mean coldness of his
expression kept her from calling out. She waited.

✳✳✳✳

Not far from Maggie's cell, General Castillo leaned back
in his desk chair and aimed closed eyes at the ceiling. His
mind was on the deputy he had cuckolded the night before. It
was the evening's only pleasant memory. The bitch had turned
uncooperative. Her screams had forced him to mollify his
attack, making the sex less than satisfactory. Now, in his
imagination he rewove the scene. New instruments and tech-

niques came into play. Conjuring up images he applied a host of subtle cruelties to the mind and body of the woman. Then he leaned forward and pushed a button to summon an aide. "Bring me the bitch in cell six," he directed.

A short time later the aide returned with Maggie. He stood, Maggie at his side, waiting for the general to recognize them.

The general appeared to direct interest at some papers. He allowed several minutes to lapse, then raised his head to the aide. "You may go," he said, and turned back to the papers. He heard the movement as Maggie, herself silent, moved to sit down. "You will stand!" Castillo ordered, not looking up.

"But General," Maggie began.

"And you will be silent!" Castillo's imagination played with the silence he allowed to go on, and on. He conjectured on its impact on the nun. His mind's eye pictured the striking, slim brunette and without looking up, he read her uncertainty, her fear. He imagined the color draining from her fair cream complexion, the blue of her eyes fading. He relished the moments.

"General," she said quietly after ten more minutes, "there must be some mistake."

"I said silence!" Castillo raised his head and stared at Maggie with dark brooding eyes. He read Maggie's startled reaction to his eyes, and turned his head down again, heat building in his loins.

"I am a United States citizen. I demand to be taken to the American Embassy." Maggie's tone betrayed her bold demand.

Again the dark eyes focused on Maggie's. "I don't give a damn if you're the whore of the United States's president. To me you are nothing more than an irritating bitch. And you will be silent if I must gag you." Castillo saw fear come to Maggie's transparent face. Again his head turned down and he again gave his imagination entrance to Maggie's head. He felt a surge of excitement. He had hurried with that other nun. He would not hurry now. He gave himself to the imaginings of the next ten-minute silence.

"Please, General..." Maggie's fear had reached her voice.

Castillo looked up, his excitement feeding on her fear. He rose, walked around the desk and stood directly in front of her, his senses alive to the many kinds of pain she was feeling. He reached out and grasped the high neck of her blouse. With a single jerk he stripped the blouse away, its back buttons yielding easily, its arms tearing. He watched her face, reading it as she recoiled from his action. Again he reached out. This time he tore away her bra. His eyes glued to her face, not to her body, not to the breasts she tried to cover with her hands. He watched feelings of humiliation and degradation sweep across her features. And then he came. Low guttural grunts punctuated the bursts of semen that oozed an irregular stain across the front of his tan trousers. With a closing grunt he swung a ceramic ash tray against Maggie's forehead. The force sent her crashing into the wall. He watched, spent and panting, as she fell unconscious to the floor.

****

Pain jabbed her throbbing head as Maggie re-entered consciousness. She was stretched out on her cell bunk face up. As she moved her hands to her temples to combat the pain, her upper arms cradled her breasts. She sat up quickly as she felt their nakedness. The remnants of her blouse and bra were on the floor at her feet. She reached for them, feeling in her face again the heat of embarrassment, anger and fear. She worked to bend the hook of her bra back to a semblance of its original shape. The loop had been ripped loose but she managed to attach the hook to the cloth where the loop had been. There was just enough length remaining to the shoulder straps to tie them around her neck. The front of the blouse was intact, and a single button survived in the back's center.

As she tucked the blouse into her skirt, the full remembrance of Castillo's cruelty filled her mind. She felt the rapid beating of her heart. Her eyes darted frantically around the cell. She tried the door and accidentally overturned the metal cup and plate. Beans and tortilla spilled onto the floor. For the first time since her imprisonment she felt completely helpless, and hopeless. She could see no way out, no escape. The hopelessness built to tears, tears to sobbing. She fought them, but the terrible imaginings and terror locked themselves to her helplessness.

Finally, when the sobbing and feelings of terror had exhausted her, Maggie knelt on the damp cement floor by her bunk and prayed. Dear Lord, I am helpless. Only your power can deliver me. If there is a back door you know the way. I remember how your angel led St. Peter to safety when he was chained inside a prison. Surely your angel can lead me from this prison if you will it. Help me have hope now even though I cannot feel it. You are my only hope. She thought of her friends in Rome, the Il Cero bunch. They're helpless too. I wonder if they even know where I am.

Later, she applied cool sulfur-smelling water to her forehead, gently swabbing the swollen skin. She tried to rest, to shut down her mind, but failed. Thoughts of Charles brought some relief, thoughts of his struggle to make sense of suffering. She remembered his story of a parishioner's pain. One summer, the man lost his barn, his cattle and most of his crops, all sucked up into the vortex of a raging tornado. Then, in the winter, on a long lonely stretch of freeway, a semi driver lost control of his truck on a patch of ice. The semi careened across the median and crashed into the pickup driven by the man's son. They were the only two vehicles on the road. A split-second difference in timing and the young man would have lived. Then, that very next summer, Charles buried the man's wife, dead of colon cancer. "It was the story of Job all over again," Charles said. "Does suffering have meaning," he asked, "Or is it just so much cosmic excrement? It seems to me..."

A key turned in the cell door. Colonel Jorge Molina stared in at Maggie and then swaggered into the cell, hurling the door shut behind him.

JORGE MOLINA

Maggie stood up from the bunk bed and backed away from the cold hardness of Molina's eyes.

Molina walked up to her. "Hello, bitch," he muttered. "How would you like to feel the Sierra Madre rumble?" He reached out and slapped her violently across the face, then grabbed her by the shoulders.

Maggie struggled, striking back without effect. "No! Don't!" she shouted at him.

A cruel smile contorted Molina's face. "Good, bitch. Fight back! Fight!" he goaded. He grabbed her by her hair and swung her from wall to wall with one hand, gouging and punching with the other.

Maggie's grunts of pain turned into screams. Her screams only broadened the savage grin on Molina's face. Suddenly, he stopped the beating and ordered her to remove her clothes.

"No, please don't."

Piece by piece, Molina tore away her clothes. Then he threw her, naked, to the cell floor and covered her with his heavy body. His knuckles poked and prodded at her face, her eyes, her ears.

Unable to resist and tormented by pain, Maggie moved in the only direction left to her, inward.

She found Charles there. She saw him clearly, his fair skin, the shock of auburn hair, the hazel-green eyes, the scar on his forearm, the familiar grin. He beckoned her to follow him and together they walked deeper. Finally he stopped and turned to her.

Maggie reached out to take his hand, but her flight into this inner refuge failed her. She found herself suddenly outside, detached, and looking down on the attack. Her breathing was rapid and shallow as she watched Molina's arms flail downward, the forced spread of legs, and the pounding thrusts of his body.

When Molina stood up at last, he stripped the last drops of semen from his penis. Maggie saw, but did not feel its sticky heat as the small jet landed on her thigh. When Molina unleashed a vicious final kick to her side she saw only the gagging and vomiting reflex it caused. At a distance she heard Molina's parting words. "Whore, you could not make an ant-hill rumble. Castillo should let me kill you. If it were up to me, I'd have you buried."

Maggie watched from above as he left the room. Then, slowly, she was rejoined with her body. An overwhelming numbness displaced her sense of detachment, and she still did not feel the pain. Who was that woman lying there under Molina's weight? she wondered. She had watched the attack, but who was the victim? Numb and in shock, Maggie sank into a torpor, and finally into sleep.

In the morning she awoke to the sound of the metal plate and cup scraping the floor. She was still lying on the floor, still naked. She felt the giant ache of her body first. Then, gradually, her memory retrieved the images of Molina's attack on her. The mental pain provoked by the images was too much to tolerate. What happened? she asked herself. What happened? A numbness encompassed her mind and her body, and mollified the anguish she felt.

She got up from the floor and reached down to retrieve several shreds of her clothing. She bundled the pieces, lay down on her bunk and clasped the bundle to her stomach, curling her body around it. She stared apathetically at the dishes on the floor. Feeling a chill she sat cross-legged on the bunk, hugged the bundle to her body, and began to rock slowly, steadily, back and forth. She heard, but did nothing to respond to, the guard who came in and retrieved the utensils from the floor. He was going to upbraid her for not shoving them out into the corridor, but stopped and stared at her bruised face and numbed eyes.

When the plate and cup rattled onto the floor that evening, she left them there. Later in the evening she began to hum, a droning tuneless hum. Finally, she ceased the listless sway of her body and the drone, and slept.

The next morning the rattle of plate and cup again woke her to both her physical and emotional pain. Memories of the attack continued to breach her defenses and bring with them the unbearable pain. Denial and the numbing grace of shock once again applied a temporary but soothing ointment to relieve her emotional anguish. She settled into a state of numbed apathy.

When her bowels began to cramp later in the morning, she felt a sort of gratitude. They were pains she could tend to. As the cramps increased in severity, she was compelled to spend much of her time on the toilet. There, she discovered dried blood on her inner thighs as bursts of watery stool pulsed from her. She was busy keeping herself somewhat clean, using the shreds of her clothing and water from the sink.

****

Early that afternoon, General Castillo arrived at his office, smacking an open palm with his riding crop. Inside, he whacked the crop across his desk several times, enjoying the sound and feel. The rounded swell of a paper weight recalled a prostitute on whose body he had once wielded the crop. When he had finished with her, welts ran in ascending tiers across the down-slope of her breasts. The remembrance engaged his lust. He summoned an aide and ordered Maggie brought. "And make sure the bitch is clean."

The aide grabbed a ring of keys from his desk and walked briskly down the hall. He opened the cell door and stopped at the odor. He looked at Maggie, closed the door, ran down the hall, and found a stout expressionless woman who pushed a cleaning cart. "The general wants her. Clean her up quickly or he'll have both our butts."

"Bah," the woman uttered, uncaring. Together they walked to Maggie's cell. "You'd better get her something to wear," the woman said. As the aide ran off, the woman pulled Maggie to her feet and led her down the hall to a common shower. She handed soap and a brush to Maggie, turned on the water and ordered Maggie into it. "Scrub," she said coldly. Then, "Hurry! Hurry!" as Maggie rubbed the hard bar of soap onto her skin.

As Maggie dried herself with a grey rag of a towel thrown at her by the woman, the aide returned with a brown prison shift. He handed the shift to the scrub woman who then helped Maggie bring it over her arms and body.

Castillo was furious. "Where the hell have you been? It's been nearly an hour." He stared down the aide, ignoring Maggie.

"Surely not that long, sir," the aide attempted. "She was not clean, and had to shower."

Castillo dismissed the aide. "Get out of here, you worthless ass."

"Yes, sir."

Castillo continued to ignore Maggie. He returned to the papers on his desk and to his imaginings.

Maggie stood quietly, hands dangling at her side. The minutes passed. Suddenly her hands went to her stomach. Spurts of stool fell to the carpet and down her legs. Yellow brown blotches widened on the rich oriental.

The odor caught Castillo's attention. He looked up and saw his fouled carpet and the vacant numbness of Maggie's eyes. He felt the ruin of his intentions, the stuff of his pleasure fouled also with her incapacity for humiliation. Infuriated, he raged from the room. "Get her out of there," he shouted at the aide, "now! And get that carpet cleaned, now! And get the smell out, now! And send that bitch to the Hole!"

****

That evening, Maggie suffered an enema given her by the same stout woman. She was handed a clean shift, and dressed herself.

"The men do not want a stinking accident in their van," the woman said.

Maggie felt numb for the ride out of the city. She saw nothing in the darkness. After twenty minutes they arrived in the quadrangle of an old, two-story, adobe structure. She was taken inside and pushed into a large cell. Three of the cell's walls were adobe. Bars, evenly spaced, made up the wall next to the hallway. The cell's floor was dirt. In one corner, a layer of straw covered the dirt, not as a bed, but to collect feces. The water supply was a half barrel, half full. There were eight people in the cell when Maggie became the ninth.

She stood just inside the door, arms dangling, apathetic to her new surroundings. An older woman, her dress tattered and blood stained, approached her.

"My name is Maria," the woman said as she looked into Maggie's eyes. She put a hand softly to Maggie's cheek. "*Loco*," she muttered to her companions.

Let them think that, Maggie thought.

"Lucky," a young man replied. He was missing an eye, and the tips of his fingers oozed blood where fingernails had been.

They were all like that in some way, she would discover. Five men and three women, all wounded, emptied by torture of their trivial knowledge, forced to create fiction pleasant to the ear of their tormenters if they hoped to see another ugly day.

Maria took Maggie's hand and led her to a spot by the back wall. She sat next to Maggie and held her hand, stroking it gently.

Maggie stiffened at the woman's touch, but then allowed it. It was, after all, a woman's touch, a gentle, caring touch.

****

That night Maria slept, her back to the wall, with Maggie's head in her lap. Maggie lay curled on her side. Suddenly, Maria was awakened by the stumble and muttered curse of a man working his way back from the straw latrine to his sleeping space. In the dim light Maria also saw the bars of the cell door begin to move in a slow sweep inward. She knew the guard by the shape of his thin body and long straggly beard. She also knew why he was here. Night duty guards regularly sped up their shifts with free pleasure taken from female inmates. In this cell it could only mean Maggie. Guards no longer bothered Maria. There was always much younger fare. Nor did they ever select either of the other two women in the cell. Their mutilations only accentuated their age, each older by far than Maria.

The guard moved a small flashlight beam from body to body. When it found Maggie, the light stopped. The guard used the light to guide him around prone bodies to where she slept. He bent to grab her wrist.

"Teniente--Lieutenant" Maria whispered, stroking the private's ego.

The guard halted his bend. "Eh?"

"Teniente," came Maria's hoarse whisper, "you must be careful."

"Stupid woman." The guard reached for Maggie's wrist.

"Teniente, listen to me. She is loco."

"You're loco. Who cares?"

"Teniente, have you not heard how dangerous it is to sleep with a loco woman?"

"I don't plan to sleep, old woman." The guard snickered gutturally.

"I am a nurse, Teniente. You know this from my records. In my village, I have seen this, not one, but three times."

The guard halted his rise. "You're a loco old woman. What do you know about anything?" Then, guardedly, "what did you see, old woman?"

"Teniente," still whispering, "when those men took this loco woman, the craziness went right to their crotch."

"What do you mean?"

"First one testiculo, then the other, Teniente."

The guard let Maggie's wrist slip free, and moved one hand to cover his crotch. "What happened to them?"

"It is horrible to see, Teniente, as brave as you are."

"What is horrible?"

"First one testiculo, then the other, Teniente. They turn yellowish green, like pus from the eye."

"You're loco."

"Teniente, I am a nurse. And worse yet, Teniente, it makes you puke to touch them. First one testiculo, then the other. They become soft like the sponge."

"Bah."

"Ah, Teniente. You are young, and I can tell you are very good with the women. It would be a great loss. A terrible smell comes from their crotch, Teniente. I know. I have smelled this smell. It is like rotting pork."

The guard stood, shuddered, then moved to the cell door, and out.

Maria settled back to the wall and relished her small triumph. She smiled in the dark as she imagined the guard's reaction. He had capital now to share with the others. It would give him a moment at the center of his peers. The other guards, too, would listen with a growing fear, unwilling to take the chance. Maria stroked Maggie's cheek. "At least from that you are safe now."

145

REACTION IN ROME

Claude Dupuis pulled the Roman collar from his neck, opened the shirt button at his throat and rolled up his shirt sleeves. He swiveled to the credenza behind his desk, reached down and booted his computer. He tugged at his broad mustache as the monitor came alive. He clicked the menu for E-mail. Routinely, daily, he scrolled all official messages coming into the secretary of state's office regardless of their intended desk. He recommended the practice to his staff so they too would keep tuned to the secretariat's activity.

On this morning, he scanned quickly, ignoring the routine. He stopped abruptly at a message to the Central American desk. *Subject: Sister Margaret McDonough -- Missing.* He read the message, swiveled to his desk and dialed the phone. "I must speak to the Holy Father immediately. It is an emergency."

"Yes, Claude?" the Pope asked when he came on the phone.

"Francis, Maggie is missing! She disappeared after meeting with General Castillo, the head of the National Police. It has been, by my calculation, over thirty-six hours."

Francis was silent. "Dear God," he said finally. "Keep her safe. What do you recommend, Claude?"

"First, that you personally call President Ruiz and urge him to make her safety a matter of national urgency. A personal call from you will convey her importance to the Vatican."

"I will do so, of course. What else can we do?"

"I'm bringing Fred in. He has friends in the US government. The American Central Intelligence Agency put President Ruiz in power -- and keeps him there. I'm confident the CIA still has a strong presence there. We will try to enlist their help. After that, I don't know. I'll keep working on it. Right now, I'll call Fred. We'll put our heads together."

Thirty minutes later, Fred sat in Claude's office in the Apostolic Palace. Claude handed him the message from the nuncio, Guerrolino.

I regret to inform you that Sister Margaret McDonough has been reported missing. She had a meeting with General Roberto Castillo on Wednesday p.m. Castillo, a stern but devoted man, was kind enough to direct his deputy to drive Sister McDonough back to her convent residence. On the way there, she asked to be left at the site where the three murdered nuns were found, saying that she wanted to pray there. She has not been seen since.

Both Archbishop Villariego and I are of the opinion that, barring an unlikely act by a solitary criminal, she has been abducted by the insurrectionists. As of now, there has been no demand for ransom.

We will keep you advised.

"We should have stopped her going alone," Fred said. "I should have gone. One of us..."

"Maggie would have seen through those courtesies, Fred. She would have rejected them. Her decision to go alone was calculated, and it was hers alone." Claude was abrupt. "Regrets don't help her now. Let's just try to help her. It is clear to me that we can expect no aggressive help from Guerrolino or Villariego. They will only wait for events to unfold. It is up to us to be aggressive. You have contacts in the US government...."

****

The next morning, Fred, feeling a chill in his gut, carried an overnight bag, his only luggage, onto an Alitalia jet bound for Dulles airport. Tourist class seats were full and he felt awkward in the spaciousness of first class, grateful though that the empty seat next to his left him free for his thoughts. He was hopeful. He had been promised the power of the U S government. Beagle O'Leary had been his grade school class-mate. They were Beagle and Ferdie back then. Fred recalled how O'Leary had become a powerful attorney in one of Chicago's largest law firms and then moved into politics. Now Senator O'Leary, he was a member of the secretive CIA over-sight committee.

"I'm one hundred percent on your side in this, Ferdie, and I've got the clout," Beagle boasted. "Get your duff over here and we'll go see the right people."

As the flight progressed, Fred's hopefulness fought a battle with deep feelings of insecurity, the secret self he had always kept isolated and hidden from the view of others. By the time the plane landed, his determination had conquered his fears. At the airport he was met by the small dapper O'Leary who led him to a spacious chauffeur-driven limo.

O'Leary briefed Fred on the drive to CIA headquarters in Langley, VA. "We'll be meeting with C. James Cartier III," he said. "He's their Central America main guy, their point man to Congress and the Administration. You give 'em the dope on Sister Margaret's importance to the Vatican. I'll lay the muscle on 'em." Clearly, Fred thought, Beagle enjoys the weight his senatorial status adds to his small frame. Still, thank God, he's the weight we need.

C. James Cartier III greeted them in a paneled conference room of the CIA headquarters. Tall, spare, with straight salt and pepper hair that moved down and over small ears, Cartier introduced a lumpy red-headed assistant, Abram Goldstein.

149

The two men listened to Fred describe Maggie's position in the Vatican and the reason for her presence in Central America. They took the dossier on Maggie that Fred brought them. Goldstein's eyes showed appreciation as he studied Maggie's picture. Both agents showed patient endurance and deference to Beagle's bombast.

"Senator, Archbishop," Cartier was aloof, but deferential, "we appreciate your handing us this problem. All too many citizens, especially those with means, barge into sensitive areas like Central America and try to solve the problem themselves. They bring attorneys or hire thugs, or whatever, and invariably end up entangled and unsuccessful. Now, obviously, I cannot reveal to you the extent of our presence there. Sufficient to say we have a presence, an effective presence I might add. We can locate Sister Margaret, I have no doubt of that, if she is still alive. And if she is alive, we can bring her out. If she is alive, we will bring her out. You can count on it. It may take time, so you must be patient. Agent Goldstein will oversee the project. He is an expert on that country, knows the powers at work there as well as anyone alive. He will report to me on a daily basis. Senator, I will keep you informed on developments. You can relay them to the archbishop. If that is satisfactory?"

The meeting ended with a final display of O'Leary's bluster.

****

When Fred and the puffed-up O'Leary left, Goldstein listened to Cartier's directive.

"I don't want any written reports on this," Cartier said. "Nothing goes to the files. We keep it strictly verbal, understand?"

Goldstein nodded. "I already know where she is, sir. Our man at Castillo's police headquarters says she's there. If we squeezed hard, there's a chance..."

"We're not going to squeeze hard. We're not going to jeopardize what we've built up there because some pious, Jesus-loving, do-gooder has her tit in a wringer."

"But, she's an American citizen." Goldstein used his only argument.

"I don't care if she's the president's mother. You get to ask them one polite question. Can we have her? If they say no, then getting her out of there would cost too many chips. We keep our chips until we really need them. You keep track of things. I'll feed O'Leary what it takes to show how hard we're working on this. The scent of that woman will grow and fade on alternate days. If Castillo says no, the trail will disappear in two weeks time."

"She'll be dead."

"So-o-o?"

Back at his desk, Goldstein threw his notepad on the desk, sent his foot in an awkward swipe at his wastebasket. "Shit! Shit! Shit!"

"What's up, Abe?" his co-worker asked. "Miss breakfast?"

"*Caveat Civis*!--Let the citizen beware. That's what's up," Goldstein replied, bitterness curling his lips. "Citizen beware" he repeated, "because your government has sold its soul to The Great American Fruit and Veggie Company. Your government doesn't give a tinker's damn for you, or your safety. Your government cares more for a sadistic bastard like Castillo than it does for you, citizen. And why? Because that sadistic bastard keeps his country safe for The Great Greedy American Fruit and Veggie Company." Goldstein slumped into his chair. "On days like this I hate this damn job, and I hate myself."

****

151

As Fred boarded the plane for his return flight to Rome that evening, he felt relieved and confident again. He recalled the quiet confidence and verbal assurances of C. James Cartier III. He felt he had accomplished his task. He had gained for Maggie the full strength of the United States government. For a few minutes, he let his imagination fill with images of that strength. He visualized great ships and submarines, squadrons of potent aircraft, armor and battalions of men. He imagined scores of secret agents ferreting out Maggie's location, paying the ransom, bringing her out, well and safe. He felt proud to be an American. For the first time since he learned of Maggie's disappearance he enjoyed a meal, even though it was the usual airline fare.

And he slept. Back in his apartment by early morning, he showered, shaved and had a cold cereal breakfast. He checked into his office for messages, and then walked down the hall in the Apostolic Palace to Claude's office to give a full report. Soon, both men were on the phone answering the many questions of Francis I. Reporting done, Fred went into St. Peter's Basilica to vest for mass and pray for Maggie's safety.

By noon Fred's confidence began to slip. He had just completed an itinerary for his next fact-finding trip when a gentle tapping at his door made him look up. Giulio Giuliano, a broad smile on his face, stood there. "Hi, Fred. I was looking for Maggie. They said she is not back yet from Central America. If you don't mind being the second choice, I will buy you the lunch."

"Come in Giulio," Fred replied, his worry holding back a natural response to Giulio's buoyancy. "There is more about Maggie."

****

Forty-five minutes later, a grim Giulio flagged a taxi in the piazza and rushed to a newly rented Villa on the *Via Appia*

152

Antica. There, he worked the phone. The first call went to Mexico City. He had friends there. Did they have friends in Central America? They did. Giulio outlined the problem. Could they help? For six hours, calls went back and forth between Rome, Mexico City, Guatemala City, San Salvador and Tegucigalpa. In that time Giulio received assurance of resources and the sure knowledge of Maggie's imprisonment in the police headquarters. To his friends in Mexico City, Giulio explained, "You understand family, my friends? She is family."

That evening, Giulio was the lone passenger on his company jet. High over the Atlantic, he subordinated his terror of flying to Maggie's plight. He did not share Fred's confidence in assistance from the US government. Perhaps, he thought, it is because we Italians have a longer experience of government, its promises, its partisan justice. He germinated a plan that flourished in his mind, and bloomed as the plane reached Mexico City.

POPE FRANCIS AND REFORM

Fred Sweeney walked into the papal office, a swing in his step. "I have good news," he announced.

Francis I, Claude Dupuis and Marco Gattone were seated around a circular table next to a window. "You have discovered a new Gospel, have you Fred?" Francis responded. "We have need of more good news. Tell us."

Fred stumbled at the carpet's edge. He caught himself quickly, his face quizzical, but still buoyant. "Senator O'Leary just called," he said. "The CIA man, Cartier, told him they are close on Maggie's trail. The rebels have her in the mountains. The CIA source says she is alive. So there is great hope. The rebels do not kill their captives. They use them as hostages or for ransom. But, so far there has been no ransom demand. Cartier has his top expert on that area, a man named Abram Goldstein, in Central America now. He is directing the search."

Claude looked at Fred, tugged at his great mustache, and spoke softly. "I truly hope it is the way you say, Fred. We must remember, however, that it was the CIA that destabilized and overthrew a legitimate government there several decades ago. And the Vatican was very much in the thick of it, abetting the CIA. It is the CIA that keeps the present government in power with their supply of arms and money. So, if it is the government that has Maggie, we may never know this. The United States will never risk losing control there."

Francis I motioned Fred to a chair. The pope's eyes were bright through his metal-rimmed glasses. "Claude has been very busy on this also, Fred," he said. "He has contacted all our allies who have influence there and asked them to use it in Maggie's behalf. We have also let it be known to President Ruiz and General Castillo that substantial monies are available for Maggie's safe return. So you see, we are prepared to pay ransom even if we acknowledge it as a reward."

The men were silent for a time, each one lost in their imaginations' sketch of Maggie's plight. Finally, Francis turned to Marco. "I wish you could have been with us at Fiesole, Marco. It was my omission that you were not. You would have been in awe at our Maggie. She taught us first the importance of understanding history, and then she taught us the history of society's and this church's treatment of women." Francis pointed toward the window and said quietly. "For me, until that moment, the scribes and pharisees were always others, out there. When Maggie finished her lesson, I began to apply the words of Jesus directly to myself. 'Woe to you, Scribes and Pharisees, you frauds! You are like white-washed tombs, beautiful to look at on the outside, but inside full of filth and dead men's bones.'" Francis looked at the others. "Because of this I must, no, we must start the process. We will examine our traditions to see if they truly expose the Gospel, or are nothing more than the unburied, rattling bones of men long dead."

"At mass this morning we will pray," Francis continued, "and my curia will pray that Maggie returns safely and quickly. I will not think that she might not return."

A papal chamberlain knocked and stood in the doorway. "The curia and guests are all present," he announced.

"Except for Sister Margaret," Francis corrected.

The chamberlain's face reddened, but remained inscrutable.

"Shall we go?" Francis said, rising. They left the office and walked down the corridor to the hall of the small throne, the *Sala del Tronetto,* where popes have traditionally given semi-official audiences to ambassadors. A portable altar stood before the throne. As he vested for mass at the altar, Francis's thoughts were on Maggie.

The sweet-smelling smoke of burning incense billowed upward from the censor as Francis spoke his prayer for

Maggie's safety. He saw some eyes harden at her name. After the Gospel was read, he walked to a middle aisle, in the midst of his curia. "My friends," he began, "this will be a homily not preached by myself. It will be a conversation among us, among friends. It is a time to speak our differences. Tell me what you are thinking. I will tell you what I am thinking. There are no recriminations. If we are to lead, we must learn the art of honest speaking. Now, please, to tell me your concerns."

From the rear, a prelate spoke from beneath respectful eyes. "Your Holiness, I wonder...."

"Not Your Holiness," Francis broke in. "I am Francis."

"As you say, Francis then. Would it not be useful to restore the obligation of a Lenten fast? It would bring people to their knees."

Francis looked at the man thoughtfully. "I think I will ask my spiritual advisor to give his opinion on fasting," he replied. He turned to Claude Dupuis. "Claude, what are your thoughts?

Claude spoke quietly. "It is my thought that when we present fasting as an obligation, we hide its benefit. Fasting should not be seen as obedience to a rule. Rather its purpose must be seen as leading toward interior personal control, the control required for the unselfishness of love. Is it not this ability we want to foster? And what is it we want people to kneel before? Is it not before Love, Himself? Certainly, not before our rules."

Francis looked around for further comment. From his right, another prelate spoke up. "Have you considered, Francis, what the presence of a woman in the curia portends? There is great danger, it seems to me, that you will give rise to women's dissatisfaction where little or none exists now. I fear you will unleash a plague of women's demands."

"Does it not flaunt centuries of tradition?" another asked courteously.

Francis beamed. "Bene, bene. We have the start of a good discussion. Let me respond so far, and then we go on. Surely, none of us can deny the explicit criteria of Jesus, that we are his disciples only if we love one another. In all of our debates, our concern can only be what constitutes this love."

"But certainly we can have this debate without women." Color climbed the speaker's wide and fleshy neck.

"We love them by excluding them?" Francis asked kindly.

"Tradition," the earlier speaker repeated, the tradition of deference and restraint in his own voice. "What about tradition? Are we forsaking it? Will people follow us if we show ourselves changeable? Will they not think us weak? Must we not be consistent and constant? Must we not stay with our traditions?"

Seated at the rear, Johann Rolf nodded in agreement but remained silent.

"Gervase, my friend," the pope responded, looking at the youngest president of his curia, "I can always depend on you for constancy. We will not abandon tradition. Neither shall we be its slave, especially not a slave to the witless opinions of men long dead, opinions that still cling like leeches to the body of the church." He turned his focus back to the group. "I ask each of you to examine this tradition of ours, our treatment of women."

Francis looked carefully from face to face and saw the question marks there. He changed course. "Forgive me," he said, "I had intended this to be a discussion. In view of this question, however, allow me to give a short homily. Let me trace for you this tradition. Follow me through a lesson in history, a lesson I confess was taught me by Sister Margaret."

"Our history begins, of course, with Jesus. Jesus lived at a time and place where women were excluded from the company of men, and from the power that men shared. Jesus, opposed to this tradition, included women in his company. Women were disciples together with men: Mary, Martha, Mary

Magdalen, Joanna, and so many more. These women accompanied him on his journeys and supported his ministry.
These women were strong disciples. They did not run away,
for example, when the men fled in Jesus' final agony. And it
was given to a woman disciple, Mary Magdalen, to be the
first witness of His resurrection. Imagine for a moment, the
magnitude of this cultural change that Jesus initiated in the
community of His followers."

"Mary Magdalen was a whore!" Rolf interjected.

"Ah, Johann, I'm glad you mention this. It leads us to the
next stage of our history. Do you know that it was not until
the fourth and fifth centuries that the men we honor as Fa-
thers of the Church slandered Mary Magdalen in this way?
Nowhere in the scriptures is this said of her. Long before
Mary Magdalen was slandered, however, the Fathers of the
Church began to do to all women what they would later do to
Mary Magdalen, defame them. We must understand that the
lesson of Jesus to include women was not long followed by
his male disciples. We do not know for sure why this is so.
Perhaps it was the pressures of the male dominated culture.
Perhaps it was a response to the philosophies of the time.
What is clear is that these Fathers of the Church began to
exclude women from the ministry. And they did this very
effectively simply by defaming them."

"An interesting theory, Francis, but surely our constant
tradition outweighs the unkind remarks of a few fathers."

"Not a few, Gervase. The attacks on woman were perva-
sive. Women were to be ashamed of themselves for being
women. The noted Clement of Alexandria said of women
that 'the very consciousness of their own nature must evoke
feelings of shame.' Can you imagine? Saint John
Chrysostom, the golden tongued orator, said of women: 'The
whole sex is weak and flighty." If such slander could be made
by a *saint*, perhaps there is hope for all of us, eh? Other fathers said explicitly that women were incapable of upright

159

morality. I have studied this and there are many more ex-
-amples. I wish I had brought my notes to give you more.
Believe me when I tell you that the record is clear. The men
of this institution have consistently, down the centuries, de-
famed, degraded and abused women and womanhood. We
have made them unclean and incapable of moral goodness,
and through this means we have driven them out of ministries and out of equality. Oh yes, I recall one more example.
Our own Albert the Great, and his disciple, Saint Thomas
Aquinas, yes, another saint, were equally guilty of this defa-
mation. Albert said that a woman is a misbegotten man and
has a defective nature. He was the man who said that women
are themselves to blame for any abuse and rapes done to them.
I tell you, my friends, this influence is with us today in the
traditions we continue."

A prelate to Francis I's right said. "But we no longer say
such things. We honor women now. We say they are equal
partners in marriage."

"That is true, Heinrich. We acknowledge they are equal
in marriage to the men, and we also no longer burn them as
witches, but we continue to exclude them from power in this
church. Should they not have equality here as well?"

The room was silent. Then another prelate said, "I still
do not see where having separate roles in the church is a bad
thing, Francis."

Francis looked kindly at the man. "There are separate
roles, of course. Only a woman can be a mother. Only a man
can be a father. But we are not talking about such separate
roles. We are talking about a voice and power in this institution. Women have no such voice, no such power. Here they
are excluded -- totally. Why? Are they less intelligent? Are
they morally deficient? Are they incapable of handling power?
I think not. The histories of women in other institutions show
this is not so."

"What are you planning to do for women?" someone

asked.

"We will return to the tradition began by Jesus," Francis replied. "We will give to women their rightful power."

At the conclusion of mass, Francis walked back to the middle of his audience. "My friends, tomorrow I leave for eastern Europe, as you know. Before I go I have instructions for you and your offices. I want you all to hear each other's instructions so that we may lead this institution with the consistency our Gervase prizes so highly. But first, let us have something to eat."

The doors opened and workmen carried in a long table. They were followed by nuns who carried platters laden with breads, cheeses, fruits and jams. Obsequiously they placed the platters on the table and left, their heads bowed.

Francis watched the nuns. Do any of these curial ministers see what I see? He wondered.

****

When the meeting with the curia was over, Claude Dupuis and Fred Sweeney walked for exercise in the Vatican gardens. Clouds thickened above them.

"Don't you think Francis is moving too fast with his reforms?" Fred asked, "too much on the table at the same time? He's been in office barely six months."

"I think he has the virtue of impatience, yes," Claude replied, "but so did Our Lord when he said, 'I have come to bring fire to the earth, and how I wish it were blazing already!'"

"But, the centuries of mistakes, so many specific instances, it's a swampland. Aren't you afraid he will get mired in the detail?"

Claude looked at the dark sky, and said, "No. I do not have this fear, Fred. Francis will do the symbols. He will address the thousand events of history with the few symbolic

161

acts. To give you the example, in Prague two days from now, when he speaks of the one reformer, Hus, he will speak to all reformers."

Rain began to fall, and quickened, soaking their clothes as they hurried toward the Apostolic Palace and the offices of the secretariat. Inside Claude's cluttered office, they wiped their faces dry with handkerchiefs. Fred continued. "I am concerned that Francis will open too many fronts to his enemies, and make himself too vulnerable."

"You are speaking of his philosophical enemies in the curia?"

Fred nodded.

"Do not be concerned about them. Francis has Marco, he has Il Cero. He is by himself more than a match for those in the curia who oppose him. And he will win some of those over. Gervase, don't you think?"

"You are not concerned?" Fred asked.

"Not about the agenda, but I am on the edge for his safety. You know him, Fred. He is not one to be kept from the crowds. He must reach out and touch them. We can only protect him so much."

"Have you been alerted to some specific danger?"

"No, no. But he goes tomorrow to not the most safe place of our globe. To give him security is not easy in the best of circumstances. In Prague he insists to walk the Charles Bridge over the Vltava river. Can you imagine how exposed he will be?"

"I think it is too early in his tenure for Francis to have that kind of enemy, someone who would try to kill him. A crackpot, maybe, but not...." Fred let the thought dwindle.

"I do not agree, Fred. The world already knows enough about our Francis to alarm those whose religion and spirituality is given to externals, and who demand it remain so, whose greed is camouflaged only if it remains so. They have reason to hate and fear him."

162

"I can feel the relief you will have when he is across that river and back in the safety of his car. Will you ride with him?"

"No, he rides alone. That is as it should be," Claude said, pulling at his chin. "I know that I should not worry as I do. It is my lack in the virtue of perspective. If I could, I would control everything about his safety, and leave nothing to God. But I cannot control the world, nor, it seems, my fear. I ask myself, do I fear for him, or for our agenda? Both, I think. If something happened to him, our agenda dies with him, perhaps for decades, perhaps for centuries."

****

Johann Rolf, Chester Pustkowski, Michael Dougherty and Gervase Janov were seated in Rolf's office.

"Did you hear him? Did you hear him?" Pustkowski almost shouted the words. "He thinks he's guilty for every crime done to women."

"Calm down, Chester," Rolf answered. " When we meet with him we'll find out what he intends to do about these downtrodden women of his. What we want to know now is how far he plans to take this insanity. What ministries he intends to parcel out to them. After two thousand years of male celibate leadership in the church, we get a pope with a queasy brain."

"We must find a way to check his sanity," Dougherty said. "Perhaps if we can show that he is mentally unstable we can force him to resign."

"There's no time for that, Michael," Rolf responded. "He's gone tomorrow on these stupid travels of his. He wants to apologize. God only knows what he wants to apologize for. He's such a weakling." Rolf looked at his watch. "We'd better go. We're due in ten minutes."

They met with Francis I and Marco Gattone in the papal

163

library.

"Your Holiness," Rolf addressed the pope, and gave the slightest bow of deference.

"My friends, when we meet like this in private, you must call me Francis. *Your Holiness* is a presumption for all of us, don't you agree?" They occupied identical chairs at the windowed-corner round table of the papal office.

"We are not clear on either the direction you are coming from, or where you intend to lead us," Rolf began.

"Bene, let us talk of where I come from first. I understand, Johann, that your Holy Office has disciplined a man by the name of Barcos. Is this true?"

Rolf nodded.

A thoughtful expression lay behind Francis' smile. "Would you say, Johann, that this man, Barcos, loves his neighbor?"

Rolf was immediately wary. "He does good to the poor: food, shelter, and all that. But, he is disobedient to his superiors. He teaches things dangerous to doctrine."

"Johann, when you die, will the Lord give you the Holy Office's catalog of doctrines and ask if you accept them, or will he ask, 'did you love your neighbor?'" Francis' voice was calm, serious.

"Both, I think. He will ask both."

Francis laughed congenially. "You are clever, my friend. Let me rephrase my question. Is doctrine to serve love, or love to serve doctrine?"

"They are to serve each other, equally. Is this some sort of test, Francis?"

Francis' laugh was generous. "You are still too clever for me. Do we not have this single directive from the Lord, 'By this will all men know you are my disciples, that you love one another?' Nowhere did he say, 'by this will all men know you are my disciples, that you assent to some list prescribed by the Holy Office'. You must admit, Johann, that our doctrines must serve love, teach it, lead to it, proclaim it. Otherwise they have little value."

Rolf maintained his outward control. "Where is this leading us?"

"Only to that one point, Johann. That everything we are about, this institution, the doctrines we proclaim, the preaching that we do, the customs and traditions that we retain, the rules that we impose, the devotions and liturgy that we establish, all, all must serve that one purpose, to bring people to love one another."

"But, Barcos! Are you saying that because this Barcos does some good things, we are to forget the rest? We are to forget and forgive the heresy?" Rolf's calm was wavering.

"Johann, it is time. It is time we sought our identity in the Lord's directive. It is time for us to make this love of neighbor the only criteria for membership. It is time for us to shed our historical preference to exclude rather than include, to attack rather than embrace. We will no longer concern ourselves if someone fails to gaze as fondly upon an abstract doctrine with the same measure of approval as we do. We will consider first the love."

Rolf showed his shock. His voice rose and took on a touch of stridency. "This institution has been constructed stone by stone on doctrines. It is the defender of those beliefs. You yourself have the title, *Defender of the Faith*. If you compromise that title you will bring chaos. If you equivocate for one instance on doctrines as if they were relative to anything, even to this insipid love, or on rules as if they permit exceptions, you will bring chaos. You will destroy this institution. You will abdicate power that has taken centuries to build. You will go down in history as a traitor."

The pope looked at Rolf's burning face. "I am pleased that you are so intensely concerned, Johann. I am happy that you feel free to challenge me. But you are wrong. The love we talk about is not insipid. It is the first truth. It is the

165

challenge to and full measure of human ability. It is the freedom of selflessness." Francis paused for a moment. "And,
we will not destroy this institution. We will only change it
from master to servant. We will not abdicate any power that
is rightfully ours. It is only that we will not claim or demand
it. It will come to us as a gift from the people whose intelligence you misjudge. We will only be doing for them what
they already know in their hearts."

Francis looked around the table. "That, my friends, is
where I am coming from, my point of departure for everything."

"You must not apologize! It will show you to be weak,"
Rolf said.

"Which is the easier thing to do, Johann? Apologize or
not apologize?" Francis asked innocently.

Rolf saw the trap and remained silent.

Francis turned to Cardinal Gervase Janov, president of
the Pontifical Council for Promoting Christian Unity.
"Gervase, my friend, which is easier?"

Gervase Janov, handsome and punctilious, swept a hand
lightly over his jet black hair. "It is easier to say nothing," he
replied

Francis turned back to Rolf. "Is it weakness then, Johann,
to do the more difficult thing?"

Rolf said nothing.

Francis answered his own query. "We are the guardians
of the sacrament of reconciliation. From the beginning we
have encouraged our people to confess their sins in this sacrament. Are we to make ourselves, like our predecessors,
incapable of confession. This institution, whose sins are now
our sins, has yet to find a voice to confess to our brothers and
sisters when we have sinned against them. It is time, Johann,
for this voice to be heard. It will be my voice."

Rolf insisted quietly, "It is a mistake."

Francis looked at Gervase. "And you?"

Janov had risen speedily in his career. He could read the wind's drift before competitors even felt a breeze. Enormous ambition lay stifled behind the youthful face that answered his superior's every expectation. He was the complete courtier. "It is said," he replied, "that confession is good for the soul."

"I knew you would agree, Gervase. And I am pleased that you will accompany me on this journey where we will begin these confessions. In Prague, I will enlarge on the apology given by John Paul II for the scandalous treatment our predecessors meted out to John Hus at the Council of Constance. We condemned him, not for his own beliefs, but for what we said were his beliefs. We murdered a man whose moral standards were higher than our own, a man who cried out against our unscrupulous profiteering from this very sacrament of reconciliation. And after doing him in, we forced his followers from fellowship. I will apologize for our shutting them out. We were the excluders. It is time to ask that we be invited back."

"You are not responsible for the sins of your predecessors," Dougherty said.

"But they become my sins if I do not confess them, Michael," Francis responded.

Rolf spoke up. "Your concern for women. It is true that they are excluded from power. But we do them no harm by this exclusion."

"I must disagree, Johann," Francis responded. "Think for a minute of the lessons we should learn from the exclusions of history. When the Jewish people were excluded from power and position by the Nazis, by this very church in the middle ages, by countries everywhere in our history, what were the results? Restrictions on the very type of work they might do, ghettos, pogroms, the holocaust -- every kind of violence, is it not so? When black people were excluded from power, for example, in the United States, what was the

167

result? Could anyone dare claim that this segregation did nothing to make them prey to poverty, to abuse both verbal and physical, to rape and to lynchings? Can anyone dare to suggest that exclusion from power, segregation of women wherever it has happened in history, whether by church or state, has not demeaned them, made them something less than human, made them seem defective, and so positioned them as targets for every kind of abuse? Is it not true that down through history men have excluded women from power and effectively reduced their status to that of property. What has been the church's response to that? The truthful answer is that we first gave men the example of exclusion, and then we collaborated with them. At best, we suggested only to men that they be kind to their property. And when men were not kind, but abusive, we simply shrugged. After all, abuse of one's own property rings no great alarm in conscience."

Francis paused and looked at his guests. "Let me ask you this: if we are truly moral leaders, should not our minds be the first to probe the history of human experience and bring greater moral sensitivity to our brothers and sisters? Or are we to be moral slugs, the last to be dragged along, our heels dug in, by the rest of humankind? Do we think for a minute that we can long impede the moral sense of people, even should we try to restrain them with our *infallible* manifestoes?"

The pope saw the troubled eyes around him. His voice took on a greater intensity. "I am saying that because we have institutionalized exclusion, this ancient, celibate, male institution is there, a participant in every blow struck, in every murder, in every rape done on women. I am saying that as long as we continue to exclude, I am there, and you are there, responsible and guilty to some degree. And I will be done with this guilt."

Chester Pustkowski, his face red and twisted, broke in. "It is God's will. He has made women subordinate to men."

168

"Do you think God will thank you for making Him the responsible misogynist, Chester?"

"What sort of power do you plan for women in the church?" Rolf asked.

"Until they are equal, Johann."

"When will that be?"

"Perhaps we should ask them to say hold, enough, when that time arrives."

Rolf turned his head down, eyes narrowed to internal visions, and swallowed hard.

The cardinals were silent, and Francis let the silence stand for a long minute. "I think always of our Sister Margaret in her captivity. Is she being mistreated? Is she being mistreated in the ways that women are mistreated? If so, how much responsibility has our church, have I, Francis, for her suffering? More that we can bear, I think."

"You will forfeit your moral leadership," Dougherty declared.

"I think not, Michael. I think I will be demonstrating moral leadership."

"You will answer to God for this," Pustkowski accused.

"Yes, Chester, I will. Happily."

GIULIO MOUNTS A RESCUE ATTEMPT

Giulio fought to contain his impatience as he sat at a poolside veranda table. Maggie had been in prison for more than a week. He was still in Mexico. The whiteness of the octagonal umbrella above him wove itself into the blue sky like a bright cumulus. He tried to relish the aroma of his thick coffee and sipped slowly, but it seemed tasteless. He watched absently as a parade of divers pierced the surface of the pool's clear blue water. The pieces come together, he thought. Now only to confirm the timing.

A short, pudgy man crossed the white tiled floor to Giulio. His chin lay hidden behind a thick white goatee. "Buenos dias, Giulio," he said as Giulio noticed his approach.

Giulio stood and hugged the man. "Ricardo, my friend, let me order for you the coffee." He started to raise a hand toward a nearby waiter.

"No, thank you, Giulio. I am already intense enough."

"You have news?" Giulio asked as the two sat.

"Yes. This has now been confirmed. The child is at her school in the capital and there are no scheduled holidays at the school for the next week. The general is also in the capital. He is scheduled to leave there tomorrow for two days in the provinces. The wife is at their country estate. It has also been confirmed that Colonel Molina visits the cockfights every Thursday evening when he is in the capital. And when the general is away, he always requires that Molina remain in the capital. So we can be confident that he will be at the cockfights tomorrow evening. Everything is as we would want it. Also, the helicopter is in place and ready."

Excitement filled Giulio's eyes and voice. "When do we leave?" he asked.

Ricardo pulled at his goatee. "Giulio, you should not do

this. Let my men do this for you. You do not know the country. You do not speak the language like a native. This task could be dangerous for you. Let me do this for you as a friend."

Giulio put a hand on Ricardo's arm. "I must be there," he said, his voice intense with emotion. "She is like a sister to me. More even. She saved my life one time. I will not lead, so I do not need to know the territory. And I will be silent. But, I must be there."

Ricardo lifted his hands in a gesture of resignation. He motioned to a man seated at a nearby table. The man, tall, solid and muscular, approached. Ricardo stood. "Let me introduce to you, Miguel Vasquez, Giulio. Miguel will be the leader. He is a native of the country and he is a trained military leader. I will leave now, and he will brief you." Ricardo looked at his watch. "You leave for the border in two hours. I will see you back in Mexico day after tomorrow. Good fortune." He motioned to Miguel to take the seat he had just vacated.

****

They sat in a one-room, rough-lumber building. The building sat in a small clearing that had been carved from the forest's tangle of dwarf oak and pines. A van, painted in forest camouflage and two dark green, open jeeps were pulled close to the building. A canvas awning, supported by tall poles at the corners, covered the building and the vehicles, its upper side painted to blend with the greens and browns of the forest canopy.

Their briefing completed, the four men, dressed in the dark green uniforms of the National Police, emerged from the building. They entered the van and drove for a few yards along a bushy lane and then down an embankment onto the dry, rocky bed of an arroyo. Several hundred yards down the arroyo the van climbed the embankment onto a rough road that had been built for lumber transport. The road took them, undetected, across the border. They drove in silence along a series of ever widening roads, turning finally onto the country's main highway, the Pan American.

Miguel wore the insignia of a captain, another that of a sergeant. The other two were privates. The sergeant drove, Miguel to his right. In the back seat, Giulio removed his cap and stared at its private's insignia, and then turned to stare out the window.

Breaking the silence, Miguel turned to Giulio. "We three were all officers in the National Police, Giulio. I do not know if Ricardo told you this about us. We were all trained by the U.S. Military in their School of the Americas. Perhaps you have heard of this school?"

Giulio shook his head. "I have not heard of this school."

Miguel continued. "When we returned to our country for duty and began to understand what our government has been doing to its people, we became sick. We came to the conclusion that we could not participate in General Castillo's brutality. We deserted and joined the revolution. Today we are wanted men, a price on our heads."

"How did you come to know Ricardo?" Giulio asked.

"You are friend of Ricardo. I know this because he told me," Miguel answered. "Ricardo wears many hats. He is friend even to the Americans who support Castillo, and to Castillo himself. But secretly, because it must be secret, he is a man for the people. He is one of us. I know also that you already know this. We do this for him."

That evening as Miguel, shed now of his captain's uniform, entered the small arena, he saw the excitement that filled men's eyes. He moved about as bets were made in boisterous voices, called back and forth over the small compound, a dirt arena open to the sky, its canvas top rolled back. The arena was surrounded by a wall-high wooden fence that kept the cleansing breezes out and the stale smells of sweat, cigars and liquor in.

A muscular, heavy-bellied guard, an armband declaring his official status, stood at the entry and checked the tickets of those entering. He bowed courteously as Jorge Molina entered. "Good evening, Colonel."

Molina ignored the guard and strutted to a row of cages at one end of the rectangle. There, his cold black eyes stared down the man whose job it was to ensure that no one tampered with the roosters. The man stepped back and Molina went from cage to cage, taking measure of each fighting cock. Satisfied, he walked to the circle of seats surrounding the cockpit and sat. His eyes held on the pit.

Miguel moved out from a group of red-faced men who were passing a bottle and smoking cigars. Curses spiced their talk and they shot streams of spittle at bare spots on the earth. Miguel walked around the pit and took a seat opposite Molina. He nodded and the civies-clad sergeant took a seat to the left and behind Molina.

Placing bets did not excite Jorge Molina, and he made none. The fight excited Molina. He had chosen his favorites as bettors do, but his selections became his alter ego, their fighting his fighting, their destruction his. For Molina, the attraction was battle, and blood.

Two handlers, each holding a cock in the crook of an arm while caressing its neck and back feathers, approached the pit, a circle about five yards in diameter. Dug several inches into the earth, the pit was surrounded by a canvas wall about two feet high. The cocks were of equal size and weight, one colored a dark red, the other white with black irregular markings. The handlers had carefully tied small surgical steel, razor-sharp knives to the back of each cock's legs.

The umpire stepped into the pit. "Attention, your attention please, Senores," he said to the forty or so men in the room. "All six fights this evening will be with the knives, not the gaffs." The men knew the difference. Gaffs are small curved needle-like steel spurs. Knives are knives, more deadly. The umpire turned to the handlers to check their readiness. They stepped into the pit and held their birds close to each other, allowing them in turn to cluck and peck at the neck and wattles of the other, but restraining the knives. The handlers then backed away, set their birds on the ground facing each other, and stepped out of the pit.

The cocks immediately flew at each other, rising as they met, knives raking. At a height of about three feet they fell back and down, knives still working. As they rose a second time, blood was running from both breasts. Midway up the second rise, their wings beating fiercely, the red cock sunk a knife into the white's throat. The fight was over. Back on the ground, the red cock clucked and pecked the loser until it lay lifeless.

A cruel smile of satisfaction crossed Molina's face. He had won. The winner's handler picked up the victor and inspected the damage. The red would live to fight again. The carcass of the loser was sold on the spot for stew meat. A worker carefully raked the pit, blending the fresh blood into the rust colored earth.

The next four matches ended just as quickly. In one fight both cocks fell, mortally wounded. The umpire decreed as winner the last to peck at the other as they lay dying. Twice, the fights' results put a scowl on Molina's face. He had lost.

The last fight of the evening pitted a cream and brown cock against a black. The cream had already survived seven fights, the black, six. After each fight their owners had nursed them back to fighting form, solid, their shaved legs strong and hard from training, their breasts and rumps muscular and barren of fat. The exacting ritual of knife tying, neck and wattles pecking, and positioning was followed. The cocks raced at each other and rose, their blades whirling. Blood streamed from, and stained the cream's tawny breast. Blood too on the black, but less of it showed.

Again they whirred upward, and again both cocks scored cuts until the blood ran freely on their breasts. The cream's handler stepped into the pit and picked up his bird, a legitimate act, examined it carefully to see if conceding defeat might save the cock for another day, another fight. Unswayed by the crowd's call to continue the fight he took his time. Then, deciding that his bird could still win, he set the cream back on the ground.

The cocks attacked again and rose with beating wings. On the way down, the black turned belly upward and fell under the cream, pumping its leg knives. The cream fell onto this whirling fury, its knives halted for the fall. It was over quickly as the cream's entrails were pulled from its belly and it lay in a pool of its own blood. The black pecked away at its vanquished foe.

Molina rose from his seat slowly. A glint livened his hard eyes and his face was flushed. He moved slowly toward the door, savoring the blood memory.

"Pardon me, Senor, I can see you understand the cocks." Miguel had moved to Molina's left as they emerged onto the street. "Would you like to see the mother of all fights? It happens this evening."

Molina turned and stared at Miguel. "You can improve on this?" he sneered. His hand gestured back toward the pit.

"Yes, Senor." Miguel was unperturbed by the colonel's scorn. "All my life I have raised the cocks. My breeding stock is from Spain, Brazil, Belgium...." Miguel waved his arm to take in the world. "All my life I have trained and fought the cocks. I know them like I know my own body. And I have this one cock, senor, so far better than those you saw tonight. And I have a friend, a competitor, who also has one such fighter. Tonight they meet. I would not mention this, Senor, but I have watched how great is your *simpatia* for the cockfights."

"Why did you not fight them here?" It was still a sneer,

but less.

"Because, Senor, we would do dishonor to these cocks if we fought them here -- to the cheap sound of jangling change, before drunks whose only interest is booze and gambling. I thought, Senor, that you are a purist, like me. I apologize profoundly if I have offended you. I thought only to...." Miguel started to turn away.

Molina stopped him. "If it is not as you say, then...." There was more than a hint of threat in his voice.

"You may ride with my friend and me, Senor, or follow in your own car as you wish." Miguel was indifferent to the choice. The sergeant moved casually into the group.

"I will follow."

"As you wish, Senor. Here is the address if you should lose us. It is a factory that is now empty. It belongs to my friend here."

Molina took the card handed him.

GIULIO'S PLAN UNFOLDS

The head mistress of Santa Clara Academy, Mother Serafia, looked out from her office window and saw the large black Mercedes drive up the entrance road. The driver opened the rear door and Luisa Angela Alvarez de Castillo sprang lightly from the car. Luisa walked quickly on long slender legs to the Academy's entrance. The dark shadows of early morning clung to the recesses of the building's giant stone face. In the tomb-like silence, Serafia could hear Luisa's heels click down the old brick corridor, past the towering marble statue of the school's patron, Santa Clara, toward her office.

Mother Serafia was not happy. The power of Castillo family donations forced her to be in her office at this ungodly hour but was insufficient to elevate her mood. I should be in the chapel, praying, she thought. She raised a disapproving glare as Luisa invaded her sanctuary without so much as a knock. Nor did Serafia discard her clear disapproval as she rose from behind her desk, her arms arching behind her as her hands crafted a proper flow to her long black veil. As Luisa advanced across the room, Serafia's arms came to rest, folded just below her starched, white guimpe. "I think it is a serious mistake, Luisa, to take Ana Alicia from her schedule like this." Her eyes, dominating the oval opening of her coif, mimicked the stern tone of her voice.

"Now, Mother Serafia," Luisa soothed, "you were young and pretty once yourself. A trip to New York will be good for Ana, educational even. When I was your student you often told us that travel was broadening."

The nun could not recall ever being called pretty. Her face lost some of its severity, though its lines still angled downward. Her hand went to the back of her head to smooth her veil. "Still," she muttered, "it is most unusual."

"I will have Ana back to the academy in a week," Luisa

assured the nun. Certainly, Mother Serafia, a week can do her no harm." Luisa looked at her watch. "We must leave now if we are to catch the airplane."

The old nun raised her hands resignedly. "Very well, I will send for the girl."

****

Not far from the Academy, Giulio drove the van slowly along awakening streets. Except for giving an occasional direction, Miguel sat silently in the front passenger seat, frequently checking his watch.

"It was not necessary that he die, Miguel," Giulio said. He let his words trail into thoughts that traced the past evening's events. Molina had been defiant in the face of Miguel's questioning, defiant until Giulio himself had withdrawn a straight razor from his back pocket, opened it, and walked out of the obscurity of the back of the room. With several swipes of the razor, he sliced open the colonel's belt and trousers. The trousers fell to the floor. Giulio's eyes, granite hard and dark, held Molina's eyes. "On the count of three, Colonel, you will lose your treasures," he said.

Confronted with Giulio's implacable set of eyes and jaw, Molina caved in. His eyes filled with terror as he comprehended Giulio's intention. At the count of two he began to talk, his mouth like an open spigot, spilling information. Giulio read Molina's eyes, sensing when the information turned from fiction to fact.

For the night, the sergeant had taken the first watch over the bound Molina. Somehow, the colonel had managed to loosen the ropes on his legs. His arms still bound, he rammed his head into the surprised sergeant, knocking him to the floor, and ran for the door. The sergeant recovered and shot Molina just as the colonel turned to grasp the doorknob with his back-bound hands.

180

Molina had died instantly. Only then had Miguel and Giulio decided to use Molina's body as a message to Castillo. Just before dawn, the sergeant and the other private had left the compound in another vehicle carrying the dead colonel's body.

Giulio braked suddenly to avoid a collision with a speeding black Mercedes that swung from a corner into their path and then past. "Crazy driver," Giulio muttered. "You think maybe he is Italian, Miguel?"

Miguel grunted. "We'd better stop for ten minutes," he said. "We want to arrive at precisely seven-thirty, when the students will have finished breakfast, but not yet started classes. The academy is only five minutes from here."

Fifteen minutes later Giulio stopped the van at the academy entrance and stayed with the vehicle.

Miguel entered the building. "There is an emergency," he announced to the portress. "I must see the head mistress at once."

"She is in her office now, soldier. Who shall I say is calling?"

"Tell her it is Captain Oscar Sturner. I have been sent on an urgent mission by General Castillo. We must hurry." His voice held the tone of urgency.

The portress picked up the phone and conveyed Miguel's message. "Follow me," she said, hanging up the phone.

"You are the second bother I have had to deal with this morning, Captain," Serafia said at the door of her office, her tone one of pique.

"General Castillo has sent me, Sister. There is an emergency. The general wants us to provide an escort for his daughter, Ana Alicia, to a place of safety. She is in danger from the insurrectionists. The general sends this message to her: *Come Ride Nevada.* Tell her that. She will know from this that it is safe to accompany me."

Serafia's eyes filled with suspicion. "Certainly, the gen-

181

eral knows that Senora Castillo has taken their daughter from school."

Miguel struggled for composure. "He does not know this, I assure you. The general is in the provinces. He personally relayed the instructions to Colonel Molina. I was nearby on another mission when I received this instruction from Colonel Molina only minutes ago."

"I will call Colonel Molina myself, if you wish."

"If the girl is not here there is no need. Are you sure she is with her mother?"

"I am certain." The nun's mouth tightened. "The mother herself was my student. She came personally to retrieve the child. I talked with her myself."

"When was this?"

"They left some minutes ago, twenty minutes perhaps."

"Do you know their destination?"

Serafia hesitated. "A vacation. Somewhere out of the country, I believe, New York perhaps. The general does not know this?"

Miguel ignored the question. "They may be in danger. I must go. Pray, Sister, that the mother and girl are safe."

Miguel hurried to the van. "She's not there," he shot at Giulio. He took the driver's seat from Giulio and gunned the van down the road. "She's not there," he repeated. "A vacation, the nun said. The nun was suspicious and would not give exact information. Somewhere out of the country, she said. I do not believe we can have such rotten luck."

Giulio shot out questions. "Where is she? Do they know? Is there time for us to catch them on the road? Can we intercept them at the airport?" He knew the answers. The black Mercedes. Twenty minutes? No chance! His eyes were wild, obvious reflections of his racing thoughts. Finally his head fell, his face filled with dejection. "Do you know where they are going?" he asked.

"Perhaps New York, or so the nun said."

"I have friends in New York. They might....but it would take so long....if it could be done at all," he rambled. "It was so perfect. We could not fail. And yet, we have failed. And there is no one else for whom Castillo would make a trade. He would permit even his wife to die."

"We must leave at once," Miguel said. "That nun is skeptical and she will be making calls. The police will know that an attempt has been made to kidnap the girl. So, we will not be given another chance here to get the daughter. That is the cold reality." Twenty minutes later, they pulled into the compound. The four men boarded the helicopter intended to carry them and the girl to Mexico. They left without their hostage. Miguel saw the despair that plagued Giulio's face. "It is true that Castillo will surely learn that a kidnapping attempt was made of his daughter," he said, "But, perhaps he will not, at least not immediately, associate that attempt with your Maggie. There is still that hope, Giulio. And we will make another plan," he said, hiding his own sense of futility.

****

At a provincial capital, General Roberto Castillo stood, hands flat on the table, and studied a map. The commander of the provincial garrison stood silently at the general's left, his manner deferential.

"How many in that village?" Castillo asked, pointing.

The commander leaned forward to read the village's name. "About one hundred sixty, General, if we include all men, women and children."

The telephone rang and the commander motioned for his adjutant to answer. The officer picked up the phone, listened a moment and then covered the mouthpiece with his hand. "It's for you, General. Major Manuel Hernandez is calling from your headquarters. He says it is an emergency."

Castillo stayed with the map. He pointed again to the

same village. "Take it out," he said. "Take it all out. We'll raise the level, throw some real fear into those bastards." He looked at a pinstripe-clad civilian across the room. "You agree, Mr. Byrnes?"

The civilian nodded. "One's as good as another," he replied.

"General?" the adjutant reminded.

"What?"

"The phone, sir. It's Major Hernandez."

"What does he want?"

"He says he must talk to you personally. It is an emergency."

"Bah." Exasperated, Castillo grabbed the phone. "What now?" he demanded.

"They found him in the park, General. The exact spot where the nuns were found," a rattled Hernandez answered rapidly.

"What are you talking about, idiot. Found who?"

"Colonel Molina, General. He'd been shot, sir. And...."

"Is he dead?"

"Yes, General, and...ah...."

"And what?" Castillo shot impatiently.

"He was naked, General, like the nuns. Someone had...ah...."

"Had what?"

"He'd been castrated, General. His testicles were stuffed into his mouth."

Castillo blanched, then banged the phone onto its receiver. He turned to the garrison commander. "They've killed Molina. I will return at once to the capital." He gave an impatient motion to his driver, a nod to the civilian, and walked to the door. There, he stopped and turned to the commander. "All of them! Men, women, children, all of them! The entire village, you understand?"

The commander nodded. "Yes, General."

****

In Mexico City, Ricardo recognized immediately the voice on the other end of the phone conversation. His face squinched into a pained look as he listened to Abram Goldstein..

"They have failed, Ricardo. Your friend, Giulio, has failed. I do not know the details yet, but they have failed. As we speak, the girl is with her mother on a plane to New York. I saw them board the plane myself. So there will be no trade for the nun. And the nun will have a very short life if she's not out of the Hole soon. Your friend is on his way back to Mexico now. I checked, and the helicopter is gone. You can tell him not to leave Mexico just yet. I have an idea. If it works, he will have his nun. If it fails, you'd better round up an army."

CIA AGENT, ABRAM GOLDSTEIN

Abram Goldstein rubbed fingers along the red stubble of his unshaved face. The nimble mind, inside his lumpy and languid frame, took in the scene: Molina stretched out in the flower bed, dead and naked. This man, Giulio, plays real hardball, he thought. If he'd got the girl, and took credit for Molina's mouthful, Castillo would get the message just how hard is hardball.

Goldstein watched as Major Manuel Hernandez stood over the body, turned and gave directions. Four policemen trampled the flower bed as they lifted the body and carried it to a pickup truck. They laid the body on the edge of the truck's bed and jumped up beside it, covered it with a canvas, and stayed there holding the canvas in place as the truck slowly drove off.

Hernandez was busy giving instructions to other policemen and didn't notice Goldstein's approach.

Goldstein recalled a younger Hernandez. Down from Washington to give a lecture on the CIA at the School of the Americas in Fort Benning, Georgia, he had met and partied with Manuel, then a captain. He recalled how ironic seemed the architecture of the school. Looking like a Spanish Church mission, the building houses what has become known to the poor of Central America as the School of Assassins. Goldstein knew that men like Hernandez, Castillo and Molina corroborated that description. "Hey, Manuel, looks like you got a problem. Can I help?" he volunteered.

The dark Latin eyes held surprise. "Abie, where did you come from?"

"Oh, I've been in town a couple days, Manuel, checking up on our guys. Planned to stop in today and pay my respects to the general. Hoped I'd run into you. Hell, you're the only fun guy in the group. Remember the good times we had up in

Georgia?"

The major's white teeth glistened below his pencil mustache. "Do I remember? I could not keep up with you. I come back here to get some rest."

"It's been awhile. How about a night on the town here? You can show me around." Goldstein saw the man hesitate. "Maybe tomorrow night? Looks to me you've got your hands full today," he added.

"Did you see what they did to Jorge?" Hernandez asked, his eyes opening wide.

"I saw it."

"Can you believe they would do such a thing? I have been here for two hours, and I still have the shivers."

"Who did it, Manuel?"

"The rebels, I suppose. Who else?"

"What's the general's reaction?" Abram asked casually.

"I called him. He was not the happy hombre, I can tell you. I do not look forward to seeing him when he gets back".

"He's away?"

"Yes, in the mountains."

"You going back to headquarters now?"

Hernandez nodded.

"Let me give you a ride, Manuel. I need to talk to you about a little problem on my side. Ride with me and you won't waste any of your time."

"Nice car," Manuel commented as Goldstein pulled out into traffic.

"Yah. Hey, with Jorge gone, that should make you number two, Manuel. Maybe I should start calling you Colonel."

"I don't know, Abie. You ever try to predict Castillo? If he decides to blame someone for this, I could end up a corporal."

"Even Castillo won't waste a good man, Manuel. You're a cinch. Wanna bet?"

Hernandez grinned, his eyes shifting back and forth. "You

really think so, Abie? You think Castillo gives me Jorge's job?"

"If he doesn't, he's crazy, Manuel. And I'm going to tell him so. The CIA's still got some chips with the general." Goldstein reached across and gave a friendly jab to Hernandez's shoulder. "You're a cinch," he repeated.

They rode in silence for a time, a glow on the major's face.

"Manuel, I need a favor," Goldstein said finally.

"For you, Amigo, anything. Except, of course, my Conchita."

"I need to interrogate the nun."

"What nun?"

"The Vatican nun, the American."

"She's in the Hole."

"I know."

"Sometimes, Amigo, I forget how much you know," Hernandez replied. "They tell me she's loco. Did you know that?"

"No, I didn't know that," Goldstein lied, and appeared thoughtful for a moment. "If she's loco, I may have to take her to our place. We're set up there to break through the loco crap. Special drugs." He looked at Hernandez for a reaction.

"You can do that?" asked Hernandez, eyes widened.

"Manuel, you wouldn't believe what some of these new drugs can do. Want to come and watch?"

"Man, I'd like to see that. Maybe next time. I'd better be around when Castillo gets back."

"Can you give me a chit to get her out, oh, say for three to five hours?"

"Sure, but the warden will want some of his men along."

"No problem there," Goldstein answered calmly. "Send the whole damn regiment for all I care."

"The warden's name is Lopez. I will call him and authorize it for you. He's a prickly bastard though, always cover-

189

ing his ass. Have your ID ready."

Goldstein dropped Hernandez at the police headquarters after agreeing on a meeting place for the next evening. He sped toward the CIA office, a drab, unimposing structure on a run-down commercial street. "You get to ask one polite question," Goldstein simpered aloud, repeating his boss's instruction. "My ass. I wouldn't give Castillo the satisfaction of saying no to 'one polite question'."

The office was deserted except for a communications operator whose behind overlapped his chair by inches.

"Have you seen Johnny?" Goldstein asked.

"He was here," the man answered, without turning toward Abie. "He just walked across the street for coffee. Said he'd be right back."

"Any word from Byrnes?"

"He called. He's on the road back to town with Castillo."

"Know when he's due back?" Abie asked casually.

"Said he'd get back to the office by late afternoon. Didn't give a time."

Goldstein checked his watch and gave a nod of satisfaction.

The door flung open and a thin, lanky, copper-headed man walked in. "Hey, y'all. Mighty perty day for flying out there. Anybody for a quick swirl around some ole volcano in that lil ole Lear baby? How ya doin Abie?"

"Johnny, I hope you got that lil ole Lear baby gassed up and ready to go. Come on. We gotta talk. Let's use the conference room." Abie led the way down the hall.

Ten minutes later they emerged and went farther down the hall to a supply closet. Goldstein came out dragging a gurney. Johnny dragged two straight chairs. They entered a vacant room where a steel exit door to the outside was locked by a steel bar. A large utility sink hung from a corner wall. After several more trips to the supply closet they had the room rigged to look like an emergency hospital room. Goldstein

190

opened a bottle of antiseptic and spilled some of the contents around the slate floor and into the sink. Soon the pungent smell filled the room. He looked around, a satisfied look on his face. "It'll do," he said. "One thing, Johnny, when this all shakes out, you were only following orders. That's an order."

"Hey, y'all. I ain't had no fun like this since Desert Storm. Don't you worry about ole Johnny now."

"OK. I'll be back in an hour, two on the outside. You take care of the airport stuff and get back here."

Twenty minutes later, Goldstein showed his ID at the Hole's gate and was admitted to the quadrangle. He moved quickly to the building and entered the administrative office. He flashed his ID to the guard at the counter and said. "I'm Goldstein, CIA, here to see Captain Lopez. He expects me."

Lopez's office adjoined the counter area. He appeared at his door before the guard had time to call him. "Who did you say you are?" he shot at Goldstein, more than a touch of insolence in his voice.

"I'm Goldstein, CIA," Abram answered. "Major Hernandez called you."

"We don't let prisoners out of here alive," Lopez replied. "Do your stuff with her in her cell, or forget it." He started to turn back into his office.

"Castillo wants this info, not me, Captain." Abram shot back.

"Come back tomorrow. I'll check you out with the general."

"Call him up right now. If you don't, I will. He wants this stuff today, not tomorrow."

Lopez turned and walked to the counter. "Let me see your ID," he demanded.

Goldstein gave him the card.

"Even so, my men go along."

"Fine with me. Only Castillo's in a hurry. Can we move

191

this along"

A woman clung to Maggie until the guards jerked them apart. Goldstein saw the woman's eyes fill with tears as she screamed her hatred at the guards. "She's a baby," she finally cried to herself as she slumped to the dirt floor of the cell.

The guards hustled Maggie to the CIA van and pushed her to a seat. One guard sat on either side. Their sergeant sat in front. As Goldstein drove, he could see the nun's numbed and lethargic look in the rear view mirror. She stared ahead and then gradually lowered her eyes to her lap.

The sergeant looked at Goldstein. "You can make such a person talk with sense?" he asked, incredulous.

"You bet we can," Abram replied. "You'll see it happen. What's your name, Sergeant?"

If Maggie heard the distinct American accent in Goldstein's voice, she failed to show it.

By the time they reached the CIA office, Goldstein knew each man by name, and had them laughing.

Inside, they walked Maggie by the communications operator who didn't even bother to look up from the science fiction novel he was reading. The sergeant gave a slight nod of approval as he scanned the room with its gurney and antiseptic odor. He stopped as he faced a tall, thin man, dressed in a white jacket.

"This is Dr. Jonathan Wilson," Goldstein said. "He will administer the drugs and ask the questions. He's the number one guy who does this stuff. Had him flown in."

"How y'all doin?" Johnny said, nodding his head.

"Now, if you guys will help me get the lady up on the gurney?" Goldstein asked. He faced the bewildered Maggie and winked.

Maggie stayed silent as two of the men helped her onto the table, strapped her on, and stepped back.

As Johnny walked to the table he lifted a hypodermic syringe and squirted a little fluid to rid the needle of air. With his back to the soldiers he winked at Maggie. "This won't hurt," he said, and injected the fluid into her arm. Slowly, Maggie's numbed eyes closed.

"It will take an hour or more for the drug to work," Goldstein announced to the soldiers. "We can wait across the hall where there's TV and refreshments. Or if you prefer, you can sit here and guard a sleeping woman."

The sergeant showed some apprehension, but shrugged and responded to Goldstein's mild ridicule. "Good idea," he said. "You have some of the...?" He raised his hand as if holding a glass.

"The best brandy in these parts, my friend," Goldstein replied with a smile.

In the conference room, Abram turned on the TV to the boisterous sounds of soccer fans. He then poured a generous brandy for each man. From across the hall he could hear Johnny whistling, "Sweet dreams, baby!"

"Straight, or watered," Goldstein asked.

"Brandy I can hold, water no," the sergeant replied, laughing at his threadbare joke.

Goldstein handed out the glasses, then poured himself a scotch. "Cheers," he said, "to the ladies."

Conversation lagged quickly and the men turned to the soccer game. Abram refilled their glasses. One by one, they nodded off. He began to get impatient as the sergeant appeared to be immune to the drug. Finally, the sergeant also went under, a strange silly grin on his face.

Goldstein ran across the hall where Maggie, unstrapped, lay quietly on the gurney. He lifted her gently in his arms as Johnny unbolted the door. "Let's go," he said.

Johnny had cleared security in advance for the CIA jet. He brought the twin engines to whirring life, called the tower for clearance and received an unexplained directive to hold. They waited, nerves on edge, for fifteen minutes. At last, they watched a large cargo plane land and lumber past them

193

down the runway, its four propellers screaming. Then, "we're cleared," Johnny yelled and raced the Lear down the runway. Aloft he gave a high five to a grinning Goldstein. "Smooth as silk, y'all."

Goldstein returned to the passenger section and waited. Maggie wakened about fifteen minutes later. The lumpy man tended to her with deft tenderness, spooning chicken soup into her mouth, and speaking encouragement in a gentle voice. "You're safe now, Ma'am. We're on our way to Mexico."

Maggie's eyes remained numb, but she attempted a smile. "Thank you," she managed to say through broken lips.

****

In Rome, Fred Sweeney put a razor nick in his chin when the phone rang. He held a tissue to the cut.

"Can you hear me, Fred? This is Giulio."

"I can hear you fine, Giulio. You caught me just in time. Five more minutes and I'd be out the door."

"I have some good news, Fred."

"Are you in Rome?"

"No, I am calling from Mexico City, Fred. Maggie is safe. She is with the doctors here now."

Fred didn't catch the strange sadness in Giuilio's voice. He was exultant and shot a prayer of thanks upwards. "How is she?" he asked.

"They were brutal to her, Fred. She is covered with bruises. I do not yet know if there are any broken bones. I will call you again when I know that."

"She's going to be all right isn't she? Who did it? How did you get her out?" Fred's questions trailed one another rapidly.

"The bruises will heal, Fred. Also, it was the government who held her, not the rebels."

"How did you get her out?" Fred repeated.

"I did not get her out. Your CIA got her out, Fred. You should thank them."

"I will thank them, Giulio. I'll bet Maggie's relieved, even with the bruises."

"Fred," Giulio replied, a deeper sadness in his voice, "I only saw her for a moment, but I think she has the deeper wound. She does not see me with her open eyes. She called me Charles."

RESIDUE

General Roberto Castillo stood at the side of his desk, riding crop in hand, and stared down on the two shorter men. Major Manuel Hernandez and Captain Egidio Lopez stood nervously at attention.

"How could you be so stupid?" Castillo demanded, his eyes blazing.

"But, General, he is CIA. He is their top liaison here. We have always cooperated." In the face of Castillo's glare, Hernandez lowered his eyes and added, "But I take the responsibility. I gave the orders."

Castillo's glare diminished. "At least you have the balls to accept responsibility, Major." He turned to Lopez. "And you, Captain Lopez, are you so incompetent that you cannot even guard a loco nun? Could you guard sheep, do you think?"

Lopez's fingers fidgeted with the visor of the cap he was holding. "I was only following the major's orders, General. And I sent guards, a sergeant and two soldiers. They were the stupid ones. This Goldstein duped them. They should have been more careful. I have admonished them."

"Admonished?" Castillo asked. "You admonished them? After you admonished them, did you tuck them into bed without their dinner?"

Lopez looked down.

"Look at me, Captain Lopez!" Castillo waited for Lopez to comply. "And who is responsible for training these men-- to make them more careful -- Captain Lopez?"

"The men were assigned to me after their training, General."

"You have no responsibility for training?" Castillo insisted.

"The sergeant trains the men, General."

"And who trains the sergeant?"

Lopez lifted his hands, palms up.

"Answer me!" Castillo shouted.

"It is my responsibility, General."

Castillo glared at Lopez until the captain lowered his eyes again, then walked to the back of his desk. "Captain Lopez, you will conduct a court-martial for the sergeant. Your court-martial will find him guilty of abandoning his responsibility. And your court-martial will have him shot. That will train your men that we do not condone incompetence." Castillo continued to glare, and spoke softly and ominously, "Are you competent enough to follow that order, Captain Lopez?"

Lopez nodded, his hands shaking now.

"I didn't hear you, Captain Lopez."

"Yes, General, I will do that."

"Thank you, Captain Lopez, Castillo sneered. "Now get out of here, both of you, so I can clean up this mess you have made." The general watched them leave, a smile of satisfaction on his face as he saw the shaky steps of Captain Lopez. When the door closed, he pushed the speaker button of his intercom. "Get me C. James Cartier at the CIA in Washington."

＊＊＊＊

Archbishop Lucas Villariego eyed the box of nougats and reminded himself of the resolution he had made that very morning while standing on his scale. A fast would be both spiritually and physically beneficial, he had decided. Now, faced with the lure of the big red box, his resolve waffled. Well, only one then, he thought, removing a single nougat. Savoring the taste he was only able to nod when his secretary appeared and said that General Castillo had called. The general had insisted that his excellency report at once to the police headquarters. It has to do with the missing nun from the Vatican.

Annoyed that an archbishop should be ordered about by anyone other than the pope, Villariego took the box of nougats along as company for the drive. At police headquarters he directed his driver to wait.

"I have found your nun," Castillo announced when Villariego was seated in the plush office. "She was in one of our prisons."

The archbishop's eyelids rose. "How is that?" he asked.

"She was captured along with several rebels in the mountains. Captain Lopez, the prison warden, says that she was brought to the prison, but is now without mental ability. I suspect she was treated severely by the rebels. In any event, she was unable to tell them who she was. It is sad that it took him this long to discover her true identity, but it is an innocent mistake, don't you agree?"

"How long was she there? I will need some details for my report to Rome."

Castillo lifted his hands and shrugged. "Only a few days, I suppose."

"Where is she now? In the hospital?"

"No. I wish it were so. But someone has removed her from the prison. We do not know where she is."

"You mean, she is lost again?" Villariego threw up his hands, imagining the Vatican reaction to that news.

"No, not lost. She was taken from the prison by a man from the Central Intelligence Agency of the United States."

The archbishop bit his lower lip and stared vacantly. "The Americans? But why?"

"She is an American. Perhaps he thought he was rescuing her. Perhaps he thought our government was unjustly holding one of their citizens. I do not know the answer myself. I have, however, talked to the CIA officer in Washington who supervises this man. He assures me that the man's action was not authorized."

"Where is she now?"

"We do not know. A CIA aircraft left the airport shortly after she was taken from prison. When the aircraft entered Mexican territory, we ceased to track it."

"What then do I tell Rome?"

"You tell them what I have told you. We captured her captors. She was with them. She is disturbed. We did not know who she was, etc. etc. etc. The CIA have her, etc. etc. etc."

Villariego felt uneasy and searched for some pleasantness to take away the feeling. "There is one thing I hope for," he said, sighing. "I hope that the Vatican will now have something to worry about besides this nun. I am so tired of their constant inquiries -- as if there was something I could do. Of all my daily irritations, Cousin General, she has made herself the most abrasive."

"Cheer up, Lucas. She is someone else's problem now." Castillo rose to show the archbishop out.

****

Abram Goldstein turned toward the door as C. James Cartier III barged into his office. Cartier ordered Goldstein's co-worker to leave. When the door closed, Cartier's anger spilled from flashing eyes, a red face, and a sharp tongue. "Who the hell do you think you are?" he yelled.

Goldstein's calm, silent scrutiny of his boss only served to further infuriate Cartier.

"I asked you, who the hell do you think you are?" Cartier repeated. "I told you to leave it alone. You went ahead and brought her out. Just who the hell do you think you are?"

"Who says I brought her out?" Goldstein asked calmly.

"Castillo says it, you meathead. He has the whole story from an aide named Hernandez. He's so pissed about this, no telling what he'll do. He wants your ass to sizzle. And he wants to do the sizzling. I've half a mind to hand you over."

200

"Oh, come on, C. James, what's one small American citizen, give or take the thousands that bastard has already massacred?"

"I told you to leave it alone," Cartier repeated slowly, hyphenating each word.

"I couldn't do that."

"Don't give me that bullshit. What are you, some bung bleeder for every poor downtrodden bastard you meet?"

"No, I just decided it ought to mean something to be an American."

"You disgust me," Cartier snapped. "If you were an American, you'd damn well follow orders."

Goldstein did not reply.

"You're done here, you goddam communist, or whatever the hell you are. Pack up your crap and get out of here. I'll see to it you never work again for the American government I work for." Cartier turned for the door, then turned back. "If you're not out of here in an hour, you'll go out ass over tea kettle, you hear me? Christ, I hate mealymouthed pieces of crap like you."

Goldstein watched Cartier's back as his former boss fumed his way from the room. I'm beginning to like you again, Abie, he thought to himself. And then he smiled. "You can keep it all, C. James." He grabbed a baseball cap from his desk and walked out.

MAGGIE AND HOSPITALS

When it was finally permitted him, Giulio entered Maggie's hospital room. He held a mixed bouquet of bright flowers in front of his face and stopped at the foot of the bed. He waited, expecting a response from Maggie. None came and, cautiously, he peeked around the flowers. She was sleeping. Quietly, he placed the flowers in a vase on the bedside table used for holding food trays and swung the table over the bed so that the flowers were directly over Maggie's midriff. She would see them immediately when she awoke.

He lifted a chair to the bedside and sat staring at the purpled bruises and scabs on Maggie's face, head and neck. She did not know me, he thought, and felt a weight falling in his stomach.

A nurse came and checked the drip of fluid dropping through a narrow plastic tube into Maggie's arm. The nurse gave Giulio a pleasant smile as she left.

Giulio's vigil lasted nearly two hours. He had closed his eyes after a time to relieve the dark thoughts that came with the sight of Maggie's face.

"Giulio."

Her voice came without life and her numbed eyes made Giulio's heart ache. Still, he felt the thrill of her recognition. "You know who I am," he said simply.

"Of course, I know you, Giulio," she answered, but in the same depressed tone.

"You did not know me earlier today," Giulio said, feeling a need to explain. "You called me Charles. I thought maybe...."

"I don't remember that. Maybe I was dreaming," Maggie said.

"You do not know how happy this makes me."

"Am I back in Rome, Giulio?"

"No, Maggie, you are in hospital, in Mexico City. I will take you to Rome when the doctors permit it."

Maggie's eyes began to close. "I'm so tired," she said, and fell asleep.

Feeling elated from Maggie's recognition, Giulio continued to sit and watch her sleep. Suddenly he realized that she had not even seen the flowers.

During the long hours of the following days, Giulio kept his watchful vigil over Maggie. She continued to sleep through most of each day and night. The doctors at first assured him that her sleep was a normal response to the damage done her body, and a sign of healing. Moreover, they had prescribed tranquilizers. Bit by bit he learned from them that she had survived the brutality without permanent damage to her interior organs. They were less certain of a prognosis from the hearing in one ear and for the damage done to one of her eyes. As the days passed they became less certain, too, of the cause for her continual sleep.

On one afternoon Giulio noticed a tremor in the sleeping Maggie's face. The tremor gradually grew in intensity and beads of sweat began to form on her brow.

Giulio quickly summoned a nurse.

"She is having a bad dream," the nurse concluded after a brief observation. "It will pass."

"Should we wake her?" Giulio asked.

"No, let her sleep."

Suddenly, Maggie sat upright, her eyes wide with terror. "No, don't!" she cried, and then, realizing it was only a dream, began to relax. She was soon asleep again.

During a waking moment, Maggie asked Giulio to inform the president of her religious order of her situation. "She might be worried."

Sister Felicity Matthews was worried, Giulio discovered when he telephoned her in Wisconsin.

"Archbishop Sweeney called last week and told us she

had been rescued," Felicity said, "but we have heard nothing since then. And I've been unable to reach him in Rome."

"That is because he is in Prague with the pope, Sister," Giulio explained. "He called me from there only this morning. But, you should know that Sister Maggie is safe. She is in a hospital here in Mexico City. She has been brutally treated, but the doctors say she will recover from her body wounds. They cannot yet speak of her mental state. I must tell you, I myself am very worried about this. I hope to take Sister Maggie back to Rome within the week -- if what the doctors tell me is correct. There I have arranged for the services of a psychiatrist, an American who teaches at the University in Rome. Her name is Dr. Susan Killips. She has the high recommendations from people I know. Perhaps you could...."

****

The lines on Sister Felicity's face tumbled upward into a fixed smile. Only her eyes showed her concern when she arrived in Mexico City the next evening. On cautiously opening the door to Maggie's hospital room she was greeted quietly by Giulio who rose from his silent watch by Maggie's bed. He walked to meet her at the door, introduced himself in whispers and then motioned her to Maggie's bedside.

Felicity stifled a gasp at the sight of Maggie's bruised and disfigured face. Her eyes tearing, she then sat opposite Giulio by the bed until Maggie opened her eyes.

"Hi, Maggie."

"Felicity?"

"It's me."

"Oh, I'm so glad to see you."

Felicity stood and reached over to embrace Maggie, letting her cheek rest against Maggie's while tears started to flow again at the flat sound of Maggie's voice. "I'll be with you as long as you're here, Maggie, and then I'll go to Rome with you."

Maggie's eyes closed.

****

Two weeks later the doctors gave Felicity and Giulio permission to take Maggie from the hospital. Maggie looked at the wheelchair, then up into the heavy face of the nursing aide. "I am perfectly able to walk," she said flatly. Dressed in a cream-colored, long-sleeved blouse and an ankle-length printed skirt, she stood between Felicity and Giulio.

"I know this may be so, Sister," the man replied, "but it is the rule of the hospital."

"I don't care if it is the rule. It's stupid."

The aide was silent, waiting behind the wheelchair.

Giulio, listening to the interchange at Maggie's side, spoke quietly. "It is not such a big thing, Maggie. Permit the man to do his duty."

"It's dumb," Maggie droned. "I'm not an invalid."

Felicity lifted her forearms, palms upward to suggest the matter was not worth an argument. "This man does not make the rules, Maggie. But he can be fired for disobeying them."

Maggie stayed peevish. "Men! They know everything. They do dumb things even when they know they're dumb."

"Our taxi is waiting, Maggie," Giulio replied patiently.

"Oh, all right, but it's dumb." Maggie moved to the wheelchair.

At the curb outside the hospital entrance, the aide pushed the wheelchair to the waiting taxi, secured the chair's brakes, and reached to help Maggie from the chair.

"I am perfectly able to stand by myself, thank you."

As Giulio moved to open the taxi door she added, "And I am perfectly able to open a door, thank you."

They rode to the airport in silence. Maggie closed her

eyes and fell asleep.

Giulio looked over at the sleeping Maggie. He clenched a fist, hoping the tight grip would alleviate his feelings of helplessness. He clenched the other fist. Somehow, you will again be the Maggie I used to know, he promised her silently.

Maggie displayed her irritability again as they wound through the line at customs. "Can you believe people can be so inefficient?" she complained to Giulio. "If I ran this show, you'd see a change in a hurry."

Giulio shrugged. "I'm sure it would be different," he replied.

On the tarmac beside his company plane, Giulio took hold of Maggie's elbow to help her up the ramp.

She stiffened and pulled her arm against her own body away from Giulio.

"After you, Maggie," he said quietly, pointing his hand up the ramp.

Felicity sat next to Maggie. The jet's seating arrangement permitted Giulio to sit opposite them. He watched Maggie as she adjusted her seat backward, avoiding eye contact with him. "I will be happy to have you back in Rome, Maggie. I have the more comfortable feeling about the doctors there. Though, I must say, I have been very impressed by your doctors here in Mexico."

"I've had my fill of doctors, Giulio."

"It is important, I think that you see the doctors," Giulio persisted. "You will do this for me, please?"

Maggie looked at Giulio with emotionless eyes. "All right, if it'll make you happy."

"It will make me very happy. One of the doctors is very famous. You will like her. Her name is Dr. Susan Killips. She is an American who teaches at the University Medical School in Rome." Giulio stopped talking. Maggie's eyes were closed in sleep and he was alone with his thoughts as the plane climbed into the late evening sky. He watched the muscular spasms of her troubled sleep.

****

Dr. Susan Killips liked the feel of the soft give in the car-pet. Her long legs carried her slowly back and forth in her university office while she read through a sheaf of papers, the report by the Mexican doctors on Maggie's physical condition, and their observations on her mental state. She read carefully, and reread segments like, "We have found evidence of rape, or of an invasion that has left traces similar to rape, or both." Finished, she lay the report on her desk and looked at Giulio who sat quietly in a leather chair. Susan sat down facing Giulio. "I would like you also to read this report, Mr. Giuliano. Perhaps you will have additional observations that might be of help?"

"Please to call me Giulio, Doctor."

"Fine, and you call me Susan."

"Bene, Susan, I will be responsible for all of Maggie's medical costs. She is like a sister to me. Your charges should be sent to me, please."

"I'll do that," Susan replied as she handed the report to Giulio.

Giulio reached for the report and in turn handed a packet to Susan. "She has been beaten, Susan, as you know. These pictures show her face at the time she was brought to Mexico. As you can see, the word 'beating' is not enough to describe the brutality."

Susan studied the pictures while Giulio read the report. She pulled in a deep breath and winced. She was silent for a long moment. "I will never become hardened to this," she said. "I hope," she added. Noting that Giulio was finished reading, she asked, "Anything else, Giulio?"

"Maggie does not talk about this beating to anyone. Once I ask her about it, and she did not hear the question."

"That helps me."

"Also, she sleeps much of the time. I know also from watching her, she has the bad dreams."

"Did she talk to you about the dreams?"

"No. Also, when she is awake, she does not smile -- ever. Before she was always smiling. I guess I would not smile either, but it is different from the way she was. Also, she is, how you say, peevish sometimes, but most often she is quiet, depressed I think."

"She was a positive person before?"

"Very much so." Giulio stopped to reflect on his observations. "Also, when I try to help her up ramp to airplane, and touch her elbow to guide her, she pulls her arm away from me and becomes, how you say, tight. I never before see this in Maggie. She always permits me to be gentleman."

After Giulio left her office, Susan resumed her walking, now with her shoes off. She ran her fingers through her light brown hair, pushing it behind her ears. What course should this treatment take? she pondered. Susan was a Catholic and knew the basics of her faith, but felt completely unattuned to the culture of a convent. Is there something unique about the psyche of a nun that would make the traumatic experience different? What implications does a vow of chastity bring to the treatment?

Her secretary opened the office door and announced that Sister Felicity Matthews had arrived. Susan followed her secretary to the waiting area and introduced herself to the president of Maggie's religious order.

"Thank you for coming, Sister Felicity. It means so much to have you in Rome. I wanted to meet with you before I meet with Sister Margaret. I expect a call from the hospital at any moment. As you know, other doctors are examining her as we speak."

"She will want you to call her Maggie, Doctor," Felicity interjected. "And please call me Felicity."

"Thank you, I'll do that. I'm Susan. Come into my office please." She led the ample nun into her office and motioned to a chair. "I'm a Catholic, Felicity , and I practice my faith, but I have little understanding of the life of a religious. To start, can you tell me your exact relationship to Maggie."

"Of course, Susan. I've known Maggie since she was a college student at Padua College, before she entered the no-vitiate and became a member of our order. We were teaching associates at Padua when she returned with her doctorate in history. Later, I was given the position of director of devel-opment for the college and no longer taught. Shortly thereaf-ter, Maggie was selected as president of the college. I must admit that I thought I deserved the job and for a time my support was half-hearted at best. But, I soon came to realize that Maggie is a creative leader, much better than I am. In less than a year I was her biggest fan. We became close friends. In her few years as president the college made giant leaps forward."

"Only a few years?" Susan asked.

"She was fired by the board of trustees. Apparently, the bishop there, Bishop Sweeney, thought that she was too much of a feminist, and he maneuvered her ouster."

"I see."

"But that didn't stop Maggie. Six months later she was hired as president of a more prestigious college, Highmount in New York City."

"I've heard of it."

"Then, about two years ago, about the time I was elected by our community to be its president, she was asked to come to Rome."

"Why? The Vatican seems so male dominated."

"The present Pope, then Cardinal Della Tevere, wanted an outspoken, honest woman to help steer a group he belonged to."

"Tell me about the outspoken, honest Maggie."

210

"Maggie is honest to the core, both intellectually and emotionally. You always know where Maggie stands, and where you stand with her."

"She's honest with others. Is she so up-front with herself?"

"Totally. She knows who she is. She'll take the blame when it's hers, and she can pat herself on the back when she deserves it. She puts on no airs. She's who she is."

"I think you should read this, Felicity. It's a medical report on Maggie by the doctors in Mexico City. You'll note that it includes a release by Maggie for her medical information to be given to you, to Mr. Giuliano and to Archbishop Sweeney. You're to be kept up to date in case decisions are required."

"Are decisions required?" Felicity asked cautiously.

"For now, only a decision I must make as to how to proceed with her treatment. Please read the report so I can ask more questions." Susan walked to the window while Felicity read.

Felicity gasped several times as she read. She stopped for a time, put the report on her lap, and closed her eyes. Tears rolled down the grooves of her cheeks when she resumed reading. She finished reading. "Oh, my God," she exclaimed.

Susan reached out and took the report. "I know," she said quietly and waited for Felicity to recover. "Mr. Giuliano tells me that Maggie is no longer able to smile. She does not, or cannot, talk about her experience. When she does talk, the tone of her voice is flat. She is apathetic. She sleeps much of the time and apparently suffers nightmares. She has been peevish with people at times. None of that seems to coincide with your description of Maggie."

"That's not Maggie," Felicity replied. "She's an upper, vivacious person, energetic to the point of needing less sleep than most of us, never petty."

"One more question, Felicity. As you've read, it appears that Maggie was raped. In your opinion, how much would a vow of chastity increase her sense of violation?"

Felicity lowered her head in thought for a moment and then looked up. "I think she would experience rape as any woman would. Rape violates the woman. It doesn't violate chastity. Maggie would be the first to argue that."

"I thought that would be the case, but I wanted your verification. Thank you," Susan said.

The door opened and Susan's secretary reported that the hospital had called. Sister Maggie was now available to see them.

"Ride with me, Felicity," Susan said. "We'll see Maggie together this first time. Your being here will mean so much to her and to her recovery."

Felicity had arranged for Maggie's room at Salvator Noster Hospital. The room occupied a corner of the convent, a segregated area of the hospital where the hospital nuns lived. The room was large enough to hold several chairs and a small table in addition to the hospital bed. When Felicity and Susan entered the room, Maggie was sitting in a chair. She stayed seated, her weak smile an effort.

Felicity introduced Dr. Killips.

Maggie's dull eyes ran a slow appraisal of the tall, attractive woman. "Another doctor?" she asked.

"I'm a psychiatrist, Maggie," Susan said. "Let's all sit down and I'll explain my place in your treatment."

From the side Felicity stared at Maggie and tried to hold back her tears.

"Maggie," Susan continued, " while you were imprisoned in Central America, you were brutally beaten. That's clear from both your internal and external bruises. It is important for you that together we examine the effects of that brutality on your mental and emotional health."

"I don't need a psychiatrist," Maggie replied sharply. "I

just need to rest, and to get my life back together."

"This is important, Maggie," Felicity interjected. "It will help you get your life back together."

Susan read the assent in Maggie's demeanor to the unassuming directive from her religious superior. "I understand that you sleep much of the time, Maggie," she said calmly. "Why do you think you require so much sleep?"

"I don't know. I suppose my body needs it to recover."

"How about your emotions, Maggie? Do you think they need recovery?"

"I don't know. Maybe."

"Maggie, if you wish, Felicity can stay with us today while we talk. Would that be helpful to you?"

"That would be all right," Maggie replied.

"Just a few questions then. We know that you disappeared after a visit to General Castillo. Do you remember going to see General Castillo?"

"Yes."

"What happened in that meeting, Maggie?"

"We talked about the murders and rapes of nuns there, and then he took me to someone else and told him to lock me up. I was completely shocked."

"Who was that other person, Maggie?"

"I...I...can't remember."

"Can you describe him?"

"I...No, I can't remember."

"Did they put you in a cell?"

"I woke up in a cell. My face was bloody."

"Was the cell at the prison called the Hole?"

"No, it was at police headquarters."

"How do you know that?"

"Because I was taken back to Castillo's office again. It was down a long hall from the cell."

"What did Castillo want?"

"He...he tore away my clothes."

"Did he attack you?"

"He struck me on the head with something. When I came to I was back in my cell."

"Who beat you, Maggie? Was it Castillo?

In reply, Maggie asked, "Would you open a window?"

"It's sweltering outside, Maggie."

"All right, but would you show me that the window does open?"

"Of course." Susan walked to the window, unlatched it and then opened it wide and closed it.

"Thank you," Maggie said softly.

Susan sat and looked again at Maggie. "Who beat you, Maggie? Was it Castillo?" she repeated.

"No, not Castillo. It was..." A flicker of panic showed in Maggie's eyes. "I...I...can't remember."

"That's okay," Susan said calmly. "That's okay for now, Maggie. Why did they transfer you to the other prison, the one called the Hole? Do you know?"

"Castillo ordered it." A hint of a smile crossed Maggie's face. "I got dysentery and soiled his carpet."

"Were you beaten before you went to the Hole, or after?"

"Before, I think..."

"That's enough for now, Maggie. We'll talk again tomorrow. Besides, Felicity has another surprise for you."

"You'll remember these young ladies, Maggie," Felicity said. "You taught them history at Padua." She opened the door and ushered in two young women.

"Jane. Barbara." Maggie said in her flat voice. She smiled a weak smile.

Felicity introduced Sister Jane Feller, a tall, thin, blond, and Sister Barbara Zarvan, a petite brunette, to Susan. "These young sisters are psychiatric nurses now," she added. "They're here to support Maggie in her convalescence."

"Wonderful," Susan replied. "I'll leave you all now so you can catch up with each other. Will you sisters meet me

214

tomorrow at 10:00 a.m. at my office?" To Maggie, "We'll be talking about you, but don't worry, we're on your side. And, Maggie, I'll see you at 1:00 tomorrow afternoon."

"Why does she sleep so much?" Felicity asked when she, Jane and Barbara met with Susan the next morning.

"There are probably many reasons," Susan replied, "but the short answer is that she's hiding the beatings and rape from herself. We call it denial. Jane and Barbara, you've seen situations like this."

The two nuns nodded.

Susan continued. "I'm sure you also noticed the flat tone of Maggie's voice and the dullness in her eyes. The trauma has caused her to unconsciously anaesthetize herself against her own feelings. In a person as strong as Maggie, the energy required to maintain these defenses is enormous. Once the memory breaks through, and I'm confident it will, she'll have all that energy for other things. Another reason for her sleep is probably the lack of rest in the sleep she is getting. Mr Giuliano said it is a troubled sleep. Nightmares most problably. On the plane ride from Mexico he observed jerky muscular spasms, pained facial expressions, and fearful sounds."

"How can we help?" Jane asked.

"That's what I wanted to see you all about this morning, the roles you three can play in Maggie's recovery. She feels safe with you. She likes you. That's obvious from her reaction to you. One or more of you will be with her through the day. I'll rely on you to give me any scrap of information you observe from her behavior. Mr. Giuliano will do the same, but I suspect that Maggie will be more on guard in the company of a man. After today, I will meet with her both in the morning and in the afternoon, at least for the next several weeks. I will meet with you each morning before my meeting with her. We will review her previous day. So, when she talks, listen. If you see that she is dreaming, ask if she remembers the dream when she awakens."

"It's so sad to see her this way," Barb commented.

"I know it's hard," Susan replied. "But I can't tell you how much it means to have the three of you here, and to know that you will stay until we resolve this. I believe there is a need for all of us to be very proactive. If Maggie's condition goes on indefinitely, there is danger of further complications. If that happens, her recovery may be compromised."

The next morning, Susan sat down opposite Maggie and studied her face for a moment. "Maggie, let's review what this is all about. Okay?"

"If you say so."

"It's important for you to remember what our goal is. Do you remember it?"

"To get my feelings back?"

"That's true, but what has to happen before that?"

Maggie bent her head in thought. "I'm not sure. I thought that was it."

"Maggie, we want you to remember the beatings, and who it was that beat you. That's our immediate goal. Sometimes people suppress memories of traumatic events -- like you can't remember who beat you. But those memories are in you some-where. Okay if we have another go at it?"

"All right."

"Did you see any other people beaten?"

"I don't think so. I did see other people in my last cell who had been beaten. That cell had eight or nine people in it. All of them had bruises and scars, even missing fingers, and eyes out."

"That was in your cell at the Hole. Did they beat you when you were at the Hole?"

"No. Both the prisoners and the guards there thought I was crazy. I let them think that and they didn't bother me."

"So you must have been beaten at police headquarters. Were you alone in a cell there?"

"That's my recollection."

"Were you alone in the cell when they beat you?"

"I suppose so. I don't remember that."

"Were you raped, Maggie?" Susan spoke the words softly.

"No." She hesitated. "But I think I saw someone else raped."

"Where did that happen?"

"In my cell, I think."

"In the single cell where you were alone, or in the group cell?"

"At police headquarters."

"So you weren't really alone in that cell. Some other woman was there with you, and she was beaten and raped."

"I...I can't remember."

Susan saw the pain come to Maggie's eyes. "Okay, Maggie. That's enough for now. Keep in mind that you are safe now. No one can hurt you here. And think about this: memories, even horrible memories, go to past events. They're just memories. They don't carry clubs or fists. They can't hurt you unless you let them. So it's okay to remember even painful things."

****

That night, Jane Feller read a mystery at Maggie's bedside as Maggie slept. The story grew tense, and just as the murderer was about to swing an axe on his victim, Jane jumped at the sound of short, hard breathing. She stood and watched the struggle mirrored on Maggie's body.

****

Maggie had entered a cave, excited and optimistic. She explored the cave floor sure that she would find the concrete historical evidence she sought. Looking back where the in-

217

verted U-shape of the cave opening allowed light to enter she saw the figure of a large man fill the opening and enter the cave. A steel door slammed down behind him, but the cave remained in shadowy light. Her breathing became shallow and rapid as she felt fear. She tried to make out his face and failed. She backed further into the cave hoping to remain unseen. He continued to approach. Then she saw the camouflage design of his uniform and felt a moment of hope. He was in uniform. Perhaps that meant safety. He had a square shape to his head, and as he came closer she saw that it was his hair, cut square on the top and sides. She could not yet see his face. He carried a flashlight, or was it a knife? in his hand. Feeling terror she turned to run deeper into the cave but almost immediately confronted the cave's back wall. There was no place to run. She turned back and now she could see his face. Only it's not a face. It's a Halloween mask, cruel and leering. The object he carries is a knife. Suddenly he was upon her and forced her to the floor. There, he repeatedly thrust the knife into her lower abdomen.

Maggie woke abruptly. Sweat glistened on her face and it took a while for her breathing to slow. "Oh, Jane, I'm so glad it's you."

"Were you having a nightmare, Maggie?"

"Yes."

"Do you remember it?"

"Some of it, I...."

FRANCIS I IN PRAGUE

The helicopter from the Prague airport carried Pope Francis, Claude Dupuis, Gervase Janov and the local archbishop. It landed in palatial gardens on the Hradcany heights where Prague and papal security personnel saw them safely into the palace residence reserved for them. Later, from a window of his suite on an upper floor, Francis looked east, over the river and down on the "city of a hundred spires," which was drenched now in the afternoon sun. Far more than a hundred, the spires poked into the skyline. Testimony to the city's antiquity, they blossomed above the rooftops: round, square, and pointed, Romanesque, Gothic, baroque and blends of architectural centuries. The sight of them cheered Francis, as if their bells and carillons were sounding a welcome. As ancient as Rome, as beautiful too, he thought. He had carefully selected this city for the start of his public agenda. Its history ran the course of the church's history, a victim of both the bad and the good of that history.

Francis turned to Claude and Gervase who were standing silent in the center of the room. "Gervase, can you think of a more appropriate place to speak of unity?"

Gervase, the president of the Pontifical Council for Promoting Christian Unity, answered with the expected, "I cannot think of one better, Francis."

"Not just Christian unity, Gervase, but the unity of all religions," Francis continued. "When my predecessors unleashed the crusades against the Moslems, the bands of crusaders also wrecked havoc with Jews everywhere -- and here. When Innocent III imposed his severe restrictions on Jewish occupations and limited them to pawnbrokers, he forced them into ghettos -- as here. The history of the Church's relation to all non-Christians is written in the history of this city just as dramatically as is our intolerance toward our fellow Christians. This is a wonderful city to say to all of them, let us begin again."

"Will we review your schedule now, Francis, or later?" Claude asked.

"Later, Claude, please. This evening you and I will review both the schedule and what we will talk about with the president. First, I want to meet with Gervase. We have work to do on tomorrow's speech. So, if you will excuse us for now?"

"Of course," Claude replied and left the room.

"Gervase," Francis said, after Claude left the room, "come stand by me at the window." When Janov had joined him, the Pope asked, "What do you see out there, Gervase?"

"It is a beautiful city," Janov replied.

"I will tell you what I see, Gervase. There is a wonderful story about how Prague was named. As in all legends, the story begins 'once upon a time'. Once upon a time there was a princess who lived in a castle on the hill where we now stand. She, too, looked out from her castle one day on the land across the river. Only there was no city there then. There was only a dark green woods. But, as she gazed she had a vision of a city standing there, a bright city, filled with churches and spires. It soon became her mission to build that city. She sent servants there with the instructions to look for a worker engaged in his labor. The servants went and came upon a man who was hewing a threshold from a great log. Upon the servants' report of this, the princess decided to name her city 'Prague,' which means threshold." Francis paused and continued to look out at the city.

"A nice story," Gervase said politely.

Francis turned to Janov, his voice excited. "Prague is our threshold, Gervase, the threshold of a new home for Christ's people, a renewed institution. We will build it, Gervase, and you will be important to its design."

"Francis, I have no skill. I cannot even pound in a nail

straight." Janov lifted his arms in helpless gesture.

Francis laughed. "You are making the joke, Gervase. I like your sense of humor." Serious then, "Gervase, since your Council for Promoting Christian Unity will be a cornerstone of our new home, Prague will also be a new threshold for your council."

Janov looked at Francis attentively.

"It has been decades now since Paul VI had his meetings with Athenagoras, then the patriarch of Constantinople. A few words exchanged between them broke down centuries of estrangement. If you remember, Gervase, Paul took the primacy away from himself and gave it back to *caritas,* to love. Athenagoras welcomed Paul's words. Then, one of Athenagoras's bishops remarked that Paul had made the papacy out of date. That was too scary for our Vatican curia. They began the backpedaling. Soon it was once again the battle between love and loyalty for primacy. It is perhaps more accurate to call it a battle between love and royalty, clerical royalty. So, Gervase, does the primacy belong to love or to Peter?"

"To love, as you say."

"Bene. We will again make it so. And this time we will not permit the backpedal. You, Gervase, will take the lead. Are you ready for this, Gervase? I promise, if you do this, it makes for you the many enemies."

"With God's help and yours, Francis, I am ready," Janov replied.

"Bene. Now, come. You must tell me if I have put all this into words for tomorrow's speech to the people of Prague." Francis led the way to a table where the papers lay. "I want to tell them only this," the pope said, "that if we but love each other, our differences are small indeed."

Janov's eyes opened wide as he looked at Francis. "I begin to see the magnitude of what you are saying," he said.

221

****

The next morning the late summer sky dawned blue and clear. Claude was awake at 4:00 a.m. and was unable to go back to sleep. His mind filled with the day's agenda and he felt a nervous tension in his stomach.

At precisely 10:00 a.m., the president of the republic met with Francis in his office in the nearby Prague Castle. They exchanged gifts and pleasantries, and Francis spoke briefly of his mission.

The president spoke of the impact left from decades of communist domination. "They were thieves," he said, "and they stole from both of us. They threatened catastrophe, joblessness or worse, against your people, Your Holiness. And with these threats they stole the religion from the people's minds. Generations of people did not hear your message. That is the problem you face. They also robbed from many people the freedom of personal responsibility. Many now expect all to be given them. That also is a communist legacy to my country. And that is my problem."

Forty minutes later, the president walked the pope to the door and parted, saying, "You understand well the power of an apology. May it work for you."

Outside the presidential office, Francis was again surrounded by his security detail. Claude was at the pope's side as Francis stopped to look up at the imposing facade of St. Vitus Cathedral, which rose above and dominated the castle compound. They walked to it. Inside, as Francis was vested for the mass, Claude went out into the sanctuary and stood, watching the great church fill with people.

The nervousness returned to Claude's stomach when Francis climbed the steps of the ambo to deliver the homily. The pope stood high above the audience, a clear target from head to waist.

"...this marvelous city of culture," Francis regaled the audience, "residence to scholars like Tycho Brahe and Johannes Keppler, home to the ancient and famous Charles University. You were home also to the great composers, Dvorak and Smetana. Amadeus Mozart made his home here for a time. You were the inspiration and home to great writers like Franz Kafka. I am indeed privileged to be here, and humbled...."

After the mass Francis spoke to the overflow crowds from a small balcony in the castle courtyard. It was the same court-yard to which, in a different time, the government herded crowds of schoolchildren and directed them to smile for vis-iting communist dignitaries.

Receptions filled the afternoon and Claude relaxed a bit. The guests were closely screened and the pope's movements were confined to the controlled space of his residence.

That night, Claude slept little, and then only after getting on his knees and begging God for the virtue of perspective, that he might see with God's eyes. A misty dawn greeted the start of his next day, as did a smiling, gregarious Francis at breakfast. While reviewing the day's itinerary they were in-terrupted by the head of the pope's protection personnel. There had been an explosion during the night along today's sched-uled route. Several people had been killed, among them, or so the police think, were the clumsy perpetrators themselves. The police have been unable to make any specific connection to the papal visit, but, for safety's sake, and because of the road's condition, today's afternoon route would be slightly altered. After the briefing, Francis and Claude finished their coffee, then parted for their morning prayers.

A car carrying a papal protection team moved slowly away from the papal residence. The bullet-proof popemobile, with the highly visible Francis aboard, followed. A second pro-tection team followed close behind the popemobile.

Claude, Gervase Janov and the local archbishop rode di-rectly behind the security vehicle, two cars behind the pope. Jitters fretted Claude's stomach once again as the caravan

223

proceeded downhill on Neruda Street, the Royal Road, through the "Little Quarter" section of the city to the Charles Bridge. There, at the two bridge towers, one old, short and Romanesque, the other a match to its medieval counterpart across the river, the cars stopped. The protection detail filed from their cars and took positions that nearly surrounded Francis as he emerged from his vehicle. The pope stopped to take in the bridge, made of hewn stonework in medieval times. The Vltava river waters moved at a lazy pace through its sixteen large, rounded arches. Francis walked between cheering crowds on either side, up onto the bridge's wide roadway. The rose-colored brick surface was bordered on each side by heavy stone parapets.

Francis beamed his kindly smile at the crowds as they continued cheering. Along the entire length of the bridge, on both sides, people stood, four and five deep, behind simple rope restraints. Protection personnel scurried as Francis breached their protective cordon and walked to the people, reached out and grasped hands as he walked. He moved from side to side of the bridge, stopping only occasionally to study the statuary that rose above the stone parapets on both sides. The statues rested on the tops of the stone piers that supported each arch of the bridge. There were thirty of them, individual statues or statuary groupings, most of them dating from the end of the seventeenth or beginning of the eighteenth centuries. Claude stopped watching the pope and turned his eyes to the skyline, the steeples, the towers, all of the nearby structures of the city that looked down onto the bridge."

Well out on the bridge, Francis stopped at the statue of St. John Nepomuc, a priest drowned from this same bridge at the orders of King Wenceslas for his refusal to betray the contents of the queen's confession. The saint was a people's favorite and the bronze panorama of the murder scene attached to the bridge below the saint's statue had its center rubbed shiny by the devout touch of thousands. Francis chose to touch it also, and the people gave way for him, two men lifting up the rope restraint. Turning, Francis invited amateur photographers to take his photo with the people beside him. Several slipped under the rope to snap the scene from the bridge's center. A sudden flap of bird wings sent a chill up Claude's back.

At the middle of the bridge, tree limbs rooted in the soil of Kampa Island, rose above the parapets. Francis paused to watch as a slight breeze brought movement to the leaves and branches.

At last, the pope made his way to the east side of the bridge. There, at the parapet of an enlargement of the bridge's surface stood a statuary grouping of the Calvary scene, the oldest on the bridge. Opposite was a surface enlargement where executions were once held. Those scheduled to lose their heads would kneel before the crucifix prior to their execution.

A man, scraggly-bearded, ragged and thin, held a violin and stood beneath the cross. His violin case, laying open on the bridge in front of him, held a few coins and bills. As the pope neared him, the man began to play Schubert's *Ave Maria*. Francis stopped in front of the man and listened intently. When the musician lowered his bow, Francis applauded and then motioned to his secretary of state. "Claude, come," he said, "I need some money."

Claude reached into a pocket, and produced several bills.

Francis folded the bills and pressed them into the man's hand. "You play beautifully," he said. "Thank you."

When Francis was again seated in the relative security of his vehicle, the procession continued along the narrow streets of the Royal Road toward Old Town Square. Suddenly, Francis stopped his car and emerged to greet a street vendor, a shriveled woman bent at the waist. Security forces again scurried to surround him as he searched her wares and selected a small inexpensive painting, a bright red rose on a dark ominous background. He motioned the three in Claude's car to join him. "I carry no money, as you know," he said simply.

This time, the local archbishop obliged.

"I saw this and could only think of Maggie," Francis said to Claude, holding the frame for Claude to see.

Soon the Gothic spires of Our Lady Before Tyn Church rose in front of them on the opposite side of Old Town Square. The Square looked to be a sea ready to boil over with people. The caravan passed the Town Hall of the Old Town and Claude checked his watch against the astronomical clock on the Town Hall's exterior. Then out into the main square, ringed with churches, open air restaurants and ancient, pastel burghers' houses.

The caravan wound slowly through the rope-lined path intended to hold back the immense crowd. Francis stopped the caravan and walked along the ropes, greeting and touching, until he reached the monument. The monument had been dedicated in 1915, on the five hundredth anniversary of the death of John Hus at Constance. The statue of Hus towers above the square and figures of Hussite supporters join him on the monument.

Francis stood, high for the crowds to see, and for him to see the crowds, on a platform erected next to the monument. He spoke without notes. "My dear friends," he began, "I have come to ask forgiveness. It happens sometimes that men lose themselves to the seductive pull of power. We lose sight of our family...."

Claude listened carefully as he looked around at the thousands of windows above them.

"I would once again sit at our family table, if you will have me...."

Claude's heart surged at the sound of a window's slam.

Then it was over. Francis was back in the safety of his vehicle, waving at cheering crowds as the caravan moved out of the square on its way to Prague's fabled Jewish Town. There it would be a private meeting with Prague's Jewish leaders, the message similar, but to Claude's relief, a safe enclosed meeting.

The cars moved slowly through the narrow streets just off the Old Town Square as Claude closed his eyes with a quiet release of breath. When he opened them, it was to a silent, dream-like world. He saw the popemobile rise, float upward, and then turn over. He saw stone blocks cascading down upon the upturned vehicle. Then only did he hear and feel the explosion as his own car was buffeted by the blast, and rubble reached and stung its exterior, shattering the windshield.

It was here, the disaster he had imagined so often. Before the horror sunk in, he was out of the car and running toward the wreckage of the popemobile. No longer a dream, no longer silence, the cries of wounded people were everywhere.

The crushed popemobile was nearly buried in heavy debris. Claude joined survivors from the protection forces and clawed at the rubble. The archbishop and Gervase knelt to the aid of the wounded. It took but minutes, but seemed an eternity, before enough debris was pulled away to reveal the crumpled body of Francis inside the wreckage. The pope's head lay caught between metal plates, a bizarre twist in his neck.

It seemed hours also, but again was only minutes, before the sirens of emergency vehicles impressed their message on Claude's consciousness. As these professionals took control, Claude sat back on the rubble, waited and wept. He raised his face to the sky, his eyes ablaze with anger.

The rescue squad worked feverishly using Jaws of Life. They spread and cut the metal that entrapped the pope. Several final cuts with the big K-12 saw cleared the final obstacles and medical personnel were quickly at Francis's side. They found breath, but it was shallow; pulse, but it was dangerously weak. They stemmed the bleeding caused by a protruding humerus bone in his right arm and a bone splinter above his left ankle. They started intravenous medications at the direction of physicians via telephone. Orthopedic and neurology physicians arrived at the scene. Under their directions, the emergency medical personnel braced and extracted Francis from the wreckage and, with exquisite gentleness, placed him carefully onto a gurney, and wheeled him to an ambulance.

The physicians rode at the pope's side. Claude was permitted to ride in the ambulance as well and stayed at Francis's feet as the vehicle moved slowly through the debris-strewn street and then quickly to the hospital. Cardinal Gervase Janov and the archbishop followed by taxi. Together in a waiting room, the three clerics paced the floor while doctors, somewhere nearby, worked on the pope.

Claude made a telephone call to Marco Gattone and after quickly briefing him, asked, "Will you ask Fred and Francis Ebowale to come to Prague, Marco? If Francis lives I will want one of us with him at all times, at least until we know from where the danger is coming, or until we have him safely back in the Vatican."

Three hours later Claude made a second call to Marco, this time with a full report from the doctors who were simultaneously reporting the pope's medical status to reporters, and to a waiting world.

"Marco, his neck is broken and there appears to be multiple damage done to his spinal cord. He is paralyzed from the neck down. His breathing was shallow and the doctors are unsure whether damage has been done to the nerves that control this function. For now they have working for him the artificial breathing. They say it is the breathing that is the biggest danger. They refuse to make the prognosis and say only that we must wait and see. But he is alive, praise God, Marco, he is alive." Claude pictured Gattone's big brown, sad eyes above the pocked cheeks. He waited for a reply.

"Claude," Marco responded finally, "I have only minutes ago received a call from Johann Rolf. He wants to see me."

"The wolves cannot be already howling?"

"I think not yet the howl, Claude, but only the poking of the nose, the sniffing. Tomorrow, or the next day for sure, comes the howl for blood."

"Let them howl, Marco. When you have all the teeth, what good is their howl?"

"Yes, but they are Francis's teeth. I will go to the chapel now and pray God to let him continue life. *Ciao*, Claude."

At 10:00 a.m. the next morning a police official held a press conference. There had been three simultaneous explosions set off electronically from a distance, one under the road below the popemobile, a second in the adjacent building at car level, and a third from the second story of the building. The building had been emptied by its owners for renovation and four workers were found in it, dead from the crushing explosions. They had been bound and gagged, presumably by the assassins.

The police now believed that the explosion of the previous night had been a diversion to damage the road bed sufficiently to change the papal itinerary to this obvious alternate route. The narrow road at the point of the explosion had been further narrowed more than a meter by the building itself, which jutted into it.

The explosions killed thirteen people: the four workers in the building, five security personnel (all four in the lead car, and the driver of the following car), and four people in adjacent shops. Moreover, the death count might rise from among the forty-three wounded. Fortunately, no crowds had lined the street at this spot because notice of the papal route had included only the distance from the Castle to Old Town Square.

The assassins were as yet unknown. No terrorist group

had claimed responsibility. The police were asking the public for assistance, any scrap of information that might be helpful.

****

Archbishop Lucas Villariego and the papal nuncio, Monsignor Mario Guerrolino sat, focused on the television. CNN followed the events surrounding the attempted papal assassination with gripping detail. Commentators walked the scene and pointed out, from outside the yellow tapes which cordoned off the area, the estimated depth of the crater created by the explosion, filled now with debris from the shattered building. They speculated also on the amount and kind of explosives used. Their cameras scanned the shredded interior of the building which housed the explosives, peering in where the exterior wall had vanished.

Villariego grabbed a handful of mixed nuts as police spokesmen reviewed known details. He watched, transfixed, as correspondents located Vatican dignitaries, Claude Dupuis in Prague, Johann Rolf in Rome, and pelted them with their usual inane questions, "How does this make you feel? Who do you think might have? Why would anyone want to?" Dupuis was factual and impatient. Rolf turned the interviews into photo ops.

"There is a man of stature," Guerrolino opined, looking at the suave Rolf. "What a picture he makes to the world. If this pope dies, Johann Rolf will be the next, count on it."

"You do not think he will die?" Villariego asked, reaching again for the nut bowl.

"I don't know that," Guerrolino replied, "but from what they are saying, should he live he will always be paralyzed. If so, he should resign. The church does not need a cripple for its leader. What image does that present? Weak, I assure you."

230

FRANCIS AND MAGGIE

Nurses wheeled the operating-room table bearing Pope Francis from the Prague Hospital to a waiting ambulance. After the short drive to the airport they wheeled it again, this time up the rear ramp of a cargo plane. Inside the plane they secured the table to the floor. Technicians checked the breathing apparatus attached to the bed, and to the pope.

The pope's doctors, the nurses, Fred, Claude and Francis Ebowale tightened their seat belts for the takeoff. Aloft, they once again attended to the pope.

The pope's eyes were alert. They moved from Fred to Claude to Francis Ebowale, as they had for weeks now. He spoke hesitantly, holding each word until there was sufficient breath to expel it. "It-will-be-so-good-to-get-home," he said.

"It will be good to have you home," Fred replied. "All of us will take hope and courage from your being there."

"The-doctors-say-I-may-live-for-years, a-full-span-of-life," Francis said.

"Your people, this church, will need you for your complete life span," Claude responded, soothing, sympathetic.

The pope's eyes pained. "Please, Claude, do not pity me. You must remember. My body is now of little use but my mind is ever young."

Claude accepted the gentle rebuke. "We will remember," he promised.

Fred and Claude left the pope's side to make way for the doctors who, routinely now, probed Francis for signs of pain and change. When their exam was completed, they medicated intravenously. Then they gave their positions back to Fred and Claude who watched quietly as Francis dozed, then slept.

"I talked with Marco by phone this morning," Claude said. "He agrees that one of us from Il Cero will be with Francis night and day. It is tragic to even think that danger to him might come from within the church, but this chance we will not take. I will confer with each Il Cero member when we return, and will then set up the schedule."

"Count on me to do my share," Fred replied, "and to take up any slack when needed."

"He sleeps soundly," Claude said, looking at Francis.

"I'll be so glad to be back in Rome," Fred said. "Maggie has been there for weeks already. Her friend, Giulio, called me early this morning. She is still at Salvator Noster. I am anxious to see her."

The pope's eyes opened at the sound of Maggie's name. "Tell Maggie I miss her and I will pray that my suffering will help her heal quickly," he said.

A group of prelates met the pope's plane when it landed at Rome's Leonardo Da Vinci airport. They were disappointed, however, when the doctors rushed Francis into a waiting ambulance, giving them no time to see more than the smile on the pope's profile.

Johann Rolf's limousine followed the ambulance.

At the Vatican, attendants wheeled the pope to his quarters. Marco had supervised its reconstruction in the pope's absence and it was now ready to receive and sustain the paralyzed Pontiff. Francis was wheeled into his bedroom and transferred from the gurney to a hospital bed. Francis would himself, with some practice, be able to operate the bed's controls. A control stick was lowered to just above his mouth. His head had sufficient movement to reach the controls and a doctor asked him to try to raise the bed so that he was sitting up. Francis took the control in his mouth and by trial and error soon raised the bed. The doctor pointed to a wheelchair, sitting vacant in a corner of the room. It too could be operated by the same type of control mechanism. "We will test your driving skills as soon as you are ready," the doctor said.

Rolf had joined Fred, Marco, and Claude in the outer chamber, and they waited while the doctors readied Francis. Rolf was exchanging pleasantries and offering polite concern when the doctors authorized their entry to the pope's bedroom.

Francis greeted Rolf with a bright smile. "Johann, how good of you to greet me."

Rolf's calculating eyes engaged the pope's. "I regret this very much," he said. "I hope you are not in great pain. It is God's will, as they say."

"Yes it is God's will," Francis replied in his staccato speech. "How strange is God's will."

"He has made a cripple of you. It is unfortunate," Rolf continued. "But, will you be able to meet the rigors of your office?"

Francis stared at Rolf and said nothing.

"If I can do anything, be assured of my willingness."

"I know your concern is for the church, Johann. Thank you. So is mine. We will talk again."

The doctors intervened. "It is time for the Pontiff to rest now."

****

Fred went in search of Maggie. At the hospital he walked down the corridor to the convent entrance and hesitated. He looked for a doorbell and found none. He felt too uncomfortable to enter the convent sanctuary without permission so he knocked on the jamb of the door. He waited, but no one answered. He turned to walk back to the hospital receptionist for help and bumped into the shoulder of a pretty young woman. "I'm sorry," he said, "that was clumsy of me."

"Can I help you?" the woman asked. "I'm Sister Barbara Zarvan."

"My name is Fred Sweeney," he replied. "I came to see

233

Sister Margaret McDonough. I was told at the reception desk that she has a room in the convent."

"I remember you now," Barbara responded. "You're Bishop Sweeney. You celebrated mass at our motherhouse in Mill City when I took my vows."

"I should remember you..."

"How could you, Bishop? We didn't meet personally. Follow me and I'll take you to Maggie."

"How is she?" Fred asked.

Barbara gave a flip of her hand. "So, so. She's not the same Maggie yet." At the door to Maggie's room she entered first. " You have a visitor, Maggie," she announced.

Maggie was seated in a recliner, wearing a white terry cloth robe over her pale blue pajamas. She looked up as Fred appeared. "Fred! How good to see you. Giulio told me that it was you who got the CIA to rescue me. I don't know how to thank you."

Barbara excused herself.

Fred studied Maggie and controlled the pain he felt at hearing the lifeless voice and looking at her dull eyes. He walked to her, bent and took her hand in both of his. "You're back," he said simply. Then, embarrassed by the tear that started to fill each eye, he turned, pulled a handkerchief from his pocket, swept his eyes, and then unnecessarily blew his nose.

They talked. Maggie remained alert as Fred gave her detail after detail of the assassination attempt in Prague, and the prognosis for Francis.

"He's so brave," she commented.

"Like you, Maggie, brave like you."

"Now tell me about you, Fred," Maggie said. "You promised me you would see a doctor about the cause of your stumbling."

"I did."

"What did he say?"

"She."

"What did she say?"

"She ran me through a whole series of tests two days before I left for Prague to be with Francis."

"And?"

"I just got back from Prague a few hours ago."

"So you haven't received the test results yet?"

Fred hesitated. "No, she called me in Prague."

"And"

"Its A.L.S.," Fred replied quietly.

"What's that?"

"Amyotrophic lateral sclerosis."

"What's that?"

"Lou Gehrig's disease."

Maggie stared at Fred. Her eyes opened wide and filled with fire. She pulled the lever to lower the foot rest of her chair and stood. "You men!" She spit the words out, her anger giving life to her voice. "You think you're immortal! You should have seen that doctor years ago. You don't care about anybody, or anything, even yourself. First you cost the life of Charles Mueller. Now you waste your own life. How dare you!" She was shouting, enraged.

Fred was stunned, unable to find a reply. The sight of Maggie helped him conquer the hurt and shock. He stood, backed toward the door and said gently. "I'll be all right, Maggie. And so will you. You get some rest. I'll be back to see you tomorrow."

****

A sense of shame kept Maggie's eyes down as Fred left the room. She felt stunned also. She dropped back into her chair and lowered her eyes to her lap. What am I doing? she thought. This good, good man. He's staring at death, and here I am judging and blaming him. My God, what's happening to me? Where are my feelings?

****

Giulio entered the hospital as Fred walked through the lobby on his way out. They shook hands. "You have seen Maggie?" Giulio asked.

"Yes." Fred paused. "What are they doing to help her?"

"I am now on my way to see her psychiatrist," Giulio answered. "Come with me. The doctor will want to meet you."

Susan and Felicity were sitting at a conference table when Giulio and Fred entered. Giulio introduced Fred and they sat down, Susan and Fred on one side of the table, Felicity and Giulio on the other.

"I'm sure you don't remember me, Archbishop," Felicity said.

"Oh yes I do remember you, Sister Felicity, though I confess the memories of my interactions with Padua College are painful and embarrassing. And please call me Fred."

"Maggie reports good things about you," Felicity said reassuringly.

"I'm glad to hear that," Fred replied. "I just visited Maggie and I'm alarmed for her. It hurts to see the lack of life in her eyes. And her anger. I've seen Maggie excited and feisty before, but never this anger. No. It's stronger than anger. All of a sudden she lashed out at me. She was livid. That's not Maggie." He looked at Susan. "What's going on with her? Do you know?"

Susan's mind quickened at the news of Maggie's anger. "I think I know," she replied. "And I think we're on the way to bring back the Maggie you know. We will need some help from God, and from you."

"I'll do anything," Fred said.

Susan looked at Fred. "I know you will, Archbishop."

"Fred."

"Thank you. You can start, Fred, by telling us about this rage event with Maggie. What brought it on?"

Fred described the event, changing only the name of his disease to the generic word, illness.

"What kind of illness, Fred? Major or minor?" Susan asked. "I don't mean to pry, but it may be helpful."

"Lou Gehrig's disease."

Susan reached a hand over to Fred's arm. "I'm so sorry, Fred. Have your doctors made any prognosis yet as to its progression?"

"Thank you. It's very kind of you to be concerned," Fred replied. "But, let's talk about Maggie now."

Felicity looked at Fred with saddened eyes. "All of our sisters will be praying for you, Fred. We'll pray for a miracle."

"Thank you."

Giulio had moved over to Fred at the news and put his hand on Fred's shoulder. "I do not pray so good, Fred. But whatever I can do, I will."

"Thank you Giulio, but Maggie now."

"On to Maggie after one more comment," Susan said. "If I can be of any assistance, Fred..."

"Thank you."

Susan continued. "I have already briefed Felicity, and Barbara and Jane, the two young nuns who came with Felicity. Fred and Giulio, you two are the closest men in Maggie's life, or so I understand."

Giulio and Fred nodded assent.

"First, I want you to know that Maggie's rage at you, Fred, is a very positive sign that she is making progress. It means that Maggie has mustered the energy to get out some of her anger. It's a good sign even if her anger is misdirected. If you imagine the prolonged brutality that Maggie has been through, you might suspect that she is not too thrilled with the male sex right now. If I'm right, she knows consciously that you are her friends, but unconsciously there is this huge reservoir of anger against the men who brutalized her. She has repressed the memory of those men and what they did. We are working to bring back that memory so she can deal with it and release her anger appropriately. In the meantime, you may be the ones to feel its force. You can take that, and not be defensive?"

Both men murmured assent.

"I know you can," Susan said, "so forgive me if I tend to beat a dead horse."

"You tell us what to do. We'll do it," Fred responded.

"Yes," Giuilio said. "And do not worry. We are not so delicate."

Susan smiled. "I suspected that too. So just stay close to Maggie. Visit her often. And please tell me of any unusual behavior on her part." Susan started to stand, then sat back down. "I almost forgot. Can one of you bring some of the mementos, pictures and the like, from Maggie's apartment for her room here. It might make her stay here more comfortable -- and she may be here awhile. I don't want her to return to work yet. Felicity supports me in that. If Maggie finds the will to energize through work, she may never remember."

"I can do that," Fred replied.

"I'd like to help," Felicity said.

That same evening, Fred and Felicity taxied to Maggie's apartment. Admitted to the apartment by the building manager, they set out to collect items that were obviously special to Maggie. Pictures of her family, one of Charles Mueller, a small Hummel figurine, a rosary that hung on the headboard of her bed, a statue of the Madonna, an oil painting of a soaring eagle, and a crucifix. As they were about to leave, Fred opened a drawer of the nightstand and pulled out a stack of letters. He recognized them, even though the envelopes were now worn and slightly tattered.

Felicity walked to his side. "What are those?" she asked.

"These are letters to Maggie from Charles Mueller," he

told her, holding them up. "They are letters he never mailed. I delivered them to her in New York when I went to apologize." He hesitated, then returned the letters to the drawer.

Back in Maggie's room, they arranged the items around the room. Fred handed the rosary to Maggie, and watched her mechanically finger the beads

****

Maggie looked out at the rain. "It seems like it's been raining forever," she commented to Barbara.

Barb Zarvan, dressed in white slacks and blouse, had her feet tucked up under her torso on a nearby chair. "It's been drizzling for a week. Dismal isn't it?" she replied as a flash of lightning brightened the room. "That lightning reminds me of a history exam you gave us once, Maggie. Do you remember the test you gave us without warning us in advance? I don't think anyone passed it. Then, in the very next class, you gave us the same test, the exact same questions. 'Lightning *does* strike twice in the same place,' you said. Do you remember that?"

"No, but it sounds like me, doesn't it?" Maggie replied flatly. She started to wander about the room, picking up and looking at the mementos brought from her apartment by Fred and Felicity. She stopped at a side table and picked up the picture of Charles Mueller. She studied the framed thoughtful face, the fair complexion, the shock of auburn hair, and the green-speckled hazel eyes. She felt the anger rise in her. How dare you die! she thought. How dare you leave me! The illogic of her thoughts struck her immediately. As if you asked for the bullet that killed you. What's happening to me?

****

Outside the convent area, Giulio caught up to Susan as

239

the psychiatrist walked toward Maggie's room. "I found these pictures at last," he said. "They were pictures we had so that we could be sure of their identities. When I couldn't find them, I was afraid I had discarded them once Maggie was out of the prison. But, here they are. This one is General Roberto Castillo," he said, holding it for Susan to view. "He is the head of the National Police there. This one is Colonel Jorge Molina, Castillo's second in command. He's dead. He was shot when he tried to escape us. It is a long story." He held up a third picture. "This one is Major Manuel Hernandez, third in command. You will see that their names have been written on the back of their pictures." Giulio handed the pictures to Susan. "I hope they will help Maggie."

Susan took the photos. "Thank you, Giulio. I'm sure they'll be useful. I doubt that many people have friends as loyal as you are to Maggie."

"She is like a sister to me."

"I'm going in to see Maggie now," Susan said as they stopped at the entrance to the convent section. "Were you also planning to see her?"

"Yes, but I will come back later," Giulio answered. "It is no problem."

In Maggie's room, Susan took a chair facing Maggie who sat in a recliner. Barbara excused herself.

"Maggie, let's start with your dream again. Does it come every night?"

"It seems like it does," Maggie replied. "It even comes sometimes when I sleep during the day."

"Is it always the same dream?"

Maggie turned her eyes upward in thought. "It seems they're the same."

"Who do you think that man is, Maggie, the one with the camouflage uniform and square head?"

"I have no idea."

"You do remember General Castillo. Is there anything

about the man in your nightmare that reminds you of him?"

"No."

"Maggie, I'm going to show you a photo. I'd like you to look at it. Is that all right with you?"

Maggie was quiet. She locked her arms and closed her eyes.

Susan waited.

When Maggie opened her eyes she said resignedly, "All right."

Susan reached into her briefcase. "Do you recognize the man in this photo, Maggie?" She handed the photo to Maggie.

Maggie looked, then looked away and closed her eyes. She looked again. "Yes, that's Castillo," she said finally.

Susan retrieved the photo and started to put it back in her briefcase, then changed her mind. "I'll leave the photo with you, Maggie. Perhaps it will jar other memories."

"All right," Maggie replied, but did not reach for the photo

Susan placed the photo on a side table. "Do you remember the beating you suffered, Maggie?"

"Didn't you ask me that already?"

"Perhaps I did. Do you remember?" Susan persisted.

"I saw someone else get a beating."

"Who was that?"

"I don't know."

"Where did that happen?"

"In my cell."

"The cell at the Hole?"

"No."

"At police headquarters then?"

"I suppose it was."

"Can you describe that cell to me, Maggie?"

"I think so. It was a rectangle, maybe six feet wide by twelve feet long. It had a strange, unpleasant smell. The walls were mostly gray. There was a sink at the back end, and a toilet with a crack in it. There was a bunk that was held to the wall by chains. The light was a bare bulb. The door was cut short at the bottom for them to shove food trays in." She paused. "I guess that's about all I remember."

"What did they feed you?"

"Tortillas. Beans sometimes."

"Did the person who got the beating get the same food?"

"I...don't know."

"Was that person a man or woman?"

"She was a woman."

"So you weren't alone in the cell?"

"No. I was alone...I think...I..." Maggie stopped, a look of bewilderment on her face.

Susan was quiet, giving Maggie time to adjust to the dilemma in her memory. Dear God, she prayed, help me take Maggie to the edge of remembering and keep her there. But, don't let my questions drive her deeper into denial. It's such a thin line I walk here. Help my steps. After a long pause, Susan changed her line of questioning. "Who are your heroes, Maggie?" she asked.

Maggie stared at Susan. "I asked that same question once of my friend, Charles Mueller," she said. "I wanted to know what do our heroes tell us about ourselves? I liked his answer."

"What was the answer?" Susan asked.

"It was in a letter. I remember it.

Dear Maggie, he wrote.

You asked who my heroes are. That's easy enough.

My heroes are people who fall or are forced into helplessness and who suffer there, enduring one or more of the afflictions brought on by life or by others.

The heroes endure, or die in the enduring. If they

live, they come through the fire enlarged as humans.
I think there are more heroes in our world
than we imagine.

Susan listened and then said slowly, "You were helpless. You suffered. And you have endured, Maggie. Can you face what you endured, and grow from it? Can you forgive the man who beat you, and raped you?"

Maggie stared at Susan, her eyes wide and questioning.

****

"I-have-been-in-Rome-for-weeks-now, Maggie. The-doctors-keep-me-prisoner-as-they-do-you." Francis had been transported to the hospital for a brain scan and had insisted on seeing Maggie. Fred had wheeled him to her room and sat now to the side.

Maggie stared at the wheelchair-bound pope and listened to his staccato voice. "I'm so glad to see you, Francis. I'm sorry about your accident," she said tonelessly. "I've prayed for you, but...but I don't feel my prayers anymore. I hope they're still good."

Fred had briefed Francis fully, but the pope still felt depressed at the sight and sound of her. "I have been praying for you also, Maggie. God will see us through."

"Where is he taking us? I'm not too happy with God lately."

"I have faith He is taking us to where Il Cero planned for us to go. They were your plans too, Maggie."

Maggie's face grew animated. Her eyes flashed. "You're infallible, aren't you?" she challenged, a bite in her voice.

Francis looked at Maggie, but remained silent, waiting.

"If you're so infallible, how come you didn't see that explosion coming, or keep me from...from...." Maggie stopped.

"That's not what infallible is about, Maggie," Francis an-

243

swered calmly.

"What's it good for then?"

"It has to do with what we believe, with truth."

"Like keeping women excluded and suppressed all these centuries is truth?" Her voice grew louder.

"No. That is not truth. It is reality though."

Her rage turned cold. "I don't think I believe anything anymore."

"You will see it when you are well," Francis said quietly.

****

A sudden sense of shame led Maggie to lower her face. My God. Look at that paralyzed man, our Pontiff. And here I am abusing him. "I'm sorry," she said weakly, but did not raise her head.

"Do not fret, Maggie. It is this fire that makes you so important to the Church. I am impatient to have you back." He paused. "Now, I must go. The doctors are waiting. We will pray for each other, yes?"

Head still down, Maggie said weakly, "Thank you for coming."

Fred wheeled the pope from the room.

Maggie's dream was always the same, and always new. She entered the cave, buoyant and optimistic, and moved deep into it. She stooped to pick up an encrusted shard and felt sure that under its earthen crust she would find a key to her research. Looking back at the cave entrance she saw the figure of a large man enter the cave. A steel door clanged down behind him, trapping her in the cave.

The dream followed its usual course until the man had thrown her to the ground and was upon her. He ripped away her clothes and sat, straddling her waist. He began to pummel her body with his fists.

Maggie woke, her eyes darting about as she took sharp,

deep breaths. She lay there a moment collecting herself and then got out of bed. She walked to the window and threw it open. A chill in the breeze made her pick up her robe from the bottom of the bed and put it on. Then she returned to the window and stared out into the dimly lit night sky. It's like looking into the shadowy dark of the cave, she thought.

Maggie did not hear Barbara as she quietly entered the room. The open door allowed the breeze to quicken and it caught the door from Barbara's light hold and slammed it shut. Maggie froze as fear stabbed needles through her body. It's him, she thought. He's come back. Molina has come back. And there before her the darkness lightened to reveal the entire scene, the way it was, the beating, the rape, Molina.

"You filthy beast!" she screamed, turning toward the door.

"It's me, Maggie, Barbara," the shadowy figure replied.

"Barbara? Barbara?"

Barbara flicked the switch and light flooded the room.

"I saw him, Barbara. I saw who beat me. I saw who....raped me. It was Molina."

Susan arrived at Maggie's room within twenty minutes of Barbara's call. She sat next to the bed and took Maggie's hand.

"You know who beat you, Maggie. Who was it?"

"It was Colonel Molina."

"Is he the man who raped you?"

"Yes! Yes! He was a beast!"

"I want to show you two more photos, Maggie. Is that okay with you? I want to know if you can identify them."

Maggie shut her eyes, but nodded her assent.

Susan retrieved the photos from her briefcase and slipped them between Maggie's thumb and forefinger. She waited.

At last, Maggie opened her eyes and looked at the top photo. "I don't know him," she said, relief in her voice. She turned the photo under to look at the second. She shuddered and closed her eyes again. "That's him. That's Molina." She held the photos out, dropped them, and shut her eyes.

Susan picked up the photos from the floor. "Yes, that is Molina, Maggie," she said. "Colonel Jorge Molina. He was reportedly a very cruel man."

Maggie reached for the picture again and studied it, a look of disgust twisting her face. Then she threw the picture to the floor and stared at nothing.

"Maggie, I know this does not feel like good news, but.."

Suddenly Maggie interrupted, "You said was?"

"Molina is dead. Giulio says he was there when Molina was shot. You can ask him about it sometime. Molina can't hurt you anymore. Nor will he ever be cruel to anyone again."

Maggie lay back, her eyes on Susan.

"There's no reason for you to ever hide from that memory, Maggie. Now, lets talk about...."

JUSTICE BEGINS

The raw, wet, wintry cold gave Maggie shivers still as she set packages down on a bench outside her apartment door and searched her purse for the key. Inside, she carried the sacks to the kitchen and unloaded groceries into the refrigerator and cupboards. She folded the empty sacks, now her supply of garbage bags, and stacked them in the cabinet under the sink. Her feelings fed memories of her childhood on a Montana ranch: the mow of the horse barn filled with hay, cords of firewood piled next to the house, basement shelves stacked high with jars of jam, syrup, the staple vegetables: potatoes, canned beans and corn, and more jars of preserved fruit. Warm and cosy now, she felt ready for the winter, and ready also for her work

She picked up the last remaining package and walked up the metal circular stairs that spiraled tightly to the apartment's rooftop loft. There, in her office, she looked out at the spires, cupolas, and bell towers of Rome's upper story. In the distance, the white-wedding-cake face of the Victor Emmanual monument stood, unshiny now in the steady drizzle. She felt a moment of depression from the dismal sky, but quickly displaced the feeling.

At her desk she pulled a stuffed envelope from the package, opened it and quickly shuffled through the photos. Then, slowly, she examined each of them. Each brought a smile and warm excitement. Giulio had thrown a farewell party for Felicity, Barbara and Jane before their return to the States. Fred was there, and Susan Killips. They had a private room at the Ristorante da Pancrazio, an underground space amid the ancient ruins of the Emperor Pompey's theatre.

"Is this not the most wonderful day?" Giulio had asked when proposing a toast. "Good health to you, Maggie, and to the happy ending of your frightening drama."

Maggie's smile widened at the picture of the tiny, pointed hat bound to Felicity's ample head by a rubbery cord.

"She is risen," Felicity had toasted, gesturing first to Maggie, and then spilling wine on them both as she gathered Maggie into a warm bear hug.

Finally, the happy, tearful farewell at the airport.

Maggie looked at her watch, then stacked the photos on her desk. She walked down to her kitchen and pulled her raincoat from the back of the chair. She buttoned the coat as she walked to the door, but stopped to pick up the photo of Charles Mueller from a coffee table. She studied his face. Now that you're back on favorite saint status, I hope you're still pulling for me. I've got a way to go -- but I'm getting there. A scrap of another of his letters entered her mind:

I've thought more about heroes. Heroes are free enough to love and do good even to their worst enemies.

There are many kinds of love. And then, there's you.

"And then there's you," she repeated, touching his face on the photo. She put the photo down gently, and walked out the door.

****

Dr. Susan Killips opened the file on her desk, Maggie's file. She began a page by page review, tracing the history of Maggie's therapy. She paused when she came to the drawing Maggie had made of the rape scene, a drawing made when she thought the event was only something she had witnessed. Susan had used the mapping strategy to bring her patient closer to the event. Studying the drawing again, Susan could see the figure of a person looking down from a corner of the drawing onto the scene below, a clear indication of Maggie's dissociative, out-of-body reaction to the trauma.

A knock on her door interrupted Susan's review. "Come in," she said.

Maggie walked through the door. "Good afternoon, Dr. Killips."

"Hi, Maggie. You're right on time." Susan stood and moved to one of two recliner chairs. She motioned Maggie to the other. "I saw Giulio yesterday," Susan began. "He told me about Maria. That might be a good place for us to start today ."

"Okay," Maggie replied as sadness filled her eyes. "You remember that I told you about Maria. She was so good to me in prison, so protective. When I started to feel better in the hospital, I wrote to her. I told her how grateful I was for her care, and I asked her if there was any way that I could help her. I don't know if my letters, I actually wrote several times, ever got to her. They were never answered."

"I do remember your description of Maria."

"Anyway, one day I told Giulio about Maria and how I couldn't reach her. He said he had friends there and perhaps they could help. The day before yesterday Giulio came to see me." Maggie began to cry. "Giulio said that she had been killed in prison. He said he had this information on very good authority, that I could trust it."

"You have always portrayed Maria as a very courageous woman," Susan replied, and reached a box of tissues to Maggie.

"She never thought about herself or her own needs," Maggie asserted, tears continuing to flow down her cheeks.

"She will live on in your memory, Maggie, and in your work."

Maggie did not respond for a time. "And I have another saint to pray for me."

Susan allowed time for Maggie to dry her tears. Finally she asked, "How's your work going?"

"Good, most of the time," Maggie answered. "I get stuck in that awful memory now and then, but I don't run from it anymore, and then it goes away."

"You'll find that the memory intrudes less and less over time," Susan replied. "Are you enjoying your work?"

"Yes, I am. Very much."

"Can you tell me about your work?"

"Yes, except for some names and cases. Our chief project has been the development of a constitution for the church. We are almost finished with it."

An hour later Susan stood to indicate the session was completed. She handed a slip of paper to Maggie. "It's a new prescription, Maggie. We'll be lowering your medication over time until it's no longer needed. And we'll set an appointment for two weeks from now. Does that fit your schedule?"

Maggie checked her calender and nodded.

Susan looked intently at Maggie. "You're a strong, wonderful woman, Maggie. I am so proud to know you."

Tears welled up in Maggie's eyes. She reached for Susan's hand and said, "I owe you so much."

"Thank you, Maggie. But I owe you equally as much. The memory of your courage will always help me through."

"Perhaps we can be friends someday -- instead of doctor/patient."

"Perhaps we can," Susan replied, and covered Maggie's hand with both of her own.

****

The next morning, Maggie sat at the large round conference table surrounded by her staff. Peter Van Antwerpen, her deputy, sat directly across the table, his forefinger repetitively pushing his spectacles back up the slope of his nose. Between them on both sides were her staff of experts: canon lawyers, theologians, scripture scholars, psychologists, lay and clerical. She felt a thrill of satisfaction as she lay the document back on the table. "Thank you," she said. "This *Constitution For the Universal Church* is your work, and that of so many around the world who provided opinions. Are you satisfied that you have all been heard?"

Words of assent sounded around the table.

"Does anyone of you see a need for further amendments, additions or deletions?"

The staff remained silent, some slowly shaking their heads.

"Neither do I," Maggie continued. Her blue eyes held a lustre of excitement. "I am so proud to have you as associates."

Murmurs of "hear, hear," "likewise," "*anch' io.*"

"Peter will send copies of the document to the papal deputy, Cardinal Gattone, and to the secretary of state, Archbishop Dupuis, this afternoon. Pope Francis has given them approval authority for this. I have already arranged with Cardinal Gattone and Archbishop Dupuis to meet with us one week from today at 1:00 p.m. Please arrange your schedule. They will have questions, I'm sure. But, with their approval the document goes to the Pontiff for signature, and then to the universal Church. We can hope for publication within the month."

The applause was controlled, but filled the conference room.

"Peter will also send a status report today to all those organizations who have provided us with opinions and recommended drafts. I think, Peter," Maggie said, looking at her deputy, "you might give a particular note of appreciation to the *Association For the Rights of Catholics in the Church* in the United States. Give them a sense of how much of their draft has been incorporated into the final draft. I would not have you do this if I did not feel so confident."

251

Peter only nodded but Maggie knew that the energetic spirit of a revolutionary inhabited his stumpy frame.

Maggie looked at her notes. "Our next item of business is tomorrow's Court Day of Decisions, our first. Let's go over the decisions to be rendered...."

****

A full-length mirror graced the back of a closet door in Maggie's office. She checked the flow of her judicial robe and turned to her deputy. "Well, Peter, do I look judicial enough?"

"You do unless you think a serious scowl is appropriate," Peter responded jovially.

Maggie laughed. "No, that may be judicial, but it's not me. Are we getting an audience?" she asked, pointing to a side door. The door led into the congregation's courtroom, and Maggie's office served as the judge's chambers on those few days each year when she would render decisions.

"I haven't checked," Peter answered.

Maggie opened the door and stepped out into the newly constructed courtroom. At the Pope's invitation, she and Peter had raided the Vatican Floreria, the name used not for a flower shop but for what amounts to the pope's attic. There, centuries of past popes' furniture and appointments are stored. Here, now, the desk and chair of Pope John XXIII had been raised on a dais to become the Judge's bench. Sides of white, ancient sarcophogi, salvaged from Vatican museum storage, fronted the desk and angled like wings to the side. Images of Christian gatherings, ichthyic symbols, and the words, *justitia, pax* and *agape* (justice, peace, love) randomly grooved their surfaces. The walls of the room were painted a plain cream color. They waited for an artist to design and cover them with judicial motif frescoes. Two plain tables stood at floor level several yards in front of the bench, one for each the plaintiff and the defendant should either desire to be present. Since all testimony was done through written briefs and depositions, a witness chair was not present.

A small marble railing separated the visitor's gallery from the participants. The gallery rose in tiers toward a cathedral ceiling. Pews, salvaged from a local church, provided the gallery seating.

A Swiss guard in full dress uniform stood at attention at the left corner of the bench. A few spectators were already in the gallery. Giulio and Fred were seated in the front row. Maggie returned their wave and walked back into her office.

Peter held a folder in his hand. "The decisions are all in order," he said. "Should I put the folder on the bench?"

"No. I'll carry it with me, Peter. Thank you."

Twenty minutes later a young staff member acting as bailiff preceded Maggie into the courtroom. His exuberant bellow ill suited the smallness of the room. "Please rise!" And as Maggie entered the room, "The Honorable Sister Margaret McDonough!"

Maggie walked up the four steps of the bench, sat and surveyed the crowd. The gallery she faced was now full. She spied Cardinal Rolf sitting near the front, a bored look on his face. He has an interest, she thought. Marco Gattone sat unobtrusively in the upper gallery, a smile lifting his pocked cheeks.

"Ladies and Gentlemen," she began. "The Congregation for Justice, with its universal jurisdiction, will render decisions today on several appeals brought to it. These decisions will be the first rendered under temporary guidelines based on the Pontiff's Apostolic Constitution, *Justitia Pro Omnibus Beata* (Blessed Justice For Everyone). I say temporary because a new constitution for the Church will be submitted to the Pontiff in the very near future for approval. Upon his approval this court will render decisions based on that constitution. Should that constitution contradict decisions made

253

under our temporary guidelines, they will be amended."

She paused and opened her folder. "Our first decision today responds to an appeal from Father Tomas Barcos against the penalty of excommunication imposed on him by the Holy Office and the subsequent termination of his responsibilities by the cardinal archbishop of Sao Paulo. As you know, this court renders its decisions on the basis of briefs and depositions presented us or requested by us from the contesting parties. At this stage of the process, further discussion is no longer permitted. However, if either party is represented here, they may step forward and occupy the tables in front of me, the plaintiff to my right. Is Father Barcos represented here today?"

A diminutive man with a gray fringe of hair and cropped beard rose from his seat and walked slowly through the railing gate to the table. He held his hat tightly against his chest with both hands as he gave a slight bow to Maggie, then stood at the table. A large younger man, furrows running along his fleshy brow, followed Barcos and stood next to him.

"Would you please identify yourselves?" Maggie asked.

The young man spoke. "This is Padre Barcos," he said, gesturing toward the older man. "My name is Phillip Michael. I am a canon lawyer from the Canadian Archdiocese of Ontario. Padre Barcos selected me to represent him from the member listing of the Canon Law International Public Defenders."

"Thank you. For the defendant?" Maggie watched Archbishop Angus Dilford get a nod from Rolf. Dilford walked to the defendant's table and identified himself nervously.

"If either side wishes to make a brief statement, they may do so now," Maggie advised. "Mr. Michael?"

Michael whispered to Barcos and the older man rose. "Thank you. Thank you," he began hesitantly. "My name is Padre Tomas Barcos. I wish only to be a good neighbor to the peoples. Thank you. Thank you." He bowed and sat

254

down.

"Thank you, Father Barcos. Archbishop Dilford?"

Dilford pulled his lanky form upright. His voice pitched higher than usual. "The Holy Office, I mean of course The Congregation for the Doctrine of the Faith, has examined the sayings of Father Barcos and found him guilty of a dangerous relativism. Moreover he has shown resistance to proper discipline. I'm confident the brief summation provided this court by the congregation has been sufficient to demonstrate the accuracy of these charges."

"Thank you, Archbishop Dilford." Maggie retrieved a document from her folder and looked out at the audience. "The decision of this Congregation in the appeal of Father Barcos is as follows." She read, "The Congregation for Justice finds in favor of Father Barcos. The penalty of excommunication is hereby rescinded and the cardinal archbishop of Sao Paulo, Brazil is hereby directed to restore Father Barcos to his former responsibilities. The Congregation for Justice finds that the arguments of The Holy Office, and their methods used in arriving at their decision, violate the very essence of our faith."

Maggie heard the surprised gasps from the gallery but continued to read. She looked up from time to time and saw the blanched face of Dilford, and the surprised face of Barcos's own attorney, Michael. She knew. This was an historic moment. Never before had The Holy Office been denied. She finished reading and scanned the gallery. Rolf's face had lost its usual urbanity. It was red and she sensed the anger throbbing at his temples. "The plaintiff and defendant may now stand down," she stated. "The next appeal is that of the New York School Teachers against the Archdiocese of New York."

When the session ended and Maggie had returned to her office, Johann Rolf strode through the railing gate, across the bench area and barged into her office.

Maggie, talking to her deputy, turned to face Rolf.

255

"How dare you publicly disgrace The Holy Office?" he demanded. "How dare you embarrass me?"

Maggie looked squarely at Rolf and responded calmly. "How dare you, Cardinal Rolf, take actions contrary to the express will of our Pontiff?"

"This is madness," Rolf sputtered, "an assault on the deposit of faith. The curia must speak with one voice."

"Not madness, Cardinal," Maggie replied. "Pope Francis has merely reiterated that love of neighbor is the core of our faith deposit. That is the one voice you should tune to."

"Bah." Rolf, apoplectic with rage, sputtered, turned and barged out the way he had come in.

Maggie turned to her deputy. "I think perhaps the good cardinal has no experience of contradiction. What do you think, Peter?"

****

Fred paid the taxi driver over Giulio's objections and the two men flanked Maggie as they walked down the sidewalk to the Ristorante Scoglio di Frisio.

"The cannelloni here is marvelous," Giulio said. He voiced a smack from pursed lips against pursed finger tips.

"And I'm hungry," Maggie asserted.

"You've had a full day. You should be hungry," Fred replied, holding open the door.

Seated at their table, Giulio repeated the smacking sound and gesture. "And you also were marvelous today, Maggie. I was so happy to be at the court proceedings. It was the big impression I got of your importance. Thank you for inviting me."

"Giulio, you know the proceedings are open to anyone. I didn't invite you," Maggie replied.

"Still, I am happy you tell me about it. You were so impressive in your judicial robe, seated up there so high. I was

256

proud to have a sister so important."

"Giulio, stop it! You are a tease." Maggie's laugh carried a lightness from of old.

"Is it not wonderful, Fred, to hear this marvelous laugh from Maggie once again?"

"It's better than wonderful," Fred answered.

"I tell you, I was so impressed at this court," Giulio persisted.

"I don't think Cardinal Rolf or the archbishop of New York were impressed," Fred added.

Maggie looked at Fred to see if he was being frivolous. No. "I think both of them fully expected a different decision," she said.

"I'm sure of that," Fred replied. "It has always been that the voice of a cleric is the voice of God. Today, you cleansed the church of that fiction and reassigned humanity to all human decisions on justice. The church will be healthier."

"Yes, I think that is so," Giulio said. "I think today, Maggie, you step upon some purple robes. The robes come off and what do we see? We see people, like ourselves."

Maggie was somber. "Justice can have no favorites."

Giulio too grew serious. "If justice has no favorites, Maggie, what then of General Castillo? If justice does not reach him, is he not its favorite?"

Maggie felt her face grow hot and she was angry at Giulio for the reminder. She quickly reasoned away the feeling. "That's different. The Christian way is to forgive offenses, Giulio. Forgiveness replaces justice."

"Yes, but does not the deed require punishment?"

"To forgive is to forget punishment."

"Yes, but what if person you forgive does not care for your forgiveness. What if he is not sorry and keeps doing bad things?"

"You still forgive. It becomes God's problem."

The waiter began placing their plates in front of them.

"We must talk more of this sometime," Giulio said. "I do not think it is fair to give to God this problem."

****

In the Central American capital, General Roberto Castillo walked briskly to his limo. His military chauffeur opened the car door and saluted.

Outside the gates of the police headquarters, Miguel Vasquez slouched at the wheel of a decaying car. Rust was its most prominent feature. Concealed by a droopy mustache, scarred cheek and bushy wig he watched through squinted eyes as the black limo emerged through the gates. He started his engine and pulled out into traffic, following the limo, but several cars behind.

When the limo parked at a restaurant, Miguel pulled to the side forty yards farther along the street. He waited, slouching again, apparently dozing.

An hour later, Castillo again entered his limo and pulled away. Again, Miguel followed, and would through each limo stop of the day.

On successive days Miguel drove different cars, but again chased and charted the limo stops through each day .

Two weeks later, the limo made a regular morning stop at a tobacco shop. The shops along the street were just opening for the day. The chauffeur left the car and entered the shop to retrieve the general's supply of fresh cigars. Castillo sat in the rear seat reading documents, paying no attention to the scant pedestrian traffic along the walk.

Miguel, still mustached and scarred, ambled toward the limo. He timed his stroll and opened the rear door of the limo just as the chauffeur disappeared into the shop. "Since you have not yet met, permit me to introduce you to justice," he announced quietly and fired a silenced bullet into the forehead of the startled Castillo.

JUSTICE UNFOLDS

Marco Gattone looked down on St. Peter's Square from his office window, his view identical to that of Francis I, one floor above. He turned as Claude Dupuis and Fred Sweeney entered. He noticed immediately the cane in Fred's hand.

"You are having trouble with the walking, Fred?" he asked. His brown eyes and pocked face showed concern.

Fred gave a gesture of dismissal to the topic. "Not much, Marco, thank you. Since the cane gives me a feeling of steadiness I've concluded the whole thing is in my mind."

They sat at a table near the window. "What are you hearing out there?" Marco asked.

Claude raised his bushy eyebrows. "You mean, about the new Apostolic Constitution?"

Marco nodded.

"*Eligendo Pontificem* (On Electing a Pontiff) has spawned a whirlwind," Fred answered. "We call them tornadoes back home. Everyone is scurrying about looking for a safe way to get through it."

Claude nodded in agreement. "Fred's analogy, it is good. The new procedure for electing a pope has only been out for several hours now. The document is also much like the earthquake. And, of course, the epicenter is right here in the curia. It brings distress to the curia and to the College of Cardinals, but joy, I suspect, to the rest of the church."

"Francis and Maggie!" Marco said. "It is I think a stroke of genius. It is so simple. They have changed the way future pontiffs will be elected. I know they have been working closely for some time now, but it has been their secret."

Claude brushed a hand through his unruly hair. "When I read it again this morning I did not think it was so much the genius. At first I think it does not go far enough. What does it do? I ask myself. It says that in future papal elections, no more than twenty-five percent of electors may come from the clergy and professed religious, and no more than fifty percent may be male. Now, if it is the intention of the document to share power in the Church with the laity, and especially with the women, I ask you, is merely changing election procedures sufficient to do this?"

"I remember a conversation I had with Maggie months ago," Fred said. "She argued that the power of suffrage would make papal aspirants sensitive to women's issues, and that over time ministerial roles would fall into place."

"I think time will show her to be correct," Marco replied. "But the document is not why I asked you to come here this afternoon. I have something else to share with you." He rose from the table, walked to his desk and returned with a manila folder. He placed the folder unopened on the table. "While you were still in Prague with Francis, you will recall that I had the papal apartment renovated to accommodate the paralyzed Francis. As is usual after such reconstruction I had our security personnel perform a careful sweep of the apartment. They found a concealed listening device. We did not remove the device immediately, but let it remain in place while our experts traced signals to the listening device. It was found in a very few days. Would you care to guess where we found it?"

Each man shook his head.

"Rolf. Our esteemed prefect of The Holy Office. The receiving device was located in his own office."

"Brazen!" Claude muttered.

"I thought of exposing him then," Marco continued, "but changed my mind after talking to Francis, who, by the way, knowing the bug was there, was able to guide conversations accordingly. After a time, we removed the bug, but left the receiver in place, useless then, of course."

"Wouldn't Rolf suspect you were on his trail?" Fred asked.

"Perhaps, but he wouldn't know for sure what happened

to the bug. Perhaps it only malfunctioned. And even if he suspected that we had found it, what could he do?"

"What happened then?" Fred asked.

"We assigned our chief of security to conduct an investigation of the Holy Inquisitor. Rolf had no need to gather information surreptiously. He could but ask and it would be given to him. It raised in our minds a question of his character."

"What is it you want of Fred and myself?" Claude asked.

Marco handed the folder to Claude. "I want you and Fred to read this. Then we will talk again another day."

****

Before the publication day of *Eligendo Pontificem* was over, a small group of curial prelates requested an audience with Pope Francis. Three days later they gathered in the small throne room of the Apostolic Palace, joined there by several cardinals from around the world. Pustkowski from Krakow was there, as was Dougherty from Armagh and Sullivan from New York. Fourteen in all.

Francis greeted them calmly. Marco, Claude, Fred and Maggie were with him.

"You are defiling a holy tradition," Pustkowski charged.

"You will recall our response to that, Cardinal Pustkowski," Francis replied in his staccato voice. "Under scrutiny, this tradition is nothing more than the bequest of self-serving men long dead, the rattle of their bones. It does not deserve the name tradition."

"The Church should be an immoveable rock," Armagh argued. "You are showing the Church as changeable."

"That is true, Cardinal Dougherty. But, we are called to be the moral leaders of mankind, not its rear guard. We must learn to distinguish the detritus of dead men from the Gospel message, and make change as the distinctions become clear."

261

"It's that woman!" Sullivan complained, heedless of Maggie's presence. "She has held out to you the apple. She has tempted you to do this, and you have allowed yourself to be seduced. I know she was treated badly, but what is that? Many suffer cruelties. But what has she ever accomplished?"

Francis looked at the man and for a time let silence be his response. Then, "What do you see on the wall behind me?" he asked.

"You mean the crucifix?" the prelate asked.

"Would you call that something Jesus did? An accomplishment?" Francis asked quietly, his voice halting and searching for the power of breath. "Or was your salvation worked through something done to Him, through suffering accepted by Him?"

"You will force the Church into schism," another argued. "It is not worth the price."

"I think not," Francis answered. "Do you plan to secede, Cardinal?"

"You are a cripple, Francis," Rolf interjected cruelly. "You are a cripple in your body, and you now show you are also a cripple in your mind. You must resign! You owe it to us who are healthy and strong. You owe it to the Church. Do it now!"

"I think not yet, Johann."

Reminiscent of Cardinals Ottaviani and Tisserant when Pope Paul VI declared that cardinals over the age of eighty were no longer eligible papal electors, Rolf and several others took to television the next day in an attempt to sway Francis. They accomplished only a public display of their wounded pride and peevishness.

****

According to the report, investigators found that only Rolf and his second, Angus Dilford, were guilty in the bugging of the papal apartment. The investigators had quickly broken through Dilford's timid denials and learned the entire story. Rolf himself had installed the bug, gaining access to the apartment on a simple ruse. The investigators learned more. They discovered the heretofore unknown aspects of Rolf's personal life, his thinly veiled alias, his mistress, and his wealth. Informed by Marco Gattone, Francis and his deputy resolved on a specific course of action.

"Francis asked that you two deal directly with Rolf," Marco informed Claude and Fred.

The two men met with Rolf by appointment in Rolf's office.

"You have invaded the privacy of the Pontiff," Claude said factually. "That is your greater offense. Ironically, by doing so, you have prompted an invasion of your own privacy. Here is the detail." He handed a folder to Rolf.

Rolf snatched the folder, opened it, and quickly rifled through the mix of documents and photos. "Privacy? Pontiff? Pontiff?" he sneered. "Someone has to track that madman," he almost shouted, looking up at Claude. "And my personal life is my business," he shouted again, arrogantly. "Get out! Get out of my office, the two of you!"

They stayed. Fred reviewed the two options available to Rolf: resign or be fired.

Rolf exploded in anger. "I will never resign," he said "and do not push me."

Claude and Fred simply sat there and waited, dissipating Rolf's attempt at menace by their calmness.

At the end, Rolf agreed to send his resignation by that afternoon.

"We want it now, before we leave," Fred demanded quietly. Then, responding to a strange directive from the Pope, he added, "And not only a resignation, Cardinal Rolf. You will also specifically remove yourself as a candidate in all future papal elections. There is no need for you to dictate the letter. I have it already prepared." He reached into his brief-

263

case, took out the letter, and handed it to Rolf.

Rolf read it with angry eyes. Suddenly, he grabbed a pen, signed it and handed it to Fred. "Now get out!" he ordered. "You both stink of this pope."

****

In his apartment that night, Rolf informed Bianca that the Vatican no longer held sufficient room for his ambitions. "I will do better in the business world. There is more challenge for a man of my ability."

"What of me, Johann?" Bianca asked, a trace of anxiety in her eyes and voice.

"What of you, Bianca? What would you want to do?"

"Be with you."

Rolf smiled at her response. His shoulders relaxed. "Then you shall be with me. We will marry, if that is agreeable with you."

Bianca's eyes came alive. She ran to his embrace. Overcome, she managed only "Oh, Johann, yes, yes."

"Pack only our suitcases. We will leave by car as soon as you are packed. We will have movers come and pack all the rest. By morning I want to be a long distance from this stinking hole."

"Where are we going?"

"To Switzerland, at least for now."

"I love Switzerland."

****

The second anniversary of Pope Francis's election was celebrated with a formal event, a black-tie equivalent party for all Vatican employees. Francis made a brief appearance and, using his tongue on the controls, playfully demonstrated a series of skillful wheelchair maneuvers to the delight of his audience.

After Francis had returned to his apartment, Maggie carried a glass of wine for herself, and one for Fred Sweeney who waited at a table.

"Has there been any progress on finding Francis's would-be assassins?" she asked as she put his glass in front of him.

"Claude told me yesterday that Interpol has some new leads and are following up on them. That's all we have for now," Fred replied.

"I hope they find them," Maggie said, taking a sip of wine.

"They will," Fred replied. "They're determined."

"Good, Now tell me, what did the doctor say?"

"She said she couldn't find any further progression."

"Does that mean it's in remission?"

"No, I don't think remission fits this disease. But I think I'm going to beat this. I think I've got a miracle coming."

"Cheers!" Maggie said. "I'll keep praying." She raised her glass to meet Fred's and kept a cheerful smile on her face. I wish we had a better reason for optimism, she thought.

At that moment, Gardinal Gervase Janov approached their table. He nodded to Fred and turned to Maggie. "Sister Margaret," he said. "I have not yet had the opportunity to know you better."

She's been here over three years, Janov, Fred thought.

"Perhaps we can change that, Cardinal Janov," Maggie replied. "I congratulate you on your appointment as our new prefect of The Holy Office. "

"Thank you. I see your hand in the new election procedures, Sister. May I say that I heartily agree."

"Thank you, Cardinal Janov. It's wonderful to know that it has your support and that of The Holy Office."

Support? Fred hid his cynicism. How ambition is so easily served when you hold the aces. Now, it's a whole new card game.

"I think this constitution is only a small, first step for

265

women, don't you agree?" Janov effused.

"We may hope," Maggie responded.

"I would be pleased to talk with you at length sometime about where we can take this from here." Janov bowed his leave taking.

"That would please me also, Cardinal Janov," Maggie replied graciously.

Give the fox credit, Fred thought. He's the first to line up. And Maggie, God bless her, saw it coming.

JUSTICE ACCOMPLISHED

The late morning air felt cool under a bright sun. Maggie, Giulio and Fred left Maggie's office and began to walk towards St. Peter's Basilica. Fred, a cane in each hand, tested each step's footing before taking another. Maggie and Giulio walked, one on each side of Fred, available to give support they each knew Fred would not take. They stopped when they neared the basilica.

"We are here now," Giulio said. "You must join the others and I will go into the basilica. I will watch your grand procession. I must tell you, I never dream such a day as this could come to be."

"We'll meet you after the ceremony," Fred said. He stumbled on the cobblestones, but managed to stay erect.

Maggie and Fred turned to join an assembling crowd. A master of ceremonies motioned them to take their place.

Maggie's eyes swept over the scene around them. "Giulio's right, you know. I never expected to see this day either."

"Oh ye of little faith."

A cross bearer and acolytes led the procession of five hundred men and women into St. Peter's Basilica. To facilitate its formation the procession had been organized in the piazza. They entered by twos, Maggie beside Fred at the lead. The interior of the Basilica dazzled in bright lighting. The pure tones of the Vatican choir filled the huge interior, singing first the majestic *Te Deum*. A large rectangle in the front center of the nave had been reserved for the five hundred, while guests surrounded them on bleachers. Giulio sat high at the corner where the nave meets the right transept. He waved as Maggie and Fred took seats below him. Looking for him in the place Fred had reserved, Maggie and Fred caught the wave and returned it.

As the choir continued its pre-mass concert, Fred's memory plowed through the prior year, turning over the events that brought them here. The health of Francis had been stable, but with little improvement. All along, though, Francis had exercised that part of him not disabled, his mind.

Immediately upon the publication of *Eligendo Pontificem*, Francis had encouraged Maggie to act quickly on the selection of the lay electors. The Apostolic Constitution dictated that lay electors be chosen by lot from the Catholic laity under the supervision of The Congregation for Justice. Maggie's staff had rapidly developed specific procedures and set deadlines for each country to conduct the drawings. Every Catholic lay person was eligible. The names of those willing to serve were certified on lottery stubs by their respective pastors. The stubs, divided between male and female candidates, were then sent to the National Bishops' Conference or equivalent. There the stubs were drawn publicly, a number to equal the electors, male and female, allotted to the country on the basis of its Catholic population.

The procedure worked smoothly. In only a few instances were the congregation's rules compromised by bishops attempting to control the drawings and thereby dictate the electors. Justice was swift in each instance. Those bishops no longer held jurisdiction of any kind.

In the meantime, Pope Francis and the Congregation for Bishops completed their selection of one hundred twenty-five clergy and professed religious electors. Both Maggie and Fred had been included in that number.

Fred was recalled from his distraction as the ministers for the mass and installation ceremony made their way up the center aisle. Francis I, wanting to be visible on this day, did not ride his motorized wheelchair up the aisle where he would be unseen by most onlookers. Instead, he had directed that the *Sedia Gestatoria,* the portable papal throne, be hauled out of storage. Now he moved slowly up the crowded Church, strapped carefully in the chair held high on the arms of strong young men and women. Unable to move even his head from side to side, unable to raise an arm in blessing, he blessed with a broad smile under warm eyes that could and did move.

Fred felt a lump in his throat and the beginning of tears at the sight of the Pope. He knew Francis's true condition, the tubes that drained his bowels and bladder, the complete physical helplessness. Since Prague, Fred had been a daily witness to the pope's bravery. He knew that Francis's acceptance of his disability and the tranquility he constantly displayed had been won painfully day by day.

Marco Gattone walked immediately in front of the pope. He would be celebrant of the mass and deliver the homily. Fred wondered at that. Francis could speak, he could deliver a homily. Why Marco? Francis had elected to speak briefly at the end of the installation ceremony.

Fred saw the moist shine of Maggie's eyes when she briefly turned to him. She put a hand on his arm as they watched Francis carried up the six steps to the main altar. There the Pope was lowered to the floor, his face to the people. The *Sedia Gestatoria* would serve him for the entire ceremony. Suddenly, Maggie's hand tightened momentarily on Fred's arm. He turned to her and saw anxiety enter, then exit her eyes. A memory?

After the reading of the Gospel at mass, Marco Gattone walked to Francis's side to deliver his homily. "The Holy Father has asked a homily of me today," he began. "You all should know that today I speak his mind and his heart, as well as my own. Future generations may look back on this day with idle curiosity while they enjoy the power and freedom Pope Francis creates for them today. It is only you, the laity of today, who will feel the weight lifted and the freedom of a power at long last shared. This equality especially goes to you women and to those of your gender everywhere. We bishops, all of us male, have grown accustomed to calling our collective self, Holy *Mother* Church. Today, thanks to Pope Francis, this irony explodes into universal consciousness.

"Universally, the bishops applaud this..."

That's a stretch, Marco, Fred thought. He recalled the fourteen cardinals who came, objecting, to Francis.

"We must all learn the lesson of love that our Pontiff brings to light here," Marco continued slowly and deliberately. "Just as love, which Christ showed us is to live for others, is the apex of human freedom, and just as trust is necessary for love, so chance is necessary for trust. Underlying this day, the trust, the love and the freedom of this day, is the way you were selected to be electors -- by chance. That makes room for us to trust one another. It makes room for us to love one another. It makes room for the Holy Spirit, the Spirit of Love, to guide you in your selection of future popes." Marco paused. "Pope Francis has chosen not to control, but to open the future to chance, to trust in your love and that of the Spirit. May you always choose in that Spirit."

Gattone returned to the altar after his homily. The mass concluded and the installation of the five hundred papal electors began. Maggie led the designees, the first to sign her name beneath an already certified signature, the first to receive from Marco the bronze medallion, the official emblem of a papal elector. The office was now the highest office in the church, higher than a bishop, higher than a cardinal.

Fred returned from his installation using both canes. He turned to Maggie who was examining the medallion.

"Beautiful, isn't it?" she whispered.

It was beautiful, and simple. A plain cross traversed by an ornately designed key, symbols of power, rose from the top half of the four-inch oval. An inscription, the elector's picture, signature and thumb print lay under glass on the bottom half.

When the last of the electors had been installed, the master of ceremonies carried a microphone and placed it in front of Francis's lips.

"My dear friends," he began haltingly. "Today is a most happy day. It is happy for you. It is happy for the church. It is my most happy day." The halting delivery could not hide the rich emotions that Francis fed into his words. "I have one more task for you. Before you return each to your own country, you will elect a successor to Francis the First."

The audience gasped. A few whispers circulated around the basilica as those who failed to hear the pope's announcement asked of their neighbors. Then silence hung until voices could no longer be still. "No! No! No!" Isolated at first, the cries grew in intensity.

Maggie looked at the frail majestic Francis, awe and tears welling up and filling her.

Fred sat, stunned.

Marco walked to Francis's side and took the microphone. He waited until the noise subsided. "So great is Pope Francis's love. Can we ask less of ourselves? Tomorrow morning precisely at 9:00 a.m., you five hundred will again come to this basilica. The Apostolic Constitution directs that one hundred twenty of you be chosen by lot, and that this one hundred twenty then elect the next Pontiff. Once again, chance makes room for trust, love, freedom and the Holy Spirit. On the day after tomorrow, the one hundred twenty will convene at the Hotel St. Martha by 8:00 a.m. You will receive further instruction at that time."

The next morning, the signature cards of the electors were deposited in a large drum brought to the altar by a master of ceremonies. The drum was then rotated to mix the cards. Marco removed the first card and handed it to Francis.

"Maribeth Preuss!" the pope announced. "You are the first elector chosen." Handed the second card, " Michelle Burg! You are the second. Please to come forward both of you and draw the remaining lots."

****

Maggie knew the two young women. They were both from the United States and she had given them a quick tour of the Vatican only several days before. Maggie's own name was the thirty-seventh name drawn. At the conclusion, sixty-four of the chosen electors were women, thirty were laymen, and twenty-six were clerics. The name of Francis I was drawn 97th. Twenty of the clerics were cardinals. The names of ten alternates were drawn to cover the possibility of an elector's incapacity.

Instructions for the conclave including a schedule were distributed to the electors before their departure in procession from the basilica.

The next morning Fred drove Maggie from her apartment to the Hotel St. Martha in the Vatican for the beginning of the conclave.

"The entire world is watching by now," Fred said. "How does that make you feel?"

"Awed," she replied. "I feel awed and humble. I wish your name had been drawn too."

Fred shrugged. "You deserve to be there. You were the force behind this, your logic and the history you brought to bear. This entire event should go down in history with your name attached. Without you, I doubt that the church would have found this new orbit -- where it will now revolve around people."

Maggie replied soberly. "And Francis, and you, and Claude, and Marco, and all the rest." And Charles, she thought. "I still wish you would be there."

"Francis will be there," Fred answered. "The two of you are worth a legion. I'll keep Giulio company. He called last night, said he had tried to reach you. We'll be there in the piazza when the white smoke rises. It will be good news.

I'm sure of that."

****

Fred returned to his office after getting help to handle Maggie's luggage at the hotel. At one o'clock he met Giulio in a nearby trattoria for lunch.

"Instruct me now, Fred," Giulio said. "Is the pope not taking the big chance with so soon a resignation? What if the new pope takes away all these changes?"

"As Cardinal Gattone said, chance is not a bad thing," Fred replied. "It leaves room for the Spirit. It's the way God worked out his creation. I'm not worried."

"Ah, you have the inside knowledge. Tell me, how many ballots will it take? Many weeks, it seems to me. All of these ladies, and even the gentlemen without collars, will they not wander about with the uncertainty for a long time?"

"I don't think so, Giulio. I'm guessing that we'll see white smoke sometime tomorrow."

"You think so? So soon? I must say I am impressed. You must know this Spirit very well. Who then will be the next pope?"

A waiter came and they both ordered pasta. Giulio ordered wine, Fred coffee.

"If I were betting," Fred answered, "I'd go with Cardinal Marco Gattone."

"You sound so sure. I am thinking you must know something."

"Not at all. I think, though, that I can see the gentle hand of Francis guiding here. You are correct that the lay electors will be uncertain and cautious in the unfamiliar conclave atmosphere. But they are enthused beyond words by what the pope has done for them. They will not elect someone who would turn back the clock."

"How do they know Gattone would not do this? Why

273

him over this Janov man?"

"Think of it this way. Francis showcased Marco when he chose him to give the homily yesterday, and to be celebrant of both the mass and the installation ceremony. By the time Marco finished his homily, despite his statement that they were Francis's words, no one doubted that the sentiments were also his own. Also, don't forget that Francis is also an elector. You can be sure that the electors will seek his counsel."

"Is Gattone not too old?"

"Is seventy-two old? Not if you know Marco Gattone. And the electors know they will be back in five, ten or so years. For now, they'll want someone who knows his way around, and Marco does, who will retain the gains made, and Marco will, and who will give them time to acquire the experience they'll need next time around, and again, Marco will."

Giulio thought a moment. "Aren't they tired of Italians? Won't they prefer someone like this Janov?"

"He'll get a few votes. But the majority of the electors will want to be more sure of him. Maybe next time. He's still young enough."

"You are so sure? I tell you what. I will wager you a bottle of your favorite wine that they will choose other than Gattone. You have the one man. I have all the others."

"Done, only let's make it cognac," Fred answered. "Let's meet again at four. We'll watch the smoke together."

The first smoke curled black from the small chimney of the Sistine Chapel that afternoon. Fred and Giulio went for dinner.

The first two ballots of the following morning also drifted upward through the chimney and billowed forth, black.

The first smoke of the afternoon was white. Fred and Giulio waited impatiently for the announcement. An hour later the doors of the Basilica's center loggia opened. The cardinal deacon appeared and declared:

Annuntio vobis gaudium magnum... I give you
joyful news... *habemus papam...* we have a pope.
*Eminentissimum ac Reverendissimum Dominum
Marcum Sanctae Ecclesiae Cardinalem Gattone...*
the most eminent and reverend cardinal of Holy
Church, Marco Gattone... *qui sibi nomen
imposuit Francesci Secundi...* who has taken
the name, Francis the Second.

Inside the Sistine Chapel, after the balloting had concluded, several attendants and nurses were admitted to tend
to Francis I. Maggie hovered nearby, worried by his blanched
appearance and the weariness in his eyes. As aides wheeled
Francis toward the door she followed them out of the basilica
and back into the Apostolic Palace. They followed a route
that led away from the papal apartments and proceeded slowly
along corridors to the place where Francis had chosen another apartment for himself.

Walking behind, Maggie tried to imagine the thoughts and
feelings that were flowing through Francis at this moment.
Already reduced to an inert body, what feelings followed this
self-made, but nonetheless precipitous fall from the pinnacle
of papal power -- and to what? Where does an ex-pope fit in?
Of this she was sure, Francis had neither counted nor fretted
about the personal costs. He had done the completely unself-
ish act. Others could wait on Marco for now. She needed to
be with and speak to Francis.

Inside, Maggie saw that his personal belongings had already been moved into this new space. Her picture rested
among others on a table, waiting for him to determine its place.

The attendants left Francis for a moment to make final
preparations for him in his bedroom. Maggie walked to him
and lifted his hands in her own. She bent to him, her cheek
touching his temple. "You will forever be loved and honored
by women," she said, emotion flushing tears from her eyes.

Moving back a step to face him, she added, "You will always be a hero to me."

Francis hugged her with his warm brown eyes, absent now of their fatigue and showing that he understood. He smiled up at her. "I am not the hero that you are, Maggie. You have suffered more than I."

Maggie demurred quietly. "Nooo, nooo, not so." She thought she detected an increase of fluidity in Francis' speech. Still aspirated and hesitant, it was less so. She wondered if the lifting of the papal burden had also released a stenosis of his lungs or their passages.

Francis continued. "It is suffering that I think about during this conclave." He pointed to a spot close to a nearby chair. "Move me there and you will be able to sit while we talk."

Maggie pushed the wheelchair to the spot, set its brake, and sat in the chair facing Francis.

"We are the fortunate ones, you and I," he continued, his eyes intent on Maggie's.

"How are we fortunate, Francis?" Maggie asked when Francis seemed to have settled into momentary thought.

"I ask myself today, Maggie, how many millions of people have already starved to death in our world, and how many more millions will starve to death before enough of our brothers and sisters awake to say, it is enough? How long until they say no more deaths by starving, and then they proceed to make it so that no one again starves to death?"

Maggie struggled to connect his thought to being fortunate.

Francis saw the question in her eyes. "Be patient, Maggie," he said. "Next, I asked myself what was the thought of just one of those starving people. Does he think, or does she think, that their starvation leads somewhere, that it has a purpose? Can they see in the midst of their hunger that their death is part of mankind's growth? That their death counts?"

The question stayed in Maggie's eyes.

"You and I are fortunate, Maggie, because we can see, through dark glass it is true, that your suffering is connected to that of so many women before you. It is this suffering that has at last awakened our conscience enough to make us try to have this church be done with the exclusion that shouts inequality, and contributes so much to women's pain. We can now hope that this church will continue to avoid the sins against women with which it has so long colluded. As you know, I have a passion for this sinful church of ours."

"I know that," Maggie replied, "and I'm beginning to understand. But what about your suffering?"

"It is the same, I think, for all suffering. I am able to see how mine is connected to all the victims of violence before me. I do not see clearly how the world will rid itself of violence in the future. Still, my suffering is a gift. It makes me feel kinship with others who are afflicted by violence. It gives me hope. And so, I am better for it. But, it is sad that it takes us so long to learn from the suffering in the world."

An hour later Maggie walked alone across the basilica's piazza to catch a bus. Recalling Francis' words her spirit lightened and then began to soar. Seated on the bus she mentally started a letter:

Dear Charles,

We talked about suffering. I know now that the moment you entered eternity you learned the meaning for the bullet that sent you there. Isn't it freeing...?

Dear Reader,

Wind-borne Publications is a very small press. Our marketing is limited to the good word passed around by our readers. If you think that this story and its theme are worth circulation, please pass the word. We appreciate it. *Wind-borne.*

Order Form

Please send____copies of *Dead Men's Bones to:*

Name:_____

Address:_____

City:_____State:____Zip:_____

Phone:(____)_____

Price:

1-4 copies:	$14.95 ea.	# copies____	$_____
5-9 copies:	$ 13.50 ea.	# copies____	$_____
10-plus copies:	$12.00 ea.	# copies____	$_____

Postage and Handling:
$3.00 first book; $1.00 each additional $_____

                                             Total: $_____

Please make check payable to Wind-borne Publications. Send order and check to:

Wind-borne Publications
P.O. Box 733
Hales Corners, WI 53130

Dear Reader,

Wind-borne Publications is a very small press. Our marketing is limited to the good word passed around by our readers. If you think that this story and its theme are worth circulation, please pass the word. We appreciate it. *Wind-borne.*

Order Form

Please send____copies of *Dead Men's Bones to:*

Name:_____

Address:_____

City:_____State:____Zip:_____

Phone:(_____)_____

Price:

1-4 copies: $14.95 ea.	# copies____	$_____
5-9 copies: $ 13.50 ea.	# copies____	$_____
10-plus copies:$12.00 ea.	# copies____	$_____

Postage and Handling:
$3.00 first book; $1.00 each additional $_____

                                    Total: $_____

Please make check payable to Wind-borne Publications.
Send order and check to:

Wind-borne Publications
P.O. Box 73ℑ
Hales Corners, WI 53130